G000123710

REG.

The Last Pharaoh: BOOK I

by Jay Penner

Series

Book I: *Regent*

Book II: *Queen*

Book III: *Empress* (final)

Prequel novella: *A Dangerous Daughter*

https://jaypenner.com

To the women of the world.

Jay Penner https://www.jaypenner.com

Printed in the United States of America

First Printing: October 2020

3.2 08-03-2023
Produced using publishquickly
https://publishquickly.com

JAY PENNER

Stay Connected!

Join my popular newsletter

My website: https://jaypenner.com

Follow me on: The Amazon author page

Or my page on: Facebook

Or write to me at hello@jaypenner.com

BEFORE YOU READ

———◇———

Writing about the Ptolemaic dynasty, including its most famous members like Cleopatra, is a very tricky undertaking. The reality is that very little of the specific period (from the Egyptian side) actually exists by way of contemporary literature or architecture. Even ancient accounts, which are based on even older accounts, don't always agree. And those oldest accounts? Even those were written decades after the lives of the dynasty. The only impactful contemporary work (from the Roman side), Julius Caesar's Commentaries on the Civil War, mentions Cleopatra briefly—that too in a dispassionate and dry manner as Caesar recounts major events. But he says absolutely nothing about personal characteristics or relationships (understandable, given his tricky situation).

One of the most important things to be aware of is that almost everything we know about the principal characters comes from a stilted *Roman vantage* written a hundred (*Plutarch*) to two hundred (*Dio*) years *after* the major events in this book!

Imagine reading a recently written book about a popular political character that lived a hundred years ago, written by an author who was fundamentally aligned to a regime that was *against* that figure, by using accounts mostly from people of that regime! I provide a detailed notes section at the end of the series to explain some of my thinking.

It is important to recognize that this trilogy is a *novel*, and at its heart, the purpose is to take you to an ancient world and entertain you. This is not an academic paper! Having said that, I have tried to maintain general alignment to major milestones of the last decades of Ptolemaic rule, and many events and descriptions of ways of life are borrowed from historical sources.

The rest, well, how do you know *it didn't happen?*

ANACHRONISMS

an act of attributing customs, events, or objects to a period to which they do not belong

Writing in the ancient past sometimes makes it difficult to explain everyday terms. Therefore, I have taken certain liberties so that the reader is not burdened by linguistic gymnastics or forced to do mental math (how far is 60 stadia again? What is an Artaba?). My usage is meant to convey the meaning behind the term, rather than striving for historical accuracy. I hope that you will come along for the ride, even as you notice that certain concepts may not have existed during the period of the book. For example:

Directions—North, South, East, West.

Time—Years, Minutes, Hours, Weeks, Months, Years.

Distance—Meters, Miles.

Measures—Gallons, Tons.

DRAMATIS PERSONAE

———◇———

Ptolemy XII Neos Dionysos Philopator Philadelphos–King of Egypt, twelfth ruler of the Ptolemaic dynasty, derisively called "Auletes" (Flutist)

Cleopatra–Second daughter of King Ptolemy XII

Arsinoe–Third daughter of King Ptolemy XII, Cleopatra's younger sister

Ptolemy XIII and XIV–Sons of King Ptolemy, younger brothers of Cleopatra and Arsinoe

Pothinus–First Eunuch of the Royal Court, Regent, Chief Advisor and Tutor to the Royals

Theodotus–Teacher of rhetoric, advisor to the Royals

Apollodorus the Sicilian–Commander of Cleopatra's army

Achillas–General of King Ptolemy's forces

Gaius Julius Caesar–Roman Consul, General

Pompey Magnus–Roman Consul, General

TERMS

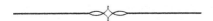

Gladius–a 1.5 to 2 ft. long sword, typically used by Roman soldiers

Uraeus Crown–the Pharaonic crown with the upright cobra in the front

Shendyt–Egyptian attire: skirt-like garment worn around the waist, falling to the ankles.

Chiton, Peplos–Greek gowns

ALEXANDRIA

AUGUST 29, 30 B.C.

———————◇———————

The cool basalt floor hid the cauldron of emotions as she waited for the man to arrive. The massive oak doors remained closed. It was dark inside, with a single column of light gliding through an open window, forming a rectangular pattern on the floor. Her two attendants fidgeted nervously. One came near her, fussing over the slightly ruffled robe, smoothing it. She adjusted her diadem and straightened a few unruly curls of her reddish-brown hair.

"Iras. Leave it alone."

"Yes, Your Majesty," Iras said, and retreated into the darkness.

From beneath the doors, the Alexandrian sunlight made a futile attempt to bathe the floor, failing after just a few inches. But movement outside signaled arrival through a play of shadows.

She waited. She had only suggested that he see her. She was never the one to seek an audience. The fine robe irritated her chest, raw from the ritual beating by her own open palms as she had previously mourned the death of the man she loved, and on whose future she had linked hers. The red welts were calmer now, with a medicinal salve applied gently over them, and then protected with a soothing rose paste.

The shadows shifted—a distinctly different pattern from that of the guards. The door creaked and opened inward. She flinched as the impatient sun, unhappy at being kept out so long, rushed in and smothered her in his warm embrace. And there, with the blinding light to his back, was the silhouette of a man.

He walked in quietly, and his men stayed back. Her eyes adjusted to the light as she studied him.

This is him?

She was surprised. The man in the purple toga looked like a gangly teenager. He was only a few years younger than her, and she was nearly forty years of age. He made no sign of respect or supplication. Here she was, a divinity of the goddess Isis, worshipped by her people, and there he stood, with no sign of reverence. She had heard much about him but had never seen him.

He shifted on his feet. He moved awkwardly. There was no confidence of a conqueror. He was not as tall as his uncle and had none of the burly handsomeness of the lover and husband who had died in her arms a few days ago.

Perhaps she could still come out victorious in this situation, like she had many times in her life, in other difficult circumstances.

His eyes refused to meet hers. They danced furtively, glancing every which way but at hers, like a nervous love-struck young boy mustering the courage to talk to a girl who waits for him.

But she knew. His eyes showed no devotion, no admiration, no affection. In fact, they showed nothing at all. The glassy-gray eyes had no mirth in them.

"Your Majesty," he said, finally. His voice was slight, hoarse, almost whispery. Heavy yet characterless, like wet sand. Like a boring tutor's.

"General," she said. She would not call him with the term he most desired. A rank higher than what he aspired to. A rank bequeathed upon him by a great man who she once loved.

He looked back. Iras pointed to a stool in the corner, and the man modestly walked over and pulled it towards him. A simple, wood-carved three-leg with a fine dark-brown cushion.

He sat. He kept his knees together. *Almost like a woman,* she thought. And then he placed his palms on his thighs. He brushed his curls to the side but continued to look at the floor.

"You walk in here like you are a conqueror," she said almost playfully. Her Latin was accented, and thus she was hampered by her inability to play with the words. In Greek, she could string words like magnificent plays or mellifluous music, appealing to the mind and the heart. She could take her voice to sumptuous highs and perilous lows, enthralling her listeners. But she knew this man responded to Latin and little else.

Should have spent more time neutralizing my accent. Speak like one of his own.

The conversation would be direct.

Simple.

She expected him to smile. Or laugh. Or retort with something. But he did none of that. He continued to stare at a different section of the floor.

He arched his back, and then stared at her feet.

How do I engage this man who refuses to look at my face or reason with my voice? she wondered.

"Your armies are finished. Your man is dead," he finally said.

"My armies stood down to avoid needless bloodshed, General," she said. "And my husband gave his life to prevent more conflict."

He finally looked at her. A cool, composed stare. The unblinking stare of a man studying his opponent's words. Measuring. Calculating. Choosing a response.

He took his time. And she knew she could not snap her fingers and have him obey her commands.

"So you say. My demands are simple."

Her cheeks reddened and heat suffused her face. "You land here, in my sacred city, threaten us, spread nefarious propaganda about our ways, and wish me to believe you?"

And you do not know that my son, borne of a great man and who, one day, will replace you, is now on the way to India, to bide his time, she thought.

He placed his palms on his thighs again. His eyes were like a crow's. "You seduced great men of my nation and made fools of them for your own benefit. You drew a sword on my sister's dignity by causing her divorce. Your man sought to break our republic while cavorting in bed with you. And you say it is I who spreads propaganda?"

His voice rose a little. It rasped more when he was excited. She liked it. That meant he *felt* something. And when a man felt something, it could be taken advantage of.

She leaned back and rested on her fine ruby-red pillow. "You are a man that knows the immense burden of rule. Your women have no voice. You think that all the impieties and improprieties are men's domain, and therefore you are threatened by the manifestation of a goddess who behaves as if she is a man."

He appraised her. The slightest smile passed his lips. "I am threatened by nothing."

"And yet, here you are. Knowing that without my endorsement, you will have little of Egypt's treasures or its people's cooperation."

"It was you who sought an interview," he said evenly.

"I only politely asked if you wished to meet me, and here you are."

He looked at a dark corner of the vast chamber. And finally he said, "Your children are under my protection."

Her heart pounded against her already hurting ribs. She was weak, having eaten less in the last two days, after recovering from a fever caused by the inflammation of the raw wounds on her chest. She allowed her attendant to wipe a sheen of sweat of her eyebrows, even as the man watched, dispassionately.

"Spare them. They seek to do no harm. They are babes in the battle between great nations," she said, her chin trembling. Sufficient to invoke pity, she hoped, even if the act was partly true. Her children were all she had left. Not her kingdom. Not her army. Not the men she loved. Not her generals.

"You defied me every step of the way. You sought an alliance with a man you knew desired to do me harm," he said. His voice had risen again. But worryingly, he had not answered her demand to spare her children.

"I did no such thing. It was ten years ago. He coerced me into an alliance–"

His hand shot up, his palm facing her, as if to say *enough!* She was taken aback. No man, except her lovers who fought with her in the privacy of her rooms, had ever demanded that she be quiet. She took a sharp breath.

"You seduced him using the most devious means. You clouded his judgment. I know all about the ship in Tarsus. Your extravagant, bacchanalian parties. He coerced you to nothing!" he rasped, and yet when he spoke, he continued to stare at a meaningless space near his feet.

She controlled her smile. "I did what a divine ruler and a Pharaoh of Egypt would do. Why do you begrudge me to do what my people expected of me when you have played politics with endless lives yourselves? I played no part–"

"You sought to entice Herod to turn on me. You provided ships to guard your lover's navy's rear and ran when you realized there would be no victory."

He speaks like a mathematician, devoid of emotion.

She looked at him with tearful eyes. "I wish to speak of your mercy to my children."

"And I wish to speak of reparations. Of payments to my men. Of peaceful transition."

"In return for the safety of my children. For assurances that they will succeed to my throne."

He raised his head, finally looking her in the eye.

What a strange man, she thought. *A conqueror. No doubt a man desired by women of all ages, and yet so awkward.*

"I assure you of nothing beyond the just treatment of yourself and your children."

A gentle wave of relief swept over her. Perhaps there was a future.

"That would–"

He leaned forward, cutting her off again.

"But you should accompany me to Rome with them."

TWENTY-TWO YEARS EARLIER

PART I

maps data: Google (c) 2021

CHAPTER 1

ALEXANDRIA

POTHINUS

The three royals walked along glorious colonnaded halls lined with sphinxes, trailed by guards, and led by their tutor.

Pothinus, the tutor, the highest-ranked eunuch of the royal court and advisor to His Majesty Ptolemy, was today taking them on a trip to one of the most respected sites in their city. Alexander's mausoleum, called the *Soma*. There, he would impart wisdom to the youngest member, the ten-year-old Ptolemy Theos Philopator—*Ptolemy, god, Father-Loving*—one who would be king in due time. The boy's two sisters came along, mischievous as they were, wishing to needle their brother while relishing the visit themselves. He knew, as he had tutored them too, that they intensely desired to be here–a location even they were not allowed to visit when they wanted.

There was hushed silence when they finally arrived in the grand sacred room, its walls made of the finest marble and painted with murals of the great conqueror's deeds, its columns decorated with vines of gold, and the floors alive with the most magnificent blue-and-orange patterns.

In the center was a sarcophagus, quite plain. The lid was thick glass, sufficiently transparent to gaze upon the mummy of a great man who had died three hundred years ago. Pothinus was always pained by the forlorn look of this sarcophagus, once glorious with lustrous golden plates and rubies, now all stripped away due to their father's mismanagement of finances and indebtedness to the bastards in Rome.

The royals stood quietly while Pothinus turned and addressed the young prince—skinny, short, wearing a fine white tunic held at the waist by golden threads.

"The first Macedonian Pharaoh of Egypt," Pothinus said. "A god to the people, a king to your great-great-great-grandfather, one who ruled the world before the gods decided he belonged in their company."

Ptolemy walked closer to the sarcophagus. The glass was higher than his little majesty's eye level. He was a slim and short boy. Pothinus raised an eyebrow at an attendant, who scurried away to bring a stool.

"No, wait," said one of the teen girls, His Royal Highness' sister, with a serious tone. The attendant froze and waited.

"You should probably bring a ladder," she said, and the two sisters began to giggle.

"Your Highness Princess Cleopatra!" Pothinus reprimanded her, as was his right as her tutor. He was perhaps one of the three people in the entire world who could raise his voice to the royal children and refer to them by names, as circumstances permitted. "And you as well, Princess Arsinoe. Behave yourselves."

While they were sometimes insufferable, as girls of their age are sometimes wont to be, Cleopatra was Pothinus' favorite. Sharp, quick-witted, willing to learn, manipulative, and stubborn, she challenged him and kept his mind fresh as a garden of roses. She was sixteen and readying herself to be a regent, though His Majesty had not yet appointed her so. For this occasion, she had dressed in a lovely white Greek gown and made sure to tie her hair in a bun, wore gold bracelets, and carried with her a bronze staff that she loved to point at things and pretend to be a tutor. Cleopatra had an oval face, a prominent nose with a slight high bridge in the middle, and beautiful glass-gray eyes. When she smiled, a dimple developed on her right cheek.

Cleopatra's sister, Arsinoe, wore a sheer blue silk drapery tied around the waist with silver threads. She wore a pearl necklace and three gold rings with ruby studs. Of the two, Pothinus thought quietly, Arsinoe was the truly pretty one, with her sharp nose, dove-like eyes, and elegant face, though she was a challenge to deal with because of her fiery temper and reckless mind.

"Yes, Pothinus, whatever you say," Cleopatra said with a smile, even as she elbowed her sister.

His Highness Ptolemy, used to their needling, wagged a ringed finger. "Father will hear of this!"

"Father will hear of this," imitated Arsinoe, shaking her head theatrically. Arsinoe was two years younger than Cleopatra, feisty and often unruly.

"Alright. Enough. My Prince, please ascend the stool and gaze upon the great conqueror," Pothinus said, even as he eyed the sisters and gestured *be quiet* while allowing a smile to escape.

They spent the next hour with Pothinus summarizing Alexander's conquests, his relation to the Ptolemies, the glory of the Ptolemies, and the children's own roles in this world. It always fascinated them, no matter how many times they heard or read about it, that their forefather Ptolemy I Soter was a companion of Alexander the Great himself, had fought by his side for years, and then had become the satrap and Pharaoh of Egypt after Alexander's death. They were also tickled by the fascinating fact that Ptolemy Soter had hijacked Alexander's body while it was on the way to Macedonia, and brought it to Egypt.

Pothinus tried to mollify the boy-prince. "You are an embodiment of a god, Your Highness, and one day you will rule this great kingdom from a throne–"

"A stool. Maybe a ladder!" said Arsinoe, and the girls dissolved into peals of laughter, causing Pothinus to admonish them again. *Should not have brought these two along!* Cleopatra had a sweet voice, like her mother's, soft and lilting, and she was adept at modulating it. Arsinoe still had the crackling voice of a young teen that broke when she laughed.

Tears sprang to Ptolemy's eyes. "I will have you both executed!" he yelled, imitating his father.

That would not be the first time, thought Pothinus, for this dynasty had no shortages of executions amongst themselves.

"No one needs to die, Your Majesty. You must pardon the insolence of your sisters," Pothinus said, even as the girls composed themselves.

"Besides, one day, one of them will become your wife and will have to listen to you," he said with a flourish.

At that, their faces fell, a sight Pothinus enjoyed somewhat.

Ptolemy grinned. "You will do as I command!"

Arsinoe crinkled her nose and Cleopatra pretended not to hear. The lectures were over, and they would return to the palace, where they would shift to loudly reading works of great Greek masters while balancing thirty-foot long papyrus scrolls. The hours could be long and grueling, their throats sore from the recitation and feet aching from sitting cross-legged. But Pothinus thought the children did well, considering the tutors could not beat them, and discipline was reserved to kneeling or being told on to the king, who sometimes thrashed them to obedience. And thrash them, he did, even if rarely. Young Ptolemy still had bruises on his thigh, and Cleopatra had permanent scarring on her forearm, the effect of a bamboo stick.

Pothinus fell behind Ptolemy and walked beside Cleopatra. "You should stop harassing him so, Your Highness. Little seeds of anger in a young mind can grow into fertile trees of revenge. One day he will be king."

"He is just ten, Pothinus. He won't remember."

"Does your bright mind not remember the days when you were ten, the games with Berenice, and your reluctance to travel to Rome with your father?"

Cleopatra fell silent at these words, no doubt remembering very well what had transpired years ago.

The young princess has much to learn, Pothinus thought.

"Your father has ordered your presence in a week's time. He desires for you to begin participating in administrative matters."

Cleopatra beamed. Arsinoe chimed in, "Why not me?"

Pothinus regarded the younger girl. "Your time will arrive, Your Highness."

"She always gets the first chance," Arsinoe pouted.

"Because I am older! Have you forgotten that Berenice ruled for two years in our father's absence? Not me," Cleopatra said. Ptolemy had walked far ahead, his little crown bobbing on his head and his gown trailing on the spotless floor.

"She was mean," Arsinoe said.

"Now she is dead," Cleopatra retorted, and they both grinned.

There are no certainties in your own lives, princesses, Pothinus thought, for in how many families had a father executed his own daughter, as His Majesty Ptolemy had done to his daughter Berenice?

There was a commotion out front, and a courtier came running towards them. He knelt before Cleopatra and Arsinoe.

"Your Highness, His Majesty has become severely ill. The royal court requests your presence immediately. Your Excellency Pothinus, yours as well."

CHAPTER 2

ALEXANDRIA

POTHINUS

Court officials had to make hasty preparations for appointing a regent due to the king's rapidly deteriorating health. Ptolemy Dionysos–the children's father–had not spoken for two days. Physicians tended to him, hopeful that he would regain his faculties and return to his duties. Pothinus, as the principal advisor and the First Eunuch of the court, had the king's ear. His Majesty had more than once told Pothinus that he valued his words. *There will come a time when I must decide who will sit beside me as regent. My son is too young. I will seek your opinion,* he had said, and unfortunately once in front of Arsinoe.

And now Arsinoe would not let it go. Of the two sisters, she was the more stubborn and hot-headed one. She was like a wild horse, untamed, and only afraid of one man–her father–who was now incommunicative. She cornered Pothinus as he hurried to the royal quarters where he was summoned. Physicians had sent word that His Majesty had regained consciousness.

"Pothinus!" she yelled, her crackling teen voice reflecting off the stone columns of the vast hall.

"Your Highness, I must see His Majesty at the earliest," he said, not slowing down. Pothinus was tall, and his legs demonstrated a sense of urgency. But Arsinoe sprang like a gazelle, her brown-black hair bouncing as she gained on him. Pothinus resisted the urge to run, for that would be the most comical scene. As much as he was the children's tutor and guide and appointed with special privileges by the king himself, there were limits to his liberties.

"Wait. I must speak to you," she said, now close. Pothinus increased his pace, fervently hoping for the distant door to appear in front of him. But that was not to be.

"Pothinus! I order you!"

The girl was unstoppable.

"Yes, Your Highness," he sighed as he stopped and turned.

"I heard he is awake," she said, looking up at him.

"As have I, Your Highness, and I have been summoned. I must–"

"He will appoint a regent, won't he?"

"It is His Majesty's decision, Your Highness. And I do not know what the king wishes to do."

"He is going to appoint a regent," she said stubbornly. "He will appoint Cleopatra!"

"Who His Majesty wishes to–"

"She is like Berenice, Pothinus, do you not see? She is cunning, and she will try to get rid of Father!" Arsinoe said almost frantically, surprising Pothinus.

"She is older than you, Your Highness, and I think we both agree that the king decides who it will be," Pothinus said, desperate to get away from this dangerous, uncomfortable conversation. The walls had ears, and not all of those ears were favorable to Pothinus.

"He listens to you, Pothinus. You should tell him that it should be me," she said, fixing her sparkling eyes on him.

Her intensity will one day burn her, Pothinus thought, but he had to defuse the situation.

"If His Majesty wishes to–"

"Of course he will!"

Let me speak, child!

"If his Majesty wishes to know of my opinion, I will make sure to mention your wonderful strength and intelligence, Your Highness," he said as he leaned forward, almost addressing her as if she were the pupil.

Arsinoe did not seem convinced. "I am not in your class," she retorted, her eyes flashing impatience. "You should tell him that Cleopatra is like her older sister, conniving and not with my father's best interests at heart."

Pothinus regarded the girl. She was fourteen and saw herself a queen. She swayed between the haughtiness of a princess with ambition, and a temperamental teen who thought they knew more than they did and were distracted by new things.

"I will convey my reservations about your sister, Your Highness, but you are gracious enough to recognize my difficulties in speaking ill of any child of His Majesty's."

"Yes, yes, I know," she clucked. "But you can use the right words. Perhaps you can get Theodotus' help. He is probably there in the chamber as well."

Theodotus. *The rhetorician, big mouth and a bigger ego,* Pothinus thought. He had nothing to learn from that bloated head, who was another tutor for the royal children.

"I will, Your Highness, and you know that I will always have your best interests at heart," Pothinus said as he bent lower to bring his eyes to the level of the feisty princess. Arsinoe was short, and Pothinus almost had the urge to lift her up, like he did when she was younger, and tell her to calm down.

Arsinoe finally smiled. She patted his shoulder. "I know. You may go," she finally said.

Pothinus regarded the energetic princess. What drove her to these swings between affection for her sister, and anger towards her? He had never really asked that question.

"Princess?"

"Yes?" she said, suddenly looking vulnerable.

"Why do you fear your sister so much? I see you both laughing and spending time together, and yet here you are, worried," he said gently, in the soothing voice of a tutor.

Arsinoe's features softened. She wrung her palms together. "I have read all our family's history, Pothinus," she said softly. "And I cannot forget."

Pothinus understood. He did not respond. Instead, he took both her hands and told her, "But you have nothing to be worried about."

"It is easy for you to say. I am sure all the tutors in the past said the same too, to the ones who died. Many of my forefathers and mothers have killed off their husbands, sisters, brothers, mothers, fathers. It is frightening. I like Cleopatra, but you know that she is clever, Pothinus! She will kill my brothers and me. I am sure of that," she said fearfully.

How could he assuage the fears of a fourteen-year-old who, in a moment of maturity, had said aloud what he had himself pondered about? Cleopatra had two younger brothers—the youngest one still a toddler.

Arsinoe took a deep breath. And then, as she turned to walk away, she paused. She stepped close to Pothinus and whispered, "I saw it."

Pothinus was confused. "Saw what, Princess?"

"Berenice," she said, still whispering, referring to her older sister.

"What about Berenice?"

Arsinoe's eyes became moist. "Father did not know I was behind the pillars..."

Pothinus' heart began to race.

"On his orders, they dragged her away screaming. She was crying and shouting when they cut off her head in the walled garden near my room. There was so much blood! I saw it all," she said, almost becoming hysterical. "She used to beat us and say hurtful things. And I heard she had her husband strangled. Cleopatra may become like my father, or her!"

"Oh, you poor child," Pothinus said, extending his arms like a father. He held Arsinoe briefly. "Your personal tutor Ganymedes and I will protect you, Princess," he said. "And I can assure you that your sister has never once, not even as a joke, ever said she wishes to rid herself of her siblings. She loves you. Now go, Princess, for I must hurry to the king."

Pothinus knew then that this fear would never leave Arsinoe—and the fear, combined with her temper, would pose a great challenge.

Arsinoe turned to her maids, who were waiting at a distance, and sprinted towards them, no doubt suddenly anxious about a different matter that was most important to girls of her age.

Pothinus sighed. He knew this was not over.

He rushed to the king's chamber. His Majesty had awakened, and he seemed to have sufficient clarity of mind. The king often lost himself in his music festivals and bouts of drinking, all of which increasingly worsened his health.

After the initial courtesies and small talk, the king prepared to discuss the question of regency.

"Cleopatra is of age and should be ready, but Arsinoe is not one to be dismissed," Ptolemy said. Pothinus knew that the king loved both his daughters, cherishing specific characters in each. "My son will have to wait."

Pothinus agreed. It was wise to let His Majesty speak some more before opining on the matter himself. There were others in the room, and no doubt some reported the happenings back to the princesses.

The king looked sickly. His large eyes had a yellowish pallor, and his ample jowls sagged, a sign Pothinus knew to be a result of excessive drinking.

King Ptolemy turned to Pothinus. "What do you say?"

"As Your Majesty indicates. Her Highness Cleopatra has the age and intelligence, and Her Highness Arsinoe has the fiery countenance fit for a princess."

Ptolemy smiled. "You say much, Pothinus, and yet you say nothing."

Pothinus grinned at the king's astute observation. "It is my honor and privilege to tutor and advise Their Highnesses, Your Majesty, and I am like a mother who cannot favor one hungry child over another."

The king nodded. "Achillas is not here," he said.

"The general is dealing with self-important mercenaries causing mischief outside Alexandria, Your Majesty," an adjutant said.

"I am tired. I wish to retreat from some of my daily duties," King Ptolemy said. "And since none of you will give me firm opinions, perhaps Arsinoe it will be. I will announce tomorrow."

Pothinus was surprised. His Majesty stared at the men around his bed, who kept their heads low and said nothing. The king's eyes shifted to Pothinus, who first squirmed, and then he mustered the courage.

"Your Majesty…"

"Yes?"

"May I take this opportunity of your presence to bring to your notice another matter of importance?"

Ptolemy gestured for Pothinus to come closer.

Pothinus leaned forward, confident that if he whispered, then no one could hear. "May I offer an opinion on the choice, Your Majesty?"

The king nodded. For all of Ptolemy's long list of shortcomings and failings, one redeeming feature of the king was that he would at least listen to his advisors, even if he ignored most of what they said.

Pothinus whispered, "Regency requires nuance and the ability to connect to the common people and listen to them, Your Majesty. Princess Arsinoe has the fire of a warrior within her, but what you need is someone who can administer, and not one who charges to battle. The lion is still on the throne," he said diplomatically.

The king broke into a smile. "What use is an advisor who does not speak when he must?"

Pothinus retreated. The audience looked to the king, who raised himself and sat upright, resting against a pillow.

"I have decided," he said.

CHAPTER 3

ALEXANDRIA

CLEOPATRA

Cleopatra entered the royal chamber with a mix of trepidation and confidence. She had walked these halls hundreds of times, and yet to set foot in them with authority was a distinctly different sensation. A week ago, amidst chants in an incense-filled sacred room, she had been appointed regent, taking over many of the administrative duties her father once carried out. She had watched him dispense justice and pronounce edicts, formulate rules and conduct negotiations, all from this magnificent hall with its soaring columns, richly painted walls, and various Greek and Egyptian statues of lions, bulls, and falcons.

Pothinus stood behind her, and the many court officials lined around her chair. Philippas, one of her new advisors, stood nearby. Her father's throne was empty, and Cleopatra seated herself on an ornate cedarwood chair with silver threading and striking blue cushions. The audience, which remained kneeling until she took her seat, now stood and made vigorous noises of admiration, raising their hands, gently slapping their cheeks, bowing to and greeting her.

"Those who wish to sit, may sit!" an announcer proclaimed, causing the older and the infirm to take advantage, while many others continued to stand.

"Her Majesty Regent Queen Cleopatra, on behalf of His Majesty, king of Upper and Lower Egypt, beloved of Dionysos, King Ptolemy Philadelphos, will administer the proceedings. We will begin," a court official proclaimed loudly.

The morning was meant for her to receive her subjects from all quarters of the kingdom: from Alexandria, Memphis, Thebes, from the remote western oasis towns, Pelusium, Siwa, all under the rule of the royal house. The first few topics were mundane—a matter of family dispute (*the daughter is entitled to the second house*), dealing with rowdy Roman rascals who cheated a local merchant (*four lashes and a fine*), a penalty for a high-handed tax official (*suspension for a hundred days*), complaints about insufficient funds to a temple (*you are too greedy*), and so on.

The proceedings paused briefly for her to rest and return.

"It was more interesting to watch," she said as her advisors trailed her.

"Such are the burdens of a regent, Your Highness," Pothinus said, and she nodded.

"I will return when I am ready," she said, and dismissed them. She retreated to her royal chamber and lay down on the luxurious, silk-heavy mattress. Her back ached from sitting on the chair for hours.

She had almost fallen asleep, fanned by her slaves, when a knock woke her.

"Your Highness, we must continue," Pothinus said from behind the curtains.

The carefree days are coming to an end, she thought, but she was eager to show her ability to rule. After all, Father may not live longer. And once he was gone, she would be the one with the last word.

Not her sister.

Not her brothers.

The next case involved a tax dispute. The collector had accused the date grower of under-reporting the quantity by half, thereby evading tax, which led to the collector falling short and being written up for his performance. The accused, a rough-looking old Egyptian man with not a hint of knowledge of Greek, maintained that the collector was a liar. After scuffles and threats, given the collector's position and the Egyptian's high standing in his town, the matter had finally reached Alexandria.

When brought forward to address the Regent Cleopatra, the accused fell to his knees and looked around frantically for how he could represent himself in a very foreign-looking court without the aid of a translator.

"Your Majesty, glorious divine Isis, I bring to you a concerning matter regarding the collector," he said in the language of his land as his eyes darted to the Egyptians in the court, unsure how his words would be conveyed. It was clear from his demeanor that he had never seen her before, or perhaps any royal.

"And I have been told briefly what that matter is," she said, her voice carrying in the room. She employed the skills taught to her by the rhetorician Theodotus. *Raise the voice, pause, let it ring in the hollows, slow it in the end, let there be weight to it.*

The man almost fell in shock, hearing her speak in his language. Cleopatra noticed the surprise in the hall, and from the corner of her eyes, the proud and beaming Pothinus and Philippas.

She prided herself on being the first Ptolemy in three hundred years to speak Egyptian. She knew that speaking the tongue of the commoners was critical to gaining their adoration–a far step from distant admiration or fear. She hoped that adoration would cause men to rise up in defense of a ruler, and a woman at that.

The Egyptian made some more gestures of supplication, and Cleopatra asked him to explain the case. Pothinus inched forward, closer to her, ready to offer any advice.

"I have been faithful and honest in my payment of tax, Your Majesty, and for every fifteen standard-carts of dates produced, I pay three to Your Majesty's collectors. I have done so for the last thirty inundations."

"He lies, Your Majesty, he–" began the collector, a burly Macedonian who seemed to have an excellent grasp of Egyptian along with Greek.

"Have I allowed you to speak?" she asked, turning to him. The man shrank to his corner, apologizing profusely for the transgression. *"You may continue."*

"The last three times, this collector has accused me of a shortfall of produce, and that I have only allowed him to collect one-and-half. But I have had no shortfall, and I have given him three. He asks me for donkeys–"

"Donkeys?"

Pothinus' beer breath warmed her ear. "Animals are sometimes demanded to make up for a shortfall."

"I only have a few, Your Majesty. What injustice is it that I must pay my dues and part with my few donkeys, and then be forced to hire workers for doing farm labor? What gods would allow such travesty!" His voice trembled with emotion, and she saw him trying to control the tears in his old, weary eyes.

She turned to the collector. "What is the tax value of the three carts?"

"Four hundred drachmas, Your Majesty," he said.

"So, the shortfall is two hundred drachmas from this man."

"Yes, Your Majesty," the Macedonian said.

Cleopatra conferred with an administrator by her side, and then she turned to him.

"I have heard you built a nice new house on the western edges," she said, causing confusion to the Macedonian.

"I, ah, yes, yes Your Majesty. A humble abode."

"And they say it cost you four thousand drachmas."

"Something like that, Your Majesty," he said, looking concerned.

"And my accountants say you have been here thrice, not before me, but before the *Dioketes*, complaining of tax under-reporting from other farmers. And each time, always keeping the values to a few hundred drachmas."

The man's face fell. He began to stutter.

"You thought I would never take the measure of a man and check his behavior. Here is what I will allow: you shall tell me the truth now, before I investigate this further, and leave with a just but small punishment—or lie, get caught, and be put to death. What would you prefer?"

The man's legs shook, and he fell to his knees. He babbled about his nefarious bribery and tax appropriation schemes and begged for mercy. The crook had threatened farmers in his region, pilfered a portion of the produce, sold it for his own profit, under-reported the tax, and then in turn tried to pin it on the hapless villagers, who usually kept quiet out of fear and the worry that the Macedonian would prevail in the court. He just had not seen that this case would end up in front of the regent, who knew the language of the villagers and took administration more seriously than her father.

"Mercy comes with penalty. Your house is forfeited to the state. You shall pay this poor man a thousand drachmas. And you shall receive three lashes. You are dismissed from service."

The man kept his head low and accepted his fate. The guards took him away, and Cleopatra addressed the accuser. *"You have come here with the truth, and the collector is being duly punished. Should you not receive your compensation, you are allowed to come before me again. May you let your people know that the regent Cleopatra brings justice."*

At that, the old man prostrated before her and his tears wet the pristine floor. They led him away gently. A powerful sense of purpose surged through her, and as exhausting as it was, she realized that she loved the process.

When she finally rose to conclude the affairs of the day, the surprise and admiration of the hall was palpable. The people knelt before her, and she dismissed the audience and prepared to return to her quarters—tired, but secretly elated at her performance.

"You were commanding and confident, Your Highness," Pothinus said.

She smiled at him. Perhaps he would also–

"Yet you were lacking at times with the projection of your voice, and the strength of your words, much necessary–"

"No queen is perfect on her first day, Pothinus, and I am not my father's age," she snapped, irritated at the criticism.

Pothinus' face fell, and he tried to recover. "I was only–"

"You were exceptional, Your Highness, exceptional," Philippas chimed in. Cleopatra's spirit rose again. She needed advisors who offered support and elevated her, instead of putting her down.

"Do I have to do this every day?" she asked to no one in particular.

A court administrator trailing nearby spoke. "Three or four times every seven days, Your Highness. Those seeking your audience have already traveled for days or even weeks in advance."

It was a strange feeling, *responsibility*. All these years, she had witnessed her father at work, her court officials and advisors show and speak of decision-making, and finally when it became real, large parts of it were just... burdensome. And yet, there was something fulfilling about it.

Why would she need to share the power with someone else?

Just then, another official sought her attention. "What is it?"

"Rome, Your Highness. There are rumblings from our western neighbors, and a messenger waits with their many demands."

CHAPTER 4

ALEXANDRIA

CLEOPATRA

———◇———

Rome had been a thorny issue. Cleopatra had spent a few years in that dirty, smelly city with its narrow roads, shit, carcasses, and narrower minds. Where her father often told her of the men with no scruples or morals. She had understood little then. But over the years, with the many briefings from her advisors and by watching her father's discussions, she had come to realize that Rome, to which Egypt was already shamefully indebted due to her father's follies, was becoming increasingly dangerous.

She granted the Roman an audience the next day, against advice—after all, it was not her advisors' call.

The genial-looking, white-haired, toga-wearing Roman was waiting for her when she arrived in the room. He did not kneel but instead preferred to bow.

The man looked surprised. His eyes shifted to the empty throne, and then towards the two men who stood by her side.

He wonders where Father is.

"You have messages from Rome?" she asked.

The man cleared his throat. "Is your father not in attendance, Princess Cleopatra?"

"I am the regent now. My father is unwell."

The Roman shifted his gaze towards Achillas, the commander of the army, who stood to her right. "Pompey has a message for His Majesty."

"It is I that you should address, unless you prefer to return with no response to Pompey," she said acerbically.

The Roman shifted uneasily, and when Achillas reprimanded him for disrespect to the throne, he finally resigned to speak to her. She knew Roman attitudes towards women were not flattering, as she had witnessed a few years ago and had read much about.

"Pompey expects Egypt to stand behind him, should there be a need. The people of Rome and Pompey count upon Your Highness."

Cleopatra turned to Pothinus and whispered, "Why this reminder now? Have they always not demanded our money and grain?"

"Perhaps they believe there will soon be a shift from His Majesty King Ptolemy to your brother. This is just a seemingly friendly reminder," he said.

Cleopatra bristled at the suggestion. *Why her brother? Why not her?*

She turned to the Roman. "And Rome will always have an ally in us. Does Pompey have a specific message?"

She remembered Pompey. The powerful general who was now immersed in the strange politics of their land, where a gang of unruly "senators" held sway rather than a king or a queen. He had spoken to her like a kindly uncle when she was in Rome, and she knew that her father had spent countless hours and coin in trying to gain Pompey's support for his reinstatement to the throne in Egypt.

The man shifted on his feet. "Nothing specific, Your Highness, except to reiterate that Pompey Magnus counts on your–"

Pothinus whispered in her ear. "This unsophisticated idiot wishes to say that we are specifically indebted to Pompey and not necessarily to Rome."

She controlled her smile. *Why not say so plainly?* These men had strange notions of decency.

"And to Pompey we are indebted," she said, causing the man to smile broadly. He seemed satisfied with the response, and she had no desire to probe him on what Pompey *specifically* counted on them for.

After the Roman left, Cleopatra engaged in a lengthy discussion about the Romans and their desires with Pothinus and Achillas. There was no question in her mind that the Romans would not go away, and that Egypt's large debt to Rome, and Rome's interest in Egypt, meant she would be asked to rule on matters that she did not understand too well.

It appeared to her that Pothinus, along with Achillas, had a good understanding of Rome and the Romans. Her father had for too long ignored interference and not paid enough attention to how Egypt should manage this looming power.

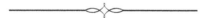

The next two weeks were full of worries; her father remained soporific and had more than once made it amply clear that he had no intention of returning to his administrative duties, and was barely coherent when Cleopatra sought his counsel.

Rome, even if far away, was threateningly near. Alexandria was experiencing grain shortages leading to small riots in certain dense quarters. And her opinionated sister–

"Cleopatra!"

There she was again. Arsinoe's demeanor had changed since Cleopatra's appointment to the regency. Her sister's playfulness had been replaced by a mix of hostility and petulance. But her advisors had assured that the temper would cool as Arsinoe grew older. For now, her sister had to be managed.

"Yes, Arsinoe," she said, smiling broadly.

"I heard the Romans were here making demands," her sister said, placing her hands on her hips as her face displayed great concern.

"As the Romans always do."

"And I heard you said we would be indebted to them!"

If only Pothinus could keep the matters of state to himself!

"We do owe them money that Father borrowed. It does no good to antagonize them."

Arsinoe looked at the skies and sighed loudly–a familiar expression of exasperation. "You should have threatened them that if they came asking again, we would cut the repayment in half!"

Cleopatra smiled. She held her sister's hand. "If it were only that simple—or perhaps if you were by my side, like the fiery sun, the Roman might have run away in fear."

Arsinoe almost smiled, and then she started something else. "You are too lenient. Kings and queens must be tough. Ruthless."

Cleopatra laughed at her sister's definitive proclamations. Unlike her, Arsinoe had not yet been schooled in the art of state, and had not spent enough time with her father to understand the burdens of a ruler. "And diplomatic. And clever. And resourceful. Have you forgotten all the lessons? Plato. Aristotle. Euripides. Homer?"

Arsinoe shook her head. "Even Pothinus thinks you are too soft."

"Did he say that?" she asked, sharply this time.

Arsinoe deftly changed the subject. "How is this new advisor, Philippas? Is he not too young to be one?"

"He is more than twice your age. He has a calm head and knows much about the administration of our countryside."

"Well, don't fall in love with him. You are supposed to be a regent."

Where does she get these thoughts?

"Arsinoe!" she exclaimed, and began to laugh. Cleopatra swatted her sister. "Why is it that you are here? I must go attend to other duties."

"Now that you are regent, you behave as if you are beyond my reach," Arsinoe complained. Cleopatra realized that she would need to speak to Pothinus to understand her sister's behavior. Surely, Arsinoe knew that as the older sister, Cleopatra was lawfully in line for the regency.

Cleopatra cupped her sister's face. "You will always be my dear sister, and just because I am busier with duties imposed upon me by Father does not mean you are forgotten. Next month, why don't we spend two days by the zoo, eating and enjoying the music?"

Mollified, Arsinoe finally broke into a smile. "Fine. If Father suspects you are with Philippas, he will have your head," she said, teasing.

Cleopatra shook her head with exasperation. Did her sister not realize that the days of teasing were over? That as a divine incarnation, she could not be associated with commoners, even if by way of playfulness?

"Be careful where you utter those words, Arsinoe," she chided her sister, even if her lips were curled in a smile. "We are no longer little children."

Arsinoe sighed again. "I was just *teasing*! Anyway, I leave your highness to her *administrative duties*," she said, exaggerating the words, and Cleopatra decided that the conversation must end before her sister picked another quarrel.

"I know you were, Sun of the Palace. I must go now to handle my *administrative duties*," she said, mocking the words herself, and turned away to walk to her waiting maids and advisors.

CHAPTER 5

ALEXANDRIA

CLEOPATRA

Pothinus took the royals–Cleopatra, Arsinoe, and the two younger Ptolemy brothers—to the grand zoo. The zoo was in the western edge, separate from the main palace but still part of the massive complex. Cleopatra knew that to maintain and run a zoo was expensive, but it was such a wonderful feature that she had made sure to continue funding its expenses, even as she looked at how her tax revenues had to be spent. They rarely came here, and all the siblings were very excited.

Cleopatra hoped to use this happy day to alleviate some of Arsinoe's fears.

They entered through a grand gate guarded by two massive granite lion statues. The menacing beasts, with their shiny-black polished surfaces, poised as if to pounce on the visitor, were a thrilling sight all by themselves.

The zoo was designed to keep in harmony with the central plan of Alexandria. A broad central pathway of cobblestones, lined with trees and small statues of various birds and animals, began at the entrance and ran straight through to the end. On either side were fenced areas or enclosures holding the animals, fanning perpendicularly from the central path. The exhibits began with parrots and other colorful birds in giant cages hung from trees.

"I really want to see the elephants and giraffes!" said Arsinoe, wide-eyed, enjoying the walk. Cleopatra held her sister's hand in her right, and the youngest Ptolemy's in the left, as the other Ptolemy brother bounced from fence to fence, shaking them and yelling wild, incomprehensible things.

"Are you a monkey, brother?" Cleopatra called to him. He pretended to behave like one while running farther away.

They walked on, watching wild dogs, antelopes, deer, camels, and peacocks. The attendants of various sections bowed to them and described the animals and their behavior.

"Did you know that wild dogs attack their victims' balls?" Cleopatra whispered to her sister. Arsinoe looked horrified, and then after a thoughtful moment helpfully suggested that perhaps the Egyptian army should recruit wild dogs and let them loose on Romans. The two giggled, imagining various obscene situations with wild dogs and their hated enemies.

Pothinus kept a respectful distance while explaining the nature and original habitats of the beasts.

They watched hippos lounge lazily near an artificial stream.

"They are the most dangerous beasts. They look lazy, but they are fast, with a terrible temper," Pothinus said. "Many of our farmers die because they are lulled to complacency around the hippo."

"Like a fat Arsinoe!" Ptolemy said, leading everyone to laugh loudly. Arsinoe chased to beat him.

With them out of earshot, Cleopatra walked next to Pothinus. "Does she still worry about me, Pothinus?"

"As it is in her nature, Your Highness. The fear and resentment are a result of the family's history," he said in a flat tone, conveying the facts.

"What can I do? Should I just ignore her?"

"Let me keep an eye on the princess. You should focus on your rule, Your Highness. The nature of men and beasts is not always easy to understand."

Arsinoe came back running, gasping for breath, having soundly thrashed her brother, who was still laughing while rolling comically on the path.

"Are you both conspiring against me?" she said, smiling.

"I am planning to marry you off to the ugliest king in all of the East," Cleopatra said.

"I am pretty enough that a handsome king will kill my husband and take me," Arsinoe retorted, and then proceeded to complain about how far it was for her to see some elephants and lions.

They were finally most thrilled when they came to the open areas, protected by giant iron-post fences, but holding the most magnificent prizes. Lions. Leopards. Giraffes. Zebras. Elephants. Many purchased or procured through conquests in Nubian lands and farther south.

Cleopatra enjoyed the shouts of glee and the excited chatter as they learned interesting facts about the animals.

The giraffe sleeps, and even gives birth, standing. (Pothinus)

Lion prides will often roar together and be heard miles away. (Pothinus)

Elephants live for over a hundred years! (Pothinus), *They still look younger than you, Pothinus!* (Cleopatra)

It is the lioness that does most of the hunting, while the male lion lazes most of the time. (Pothinus)

I am a lioness. You are just a lazy lion! (Arsinoe to Ptolemy)

You are so proud of being regent that your neck is now like a giraffe's! (Arsinoe to Cleopatra)

I swear I will set wild dogs on your little balls! (Arsinoe to Ptolemy)

Once there was a fat hippo, its name they say was Arsinoe, she was such a beast, all she did was eat, and shit and fart, ho-ho-ho! (Cleopatra to Arsinoe)

They were exhausted by the time the trip was complete, but the walk back was filled with laughter. Arsinoe and Ptolemy uncharacteristically thanked Cleopatra for the trip. "You are not a terrible regent," Arsinoe said as she hugged her sister.

How long will her affection last? Cleopatra wondered.

"And you should stop worrying about me," Cleopatra said as Pothinus watched quietly.

But Cleopatra's mind was becoming restless. She had to decide the roles and responsibilities of her advisors—and Pothinus could not be the one for all matters. She needed his experience for what she perceived to be the larger, more complex problems—like Rome, and Alexandrian mobs. Pothinus had a fine mind and a wealth of experience, having dealt with Romans for decades. When Rome came knocking, she thought, the knocks would only increase in frequency and urgency, until they rammed the door in.

She would make Pothinus the chief advisor for all western affairs and Alexandrian administration, whereas Philippas would counsel her on all other matters of Egypt, some of which were more urgent because of the recent drought.

CHAPTER 6

ALEXANDRIA

POTHINUS

"Surely I am capable of advising you on all manner of subjects, Your Highness. To split the chief responsibility in two will take away an advisor's ability to see intractable problems as a whole, incorporating Egypt and outside," Pothinus protested.

Cleopatra would not budge. "The challenges are too many, and I need your counsel on matters most dangerous, Pothinus. Do you not see it? You are the ears and voice of reason to my brother, you manage my sister, and you advise me. There are only so many things an advisor, even the First Eunuch, can handle. Besides, father still seeks you when he is awake."

"And I can delegate my responsibilities, Princess Cleopatra. Your young regency needs–"

"I have decided, Pothinus, and we will speak no more of it," Her Highness said. Her eyes flashed a warning.

Pothinus bristled at this curtness. *The child has grown her wings, and the goddess is manifesting herself,* he thought. How much had changed so quickly–it was not too long ago that she would come running to him for all manner of problems, from broken terracotta dolls to 'men looking at her funny.'

He bowed to her and knelt. "As you wish, Your Highness. I will be the hawk that watches over Rome and the unruly thugs in our streets, and should you ever seek my thoughts on any other matter–"

"I will not hesitate to find you, should Philippas' experience fall short," she said, smiling this time.

When she dismissed him, Pothinus, deeply upset, left the quarters. On his way out, Arsinoe, who was probably observing from a distance, made sure to join him and complain some more. And she too was unhappy about Philippas taking a principal role with her sister, cutting her and Pothinus off.

Pothinus reflected on his own life. Born to a pious Egyptian family and gelded at a young age for priestly duties, he knew the pain of a searing hot knife well before most of his kind. Pressed into the service of temples, and then to tutoring and administration, he had risen from Her Majesty's grandfather's time and knew the complexities of governing Egypt. He was sure through his observation that for an immature girl, no matter how intelligent, to seek control at so young an age would be a disaster. He had given his life to the kingdom and had amassed no less influence and power for himself. For him, the company of women afforded no pleasure, but the company of power offered succor—and she was trying to take that away.

He could not let that happen.

CHAPTER 7

ALEXANDRIA

PHILIPPAS

———◇———

Philippas separated the curtains and walked out grinning from the congested confines of the whorehouse. All the wine had made him lightheaded, and he wobbled. It had been a great two days—he had gone from 'one of the many advisors to the court' to the principal advisor for Her Highness Cleopatra! The position brought with it prestige, power, higher pay, and the chance to enrich oneself quickly. It had taken Philippas' considerable charm, looks, and intelligence to get noticed, and he had been exceedingly careful never to step out of bounds.

It was getting late. Her Highness would return from her jaunt in a day or two, and he had to be ready by then with some impressive reports and advice. He wobbled on the narrow, poorly lit cobblestone street. Only a few people walked around. Lamps hung from the low wooden poles jutting from brick walls. The street smelled of cow dung, and dust coated everything.

It was dirty. Musky. Exhilarating.

He stretched his back and cast his eyes at anyone who looked at him. *I am now the principal advisor, be careful of me!*

At a distance, he could see the gates to the magnificent, falcon-lined avenue that led to the palace.

He had to keep an eye out for those filthy coin thieves who knew how to distract a man and steal his money. The recent droughts had created more unrest in the city, and thieves came out of the shadows—bolder and meaner. The last time one of them tried to steal from him, he had caught the boy, dragged and tied him to a tree, and had his men chop the boy's arm off. He did not have his guards with him this evening–he preferred not to advertise his indiscretions at this sensitive time.

A slight, mousy man bumped into him, and Philippas grunted in irritation.

"Watch where you walk, you oaf!" shouted the man, catching Philippas by surprise. It was a Macedonian voice, without a doubt. He turned to face the man but could not see his face in the darkness.

"Watch who you are talking to, you son of a whore, or I will smash your face into the ground." Philippas took an unsteady step toward the hooded man.

The man stepped to the side, and at that moment a pair of strong hands gripped Philippas' right hand and waist. In his drunken haze, Philippas wondered why they were not reaching for his coins.

"Keep your hands off me!"

He swung and missed. From the corner of his eye, he noticed another figure emerge from the darkness, and an intense, searing pain ripped through his torso. Philippas' military instincts now took over, and he tried to assess his situation. He had once served in His Majesty's battalions and had a modicum of training.

There were three men. One was in front but not in contact, and two were behind him—of which one had stabbed him.

Philippas crouched and turned, facing his attackers.

Now he could see them in close quarters.

The two men were large and appeared fit, and had the stance of soldiers. And each had distanced himself smartly in a wide arc so Philippas could reach one but not the other at any time. Philippas lunged at the man to his right, but he stepped back. A blade sliced him below the chest, and Philippas screamed as a warm gush of blood stained his tunic. He stumbled and fell, and his back hit the protruding cobblestones.

He raised his hands to cover his face and shouted, "What do you want?"

There was no reply.

As Philippas flailed about, the first man stepped forward and plunged a short knife into his chest, stabbing him several times in quick succession, each thrust making a soft squishy sound until it scraped the ribs.

Philippas' mouth opened wide in a silent scream, and he began to choke. The taste of iron and salt filled his mouth. His body jerked as he tried to sit up, attempting to relieve the drowning sensation as his lungs filled with blood.

A hand covered his mouth, and a cold blade pressed against his neck.

The attacker sliced his neck open.

In the last few moments, Philippas' mind tried to comprehend the attack—what had he done? Were they somehow related to the whores he was visiting? Did he owe money to someone? Was this related to his new role?

At a hazy distance, he thought he heard a soft, deep voice: "Rule the heavens, Philippas."

And then the lights in front of Philippas dimmed to utter darkness.

CHAPTER 8

ALEXANDRIA

POTHINUS

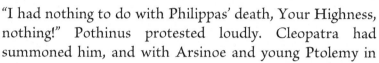

"I had nothing to do with Philippas' death, Your Highness, nothing!" Pothinus protested loudly. Cleopatra had summoned him, and with Arsinoe and young Ptolemy in tow, recriminations were flying high, like sparks from a tree struck by lightning.

"In two days—just two days, Pothinus, since I appointed him—the man is stabbed in an alley of ill-repute. How is it that Philippas lived to see thirty years and died as soon as I appointed him?" Cleopatra asked. Her cheeks were red with anger.

"Maybe Philippas decided to go to the whores in celebration, and got himself killed," Arsinoe yelled, jumping into the fray.

Ptolemy, only eleven, had to put a word in. "Why do men go to the whores? Maybe he likes the whores."

"You be quiet, what do you know about whores?" Cleopatra admonished her brother.

But young Ptolemy stared back defiantly. "I know *everything!*"

Pothinus glared at His Little Majesty, who shrank back.

"Your Highnesses, may I speak in private with Her Highness Cleopatra?" Pothinus asked Arsinoe and young Ptolemy.

"No, I wish to be there!" Arsinoe declared. "It is better for me to know if there are conspiracies."

Pothinus looked at Cleopatra with imploring eyes. *I need to speak to you alone, Your Majesty, not with these two interrupting on matters beyond their comprehension.*

She took the hint. She signaled her guards and asked Pothinus to follow her. "I will speak to him alone," she said icily. And over her siblings' protests, she led him to a room where they could speak alone.

"Why, Pothinus, you had no reason to be threatened," she said a little more gently.

Pothinus was exasperated. "May I speak my mind, Your Highness? Have you ever seen me not have your best interests at heart?"

Cleopatra leaned back and crossed her arms—something she did when she was willing to hear, but not willing to *listen*. "Go ahead," she said.

Pothinus placed his palms together in imploration. He hoped to convince her that he had nothing to do with Philippas' death. If the princess would not step back from her insinuations, then he would have no choice but to go to His Majesty with a not-too-favorable opinion of her Regency.

"What would I gain from having Philippas killed?"

"You were unhappy at the split responsibilities, and I know that you left the palace angrily, disguised, and vanished into the crowds," she said, her lips curled in a knowing smile.

She had me followed?

"As I sometimes do, Princess! Even an old eunuch needs to lament his misfortunes in the privacy of a dark tavern."

"...And then Philippas gets killed."

"Which would make no sense! Even if I were to plot his death, it would be foolish to attempt it so quickly, when the fingers would so obviously be pointed at me. I had absolutely nothing to do with this travesty," he said forcefully.

She relaxed somewhat. She pulled on a strand of errant hair that had escaped the confines of her bun. "You are certainly too clever to do something so stupid," she finally said, smiling. "The brilliant Pothinus, hiring half-drunk assassins to murder a royal advisor."

Pothinus let out a breath. Cleopatra turned to look at a mirror. She was slightly taller than her sister, slimmer, and had a habit of tugging at her earlobes when something bothered her.

"What did you mean when you said that the Romans expected power to shift from my father to my brother?" she said suddenly, fixing her stare at him.

Pothinus stammered, unable to quickly recollect what she was referring to. "I beg your indulgence, Your Highness. What do you mean—"

"When we were addressing the Roman, you said—"

He remembered. Pothinus reprimanded himself for the remark, but there was truth to it. "I meant no implication to your authority, Your Highness. As it is customary and is dynastic law, the first male heir assumes kingship, with Your Highness taking over as Queen. You know the Romans; to them, power flows from the arms of a man."

She shook her head. "Was it not you who taught me about the great Queens of my past—for example, the second Cleopatra, who stood on her own and exercised power that flowed from her breasts?" she said sarcastically.

Pothinus knew that to show weakness in argument would be seen poorly. After all, the First Eunuch would not hesitate to offer frank advice, even to the king himself. Handling a princess coming to terms with her power would be a different matter.

"That may be true, Your Highness. Your authority is not compromised, but it is paired with that of a man in the dynasty. Such are our customs, such is our law, and unlike the barbaric Romans, the great women of the Ptolemies exercise influence by sitting beside the king, rather than behind him."

She had a point. After all, not too long ago, Queen Berenice had one of her husbands strangled because she did not like him.

"My brother is a child. And he is not too bright. When he is made king, what stops him from proclaiming stupid and ill-thought edicts that harm the kingdom?"

Pothinus did not have a good answer. A king's proclamation was just that: *a king's.* There were not many checks against that power–except, of course, the threat of an Alexandrian mob, or strong words from one of the many Roman warlords.

"A co-rule with you as the Queen allows for the checks, Your Highness. Besides, with me behind you and Achillas by your side, His Highness young Ptolemy will make decisions that are collaborative and cooperative. Of that I am certain."

Cleopatra walked closer to him. Close enough to feel her breath on the base of his throat.

"I intend to make the decisions, Pothinus. You and Achillas will advise. But I will be the one who will decide. Not a cooperative. Not a collaboration. Not a council. If the great Alexander did everything by council, he would never have gone against the Persians or reached the borders of India."

You are seventeen, Your Highness, and you are no Alexander.

He bowed to her deeply. "As is your right and divine authority, Your Highness. I shall never forget that."

"I will not replace Philippas. But I will seek you as I see fit, and you will continue to handle the subject of Romans. I will speak no more of the matter of his death, whether you had a hand in it or not."

Pothinus knew that to continue to stress his innocence would do no good and might even raise further suspicion. He dropped the matter.

He would need to speak to both His Majesty and the son, young Ptolemy.

CHAPTER 9

ALEXANDRIA

POTHINUS

Pothinus found the right opportunity to speak to the Little Highness during the next tutorial. The royal children indulged in a rigorous education that lasted for hours each day. The day began with the recitation of Homer, and then, depending on the age of the pupil, progressed to matters of history, mathematics, astrophysics and astrology, administration, medicine, zoology and botany, philosophy, rhetoric, geography, and politics. They sat cross-legged on a hard wooden plank, closed their ears with their palms, and either read loudly or repeated after the teacher. They practiced writing on wax-coated wooden slates. They read, balancing long papyrus scrolls on their thighs. They recited mathematical tables. They remembered countries and trade arrangements. Pothinus was proud of the quality and rigor of the education imparted to the royal children. He was sure that it was the best in the world.

Sometimes much to his own detriment, Pothinus thought.

Young Ptolemy strolled in, followed by his attendants and slaves, and made himself comfortable on a cushion. He had been told that today would be a relaxed day of discourse.

Ptolemy looked quizzically around the room. Pothinus had asked Theodotus, the teacher of rhetoric, to join him. He did not personally like Theodotus, the arrogant big-mouth who thought that just because he was a rhetorician, he was an expert in all matters of governance. But Theodotus had considerable influence in the palace.

"What are we learning today, Pothinus?" he asked. "Are my sisters not joining in the morning?"

Of the four Ptolemy children, three often began the day together. The fourth, the youngest, Ptolemy XIV, was too young to be in these sessions.

"They have matters to attend to, Your Highness," Pothinus said. "I have decided that with the rapidly changing situation, it is time for His Highness to be well-versed in the subject of politics and rule."

Ptolemy was suddenly very interested. "You will tell me how to rule as king?"

"…among other things," Pothinus said.

CHAPTER 10

ALEXANDRIA

POTHINUS

The unrest began small. Just a few angry people arguing with the local granary official, who would not open the warehouse and release additional supply to local shops. But the shouting turned into a scuffle, and soon mischief-makers and others with a propensity to jump into any fracas, no matter whether they had any interest in it or not, joined and amplified the fight. The narrow lane filled with a boisterous and violent crowd that began to break shop doors, set fire to government offices, and steal and loot from homes on the street that eventually led to the Canopic Way and the royal quarters.

The garrison commander, acutely aware of how quickly these events spiraled out of control (not too long ago, the crowds had even managed to make the king flee the town, such was their power), sent a small detachment to put an end to the growing unrest. But they returned, after having lost two of their men, with the rest in tattered robes and with bloodied bodies.

The news reached the palace. While these scuffles were typically handled by Pothinus or Achillas or one of the many regional administrators, Cleopatra heard about the disturbing news and decided to react in the most inexplicable way–she decided to lead a military contingent, along with Alexandria's western administrator and two priests. The area was known for its busy Jewish quarters and a large concentration of Egyptian fishers who went out to the sea, and also Lake Mareotis.

Pothinus begged her to reconsider. "This is a matter for the military, Your Highness. Your father trusted the garrisons with this task, and you have not been trained in urban conflict or riot control."

"This is not a war, dear Pothinus," Cleopatra replied. "These are our people. They riot because they cannot feed their children. What kind of a regent would I be, if I were to send swords their way instead of kindness, as you often told me? Was it not Heraclitus who said that *what you choose, what you think, and what you do is who you become?* And this is who I choose to be."

Pothinus was proud of both her mastery of the classics and how she brought them to bear in her thinking, but also frustrated at her immaturity of thought. Cleopatra had never seen a riotous mob, nor led a small unit on a skirmish—much less led a contingent to tame an Alexandrian mob!

But she would not reconsider. Pothinus was forced to join her as she was carried on a magnificent litter, lifted by thirty slaves, and surrounded by the elite royal regiment dressed in an array of red, green, and gold. The news of her arrival traveled quickly to the riotous areas, causing much confusion and awe. Pothinus watched as the heavily armed regiment began to quickly surround the alleyways, corralling the people and clubbing them into obedience when needed, and began to announce loudly for the troublemakers to halt. But it was not the military action that quelled the unrest, but the sheer spectacle of the future queen herself supervising the calming of the crowds. When she stood, wearing bracelets made of malachite and amethyst, and a crown that cleverly mimicked the sun and ram's horns of a Pharaoh, subtly telling the people that she was *the queen* even if not yet the queen, the rabble-rousers had no reaction but to drop their bricks, poles, stones, crowbars, knives, and swords, and instead gape at the spectacle unfolding before them.

What caused even greater astonishment was when she addressed them, in Egyptian, and then in Aramaic, and then in Hebrew, causing loud exaltations. Pothinus was both transfixed and worried.

"My people," she said, extending her slim arms towards the bruised and riotous crowd, now bunched and pushed against walls and compounds beyond the shield-linked soldiers, "I have heard your complaints. You need more grain to feed your families and to gain strength for your hard work."

There were murmurs in the crowd.

"I have ordered new supplies from the south, and the carts will arrive soon. Go home with the confidence that your bellies will be full!" Her voice rose theatrically, piercing the warm Alexandrian air.

The crowds were suddenly still.

"Let your grandfather's shop thrive as it always did, and your father's carts be unharmed, and your sister's house remain unmolested from these riots."

Many shouted, "Hear! Hear!"

Pothinus, who was on an elevated platform himself, angled behind Cleopatra's litter, eyed the surrounding. They were at an intersection of four crowded streets that converged, and all those streets were full of people. Fires still burned in small pockets at a distance, and there were still plenty of projectiles lying on the ground.

"Scan the peripheries, tell some of your men to discard their uniforms and meld with the crowd. Pay attention to–"

And just then, a brick came flying from the right, barely missing Her Highness' head but knocking off the crown.

Pothinus shouted in alarm, but Cleopatra barely flinched. He saw her eyes reflect fear, but she quickly composed herself and smoothed her hair. Several soldiers pushed their way into the area from which the weapon came, and a group broke into a fight. Someone screamed "liar!" but at the same time, a wondrous thing happened–large sections of the crowd formed a protective outer ring, with men linking their arms as a shield, and many imploring for the princess to return.

Pothinus jumped from his carriage and clambered up Cleopatra's, supported by two slaves who hauled him up.

"Your Highness, you must return. Return now!"

She was breathing heavily, her cheeks were flushed, and sweat covered her face. "See them! They listened to me," she said, showing strange excitement at her power over the crowds, even as she unconsciously rubbed her head.

"They did, Your Highness, but there will not be many more opportunities if they bash your head in!" he said, almost shouting her down like a teacher, and this time she listened.

"Take me back," she commanded. "And bring the troublemakers to me," she said to the commandant by her side. As her litter turned, she stood tall again, waving to the people, some who had now congregated on balconies to see her. Amidst the clamor and the noise, the litter bearers trotted first through the alleyways, and then onto the majestic Canopic Way lined with sphinxes and falcons, until she was returned safely to the palace. Pothinus stood by her side throughout, alarmed and angry.

Recklessness may bring some popularity, but such populism also threatened existing power structures.

Pothinus was beginning to feel very vulnerable.

"You cannot put yourself at such risk, Your Highness," Pothinus argued, now joined by Theodotus. They had sent word for Achillas to join if he could, as he was returning from his mission in the East.

"As regent, am I not entitled to my decisions?" she argued. "Alexander was a general at sixteen!"

Oh dear, not Alexander again. You have breasts and he did not!

"If something happens to you, Your Highness, His Majesty will have our heads on a pike. I am responsible for your well-being, and you should be discussing it with me before you put yourself in dangerous positions!" Pothinus said.

Cleopatra turned away. Pothinus thought he saw tears, but whether that was from fear or rage, he could not make out.

"I will speak to Father to grant me more autonomy. Egypt and Alexandria need a new approach. The people should see more of me. They must feel comfortable knowing that their best interests are being protected. We cannot be sending armies at every sign of unrest."

New approach based on what learning? Pothinus wanted to counter, but now was not the time. Unlike Arsinoe, with her fickle nature, Cleopatra was more measured; eloquent, but more stubborn.

They argued some more, with each side unwilling to concede much. Cleopatra reluctantly agreed that exposing herself in a riot was not the most intelligent of actions, and Pothinus nodded acceptance that her presence had calmed the crowds much faster than otherwise. Theodotus hemmed and hawed and danced on his feet, agreeing with everything and everyone until his words meant little to anyone.

Eventually, Achillas came rushing to the chamber, looking very worried, but with several bound and dragged men behind him.

"Your Highness, why would you–"

"I have heard enough already," she retorted, cutting him off. "Are these men from the riots?"

"Yes, Your Highness," Achillas said. "I have been told that these men set fire to the granary, and were also behind the instigator who hurled a brick."

"Who is the instigator?" she asked.

"We are looking for him. A troublemaker from the Hebrew quarters, I am told."

The men looked on defiantly, even as they knelt. Dealing with Alexandrian ringleaders had always been tricky business. Often, the palace used bribes and enticements for the leaders to buy them off. Rarely were they ever publicly punished, for fear of instigating more trouble through their henchmen. It was a delicate balance–maintaining order and discouraging further mischief. Executing troublemakers was good for the countryside, but not for volatile Alexandria. Once in a while, the men were privately warned that they would receive some lashing to prove a point while being secretively paid to be quiet.

"We will deal with them, Your Highness," Pothinus said as he glared at the men. Achillas nodded–there was a silent understanding of how this would work. Thankfully, the royal children rarely, if ever, dealt with these matters, for the lessons usually brushed away topics on riots as concerns beneath royal consideration.

"How certain are you that these men played an important part in instigating the riots?" she asked, not willing to abandon the subject.

At Achillas' prodding, the men confessed to the attack on the granary and encouraging the looting, with some of the men proudly proclaiming that they were the voice of the people and that Her Highness should be aware of the anger of the commoners.

"You say the commoners are angry, and yet you set fire to their granary and loot their shops," Cleopatra said, her voice now cold.

The leader stuttered and looked at Achillas and Pothinus. Suddenly things were not going to plan. Pothinus knew he had to intervene. He stepped forward and struck the man on his face, causing him to topple from his kneeling position. "You stutter because you have nothing of substance to say!" he screamed. "You will receive a sound thrashing, and may you not forget Her Highness' mercy—"

"Who said anything about mercy?" Cleopatra said, fixing her eyes on Pothinus.

"Your Highness, may we speak—"

"No. We may not. Put him and his two henchmen to death. Then hang their bodies where they threw the brick at me. Post a board that says we will not tolerate attacks against the hardworking people of the quarters and will not allow their supplies to be interrupted by rioters."

Pothinus' blood rushed to his cheeks. Not only had she completely ignored his suggestion, but she was now going against established, unspoken protocols. This would create difficulties for him and the local administrators. The kneeling men began to shout their innocence, saying that they were forcibly brought here without evidence.

"Your Highness, the people see these men as their own! We will enrage them and bring more violence to the streets," he implored, and Theodotus too weakly joined the chorus.

Achillas said nothing, but Pothinus understood his predicament.

"That is how you have always done it, Pothinus," she said, "but that is not how I intend to do it. Was it Parmenio–" and she abruptly stopped, perhaps perceiving Pothinus' reaction to her bringing up another 'Alexander example.'

Cleopatra turned to Achillas. "Let it be done," she said, and walked away from the shouting men and a hapless Achillas.

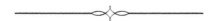

Theodotus hissed under his breath, "If she is this way now, imagine her once she is proclaimed queen!"

"Just look at what she did today. She has no value for any of us. First, it was Philippas. Then, it was her idiotic decision to rush into a riot. And now, she leaves us cleaning the shit she left behind!" Pothinus exclaimed, certain that they were all finally alone in the open hall.

Achillas stood uncomfortably, unsure of what to do. Pothinus goaded him. "What do you say, Commander? Do you think you will have a good night's sleep with her lording over you? She listens to no one!"

"That may be the case, Pothinus, but she is young and is a new regent. Perhaps once she realizes the complexity of rule, she will turn to us? At least she decides, unlike her father," he said.

Pothinus was irritated. "The danger is that power goes into her head, and she gets worse. Her father left the difficult decisions to us, and we men know what is best for this city and kingdom."

"By men you mean…" Theodotus sniggered.

"I have heard every insult and every joke there is, Theodotus, so watch your words," Pothinus said. "It is the mind that thinks, not the balls, even if I do not have two." Theodotus shrank under Pothinus' withering glare.

He turned to Achillas. "You know as well as I do that it is the adults who have managed to keep Egypt from crumbling into dust. His Majesty's lack of leadership and Cleopatra's hasty behavior are both dangerous. A woman with such a mind will bring us all to ruin, and any fool with a sense greater than a donkey's knows that the Romans will get an erection at the thought of a woman at the helm. They will take over us completely!"

"They are preoccupied with their own miserable affairs. Caesar makes noise in Gaul, and Pompey is thumping his chest. I have heard of trouble brewing between them. They will be busy for a while," Achillas said.

Pothinus slapped his own head repeatedly and theatrically. "Are you a fool, Achillas? Do you really think that their quarrels will not touch us? Any one of them will come running to us like a bitch in heat, asking for money or supplies. Take that stupid shining helmet off your head and *think!*" Pothinus yelled at the general.

Theodotus concurred with Pothinus. The man's rhetorical abilities had failed him, but he was clever enough to see the risk of being sidelined. "His Majesty gets worse each day. Have you seen his eyes? They are yellow as honey. They say that it is a sign of his liver dying."

"What is His Majesty's inclination? Do you know what he has promised the Romans, should he die?"

Pothinus shook his head. "I do not. His Majesty has shown no desire to share his thoughts on the matter."

Theodotus adjusted his tunic and rubbed his curly beard. "The question, Pothinus, is will Cleopatra ascend the throne along with her brother if we have no say in the matter?"

"Whether she ascends the throne or not is not the pertinent question," Pothinus said, looking at Achillas and Theodotus. "It is whether we have sufficient control over his Little Majesty who will be king."

The men contemplated their situation.

Achillas was suddenly bolder. The general removed his helmet and rubbed the polished bronze surface. "Might there be a whisper in His Majesty's ears to nominate Arsinoe? Hot-headed as she may be, we can control her."

CHAPTER 11

ALEXANDRIA

POTHINUS

---◇---

The king had worsened significantly. Access to him was difficult, and whenever Pothinus had audience, Ptolemy was barely comprehensible and never in the right mind for nuanced conversations. Finally, Pothinus bribed the royal physician handsomely to alert him should His Majesty be awake and demonstrating clarity of mind.

Pothinus, Theodotus, and Achillas had spent days expressing their frustration with Cleopatra. The display of three dead rioters in the Hebrew quarters caused quite a stir, and Pothinus lost the confidence of a few local leaders, though news was that people were pleased at this action. Then, Cleopatra ignored Achillas' recommendation and imprisoned several *Gabiniani*—mercenaries who had years ago come to instate His Majesty to the throne, courtesy of Pompey Magnus, and stayed behind in Egypt—for stealing several olive carts headed to the port. She also cut Theodotus' hours engaging with her and reduced his pay, stating that all senior servants of the palace had to bear some financial hardship along with the people. Pothinus egged them on, greatly exaggerating these transgressions and causing each man to feel like they had been grievously wronged by Her Highness.

On this day, the messenger who came running had favorable news: The king was speaking and was in good spirits. Pothinus gathered Theodotus, pulling him out of a lecture, and then Achillas, who had remained in station in the palace. The three rushed to the royal chamber where, surprisingly, the king was sitting with his back to the pillows and holding a cup of a hot brew made of lemon, honey, and salt.

The men bowed and came to his bedside. Ptolemy seemed like he had aged significantly in the last year. He was now sixty-six years old. His once thick and generous hair had turned snowy white. His face had puffed up and had an unhealthy pallor. His jowls sagged, and the skin beneath his neck was loose and mottled like a hyena's. The king's hands shook as he balanced the cup. He was wearing a brilliant blue silk robe that hid his now corpulent body.

"You look well, Your Majesty," Pothinus said, and Theodotus joined the chorus.

Ptolemy acknowledged them. "I feel a little better today. So, what brings the three of you to me?"

Pothinus cleared his throat when neither of his companions ventured into the sensitive topic. "Her Highness Cleopatra has been making a mark as a regent, Your Majesty, and we are all awed by Her Highness' mastery of the kingdom's complexities and deep understanding of people's desires."

Ptolemy shifted on his bed. He looked at the three around him, finally resting his calm eyes on Pothinus.

"But?"

The king may be ill, but he is still perceptive.

"You have entrusted us with the safety of this great land, your legacy, and the comfort of our citizens," he said slowly, and his eyes wandered towards Theodotus.

Theodotus took the cue. "It is not just the poor harvest, rising crime, and devalued currency that we have to contend with, Your Majesty, but the unrest in Rome will arrive at our shores."

Achillas joined in. "Alexandria is showing signs of unrest as well. The Gabiniani were—"

"I have heard," Ptolemy said. He pushed himself back and sat straight. The king was a big man, much like his ancestors, and was an impressive figure in his younger days with his broad shoulders, trunk-like biceps, and elegant face. Of course, no man would guess that one day those powerful arms would hold a flute and drown his belly with wine.

The king's voice was raspy. "You have concerns about Cleopatra," he said, almost as if it were a statement.

Pothinus bowed low. "We have no standing or authority to question Her Highness' rights to her decisions, Your Majesty, and I apologize profusely for any such inference. We are deeply worried for her safety, and that of the other royals, and you know that I have never hesitated to voice my fears to you."

"Speak your mind, Pothinus," His Majesty finally said as he handed the cup to an attendant.

Pothinus bowed to the king again. "Your grace is unparalleled, Your Majesty, that you allow advisors like us to utter our views. We," he said, making it a point to sweep his palms towards Achillas and Theodotus, "are of the view that a regency that considers the opinions of the senior advisors on matters of state is a safer, secure bet than one which functions independently."

Ptolemy smiled. "So, she is doing what she wants and is not seeking your counsel."

Pothinus did not show the relief that coursed through him. The king's mind was functioning astutely this day, and he had simply said out loud the thought that Pothinus and Theodotus had carefully crafted through a roundabout choice of words.

"Her Highness displays the individualistic strength of your first daughter," Pothinus said, bringing up the name of the girl whom His Majesty had put to death for her role when he was away in exile.

Ptolemy shook his head. "They are not the same. But Pothinus, is Arsinoe ready? Were you not the one to suggest Cleopatra to the regency?"

And I regret that, Your Majesty. "I am no oracle, Your Majesty, and I erred in my recommendation. An uncontrolled fire may burn a forest."

Ptolemy scoffed. "And you think my Arsinoe has no fire?"

"Her Highness has much in her, but hers is a fire that can be supported and directed to kill the weeds and poisonous vines. She will make an exceptional regent and queen, alongside His Highness Ptolemy, as we navigate these treacherous times. We are all certain of that," he declared. Theodotus and Achillas nodded vigorously.

If any of this conversation traveled to Cleopatra, their lives could be in danger. But they had to take the risk.

Ptolemy sighed loudly. "I know that the gods seek me, and it is a matter of time."

When Pothinus and others made loud objections, Ptolemy waved dismissively. "You all know that to be true. My desire is for Egypt to find a way forward and escape Rome's hold. I agree that the situation is extraordinarily difficult, and I hope that those after me will not make my mistakes."

Your many mistakes, Pothinus did not say, but it was Ptolemy's actions that had put Egypt in a terrible position with Rome.

"The people and we, the advisors, miss your wisdom every day, Your Majesty."

"I have no desire to return to rule. To try to remove Cleopatra now will cause significant unrest, but I will appropriately address the question of succession in my will. Is there anything else?"

That was a sign that His Majesty did not want to engage further on this, but Pothinus was secretly pleased at how the conversation had ended. The men discussed a few other matters, not of as great import, until His Majesty's eyes began to droop. Soon, his chin rested on his ample chest and he began to drool. The physician asked them to leave.

"You are masterful, Pothinus," Achillas said. Pothinus was pleased.

Theodotus went a step ahead. "You may have successfully saved Egypt by placing it in our hands!"

CHAPTER 12

ALEXANDRIA

POTHINUS

The month before the Alexandrian sun would bring a new season, His Majesty Ptolemy succumbed to his illness. His last few months were with little to no communication with his advisors or children, and finally, on a warm afternoon, the royal physicians declared him among the beloved gods. Unfortunately, the king seemed to have thought he would live longer, for he never clearly announced his successors verbally, leaving it to the reading of the will.

The weeks of mourning began, but the palace was tense about what would come next. The Alexandrian people, too, decided to be quiet and await news of succession. Out of an abundance of caution, the royals were placed in separate secure areas, under the security of different commanders with control of different legions. An envoy of Rome, Tribune Publius Cornelius, who had arrived just a few weeks prior on news sent months ago that the king was dying, issued dire threats that any shenanigans that might prevent the reading of the will and peaceful transition of power would be seen very poorly by the Roman Senate. Achillas took over the protective details of Arsinoe and the young Ptolemy, a clever move by Pothinus to ensure that the likely rulers remained in strong hands, while an officer named Apollodorus the Sicilian took charge of Cleopatra and the youngest Ptolemy's protection.

The augurs chose a date for the revealing of the will in the magnificent temple of Taposiris Magna, on the western end of Alexandria. The streets were cordoned off, and the royals; senior advisors; all commanders of the army; the Roman representatives; and the chief priests of Alexandria, Thebes, Memphis, and Ammon, all arrived at the beautiful sandstone temple with its glorious statues of Osiris, Isis, and her child Horus. At the appointed hour, Cleopatra, Arsinoe, and the young Ptolemy XIII knelt in front of the gods' idols and waited for the priests.

Much to most people's frustration, the agreement His Late Majesty had with Rome was that a Roman representative would read the will. This was to ensure the integrity of the process and minimize palace intrigue, and Publius Cornelius was handed the wax-sealed scroll tied with silver threads. Throngs of people waited outside the temple, beyond the tall compound and the gate guarded by two sphinxes.

First, the priests burned incense in the sacred inner chamber in the center of the vast complex, filling the room with a mystic aroma. They chanted various invocations to the gods. Then, they bathed the idols with milk and offered food. This went on for a good portion of the afternoon, creating a heady atmosphere of suspense and anticipation. Pothinus watched with apprehension, waiting for the announcement that would put the kingdom firmly in his control. Publius Cornelius, unaccustomed to these rituals, sat sweating in a corner, looking distinctly uncomfortable.

If only I could snatch that scroll and read it first! Pothinus thought.

Finally, an announcer called to end the ceremony, and asked the people to rise and listen to the will. The priests made a prayer and lit several lamps in the dimly lit chamber. Pothinus' heart stomped on his ribs, and he strained to see Achillas standing on the other side.

Tribune Publius Cornelius finally made his way to the wooden podium. His toga was stained with sweat, and the aristocratic Roman wiped his forehead as he stood on the podium, looking at the distinguished members of the royal family and the senior officials of the court.

He placed his hands in the front, while gently gripping the papyrus scroll, and addressed the audience. "His Majesty Ptolemy has entrusted the People of Rome to protect the interests of Egypt. In my role as a voice of the Senate, I hereby prepare to read the will of the late, glorious King Ptolemy Dionysos Philopator Philadelphos. It is expected that whatever the will may state, the children of the family, the commanders of the army, and the revered priests of the great temples of Egypt shall accept it as written. I will now ask acceptance by each."

Lucius then asked each royal, starting with the eldest, Cleopatra, if she understood the requirement and would adhere to the contents of the will. Each royal accepted, followed by the administrators, Pothinus, Achillas, Theodotus, Metjen (an advisor of Cleopatra), and the senior priests. Pothinus was pleased at the robust nature of the transition, partially made possible by Rome's intervention. But his steps would be to decide a long-term plan to extricate Egypt from Rome's hold.

Once the acceptances were complete, Lucius gently cut the thread on the scroll, and in front of anticipating eyes, unrolled it with a flourish.

He began to read.

The first few paragraphs talked of the king's love for his people, wishes for their prosperity and so forth, none of which excited the audience. Then, there were several awards–free grain to specific families, short-term tax exemptions to certain towns, monetary awards to individuals favored by the king, offerings to gods and so on, some of which had direct impact on the audience; some were happy, and others disappointed. There was not much for the king to offer, for it was his mismanagement that had led to a difficult situation in Egypt. *At least he did not give away what he did not have*, thought Pothinus.

But so far, the king had not hinted at succession.

Lucius slowed down and took a deep breath. The audience was suddenly aware of what was coming next, and an absolute silence descended on the sacred room.

"As king, it is my divine responsibility to ensure peace, strength, and prosperity in this great land. Each of my children is eminently capable of ruling, with the right wisdom and watchfulness of their advisors."

Pothinus smiled at Achillas. Theodotus nudged Pothinus from behind.

"I have entrusted the people of Rome to act as protectors of Egypt–"

Pothinus was irritated at this explicit announcement, but that was something they would need to deal with in time.

"And to bring balance to the rule, I hereby announce to the throne, my son Ptolemy XIII–"

Yes!

Lucius nodded at the young Ptolemy, who seemed overjoyed at this official proclamation. He was now nearing thirteen years of age, and king of an ancient kingdom under threat.

"And by his side, as Queen consort and co-ruler, my daughter Cleopatra. And my will shall be done."

It was as if the dead king had risen from his tomb and punched Pothinus in the gut. He saw Achillas flinch and heard Theodotus curse under his breath.

That fool condemned Egypt even as he died!

Lucius looked at a beaming Cleopatra and nodded at her. Ptolemy looked deflated. Pothinus hoped that the little drops of poison he and company were dropping in his Little Majesty's ears would work to their advantage. The question, he wondered, was how to now deal with this delicate situation where Cleopatra wielded equal power.

As the ceremony came to an end, late in the evening, an unusual storm developed in the sky, with slashing rain and lightning. Pothinus wondered if the weather gods were portending his future.

The coronation of Cleopatra and Ptolemy was a magnificent affair. The king and queen traveled down to Thebes to make offers to gods and the great temples. The procession started from the western edge of the palace, proceeded to the end of the grand Canopic Way, and then embarked on a beautifully appointed boat that took them to Lake Mareotis through a canal. They went by land from the eastern edge of the Lake, and then again on a boat down the Nile. Once in Thebes, they sat on gold-and-gem studded thrones on exquisite chariots drawn by four horses each. Throngs of people cheered from pharaoh-statue lined pathways to the great temples. They watched glorious performances of dance and music, cheered for athletic demonstrations, and then participated in the worship of the sacred bull.

Cleopatra enthralled her audiences with her mastery of their language. She addressed her people, dressed in the classic garb of Pharaonic queens and the embodiment of Isis, and spoke of her love for them and the land, and how she would rise to protect them from the dangers from below, above, far, and within, and they wept and shouted for her.

Every display was designed to overwhelm the senses and enthrall the audience with divinity and complete submission to the royals. Fire performances in thick incense smoke; harp and lyre players sitting inside a ring of fire; women dressed as swans swimming in the river; mesmerizing dramas with Anubis, Seth, and Re; archers who shot arrows adorned with lotus and rose into the sky–every act was designed to awe. The women—many of whom were influential in their own ways, owning farms and vineyards, grain mills, food stalls and perfume factories, papyrus shops and orchards—were overcome by emotion seeing a goddess speak their tongue and talk of their contributions. The boy-king suffered through it all, often resentful and sometimes petulant that he was not getting the same devotion, which forced the administrators to create circumstances and elaborate ruses that massaged his ego.

At each stop, they met delegations of farmers, tradesmen, administrators, and tax collectors, taking their petitions and dispensing justice or granting clemencies, exemptions, and extensions. The acts were designed to mollify the people frustrated by the devalued currency, trade troubles, bad harvest, and general administrative mismanagement in the last years of His Late Majesty's rule.

The couple finished the exhausting trip, successful by every measure, and returned to Alexandria. Ptolemy fell ill with dysentery and Cleopatra lost weight. Arsinoe, who was a silent traveler, was not too happy at being seconded and not receiving the same level of adulation as her sister, but she behaved reasonably all things considered, for her advisor, a eunuch named Ganymedes, had told her that dignified behavior was essential to a *future queen*—and Arsinoe very much saw herself as a serious contender for the throne.

Such was the beginning of Cleopatra's rule as Queen.

CHAPTER 13

ALEXANDRIA

CLEOPATRA

Cleopatra was frustrated at the developments in the countryside. Beer, grain, and fruit exports were suffering due to the devaluation of currency, poor inundation was causing production problems, and the high-handed behavior of some tax collectors was leading angry villagers to chase and beat them. Her brother's solution to every unrest was arrest and death, and she often had to intervene to find new tactics. The "Gabiniani," soldiers of Rome, many who were Celts and Germans but entirely "Egyptianized" after years here, were becoming a thorn due to their lawlessness. She thought that while Pothinus listened to her, or was aligned with her recommendations, he subtly sided with her brother and often used language that suggested Ptolemy had the greater power in the co-rule.

She had summoned Pothinus and Achillas for discussion of certain important matters. Achillas and two royal guards waited with Cleopatra. Pothinus hurried into the chamber, followed by Theodotus. The men were sweating profusely–it was sweltering in Alexandria, and she had made sure to make the message urgent enough, and had chosen a distant corner of the palace, forcing them to cover much ground.

"Your Majesty, you summoned us?" Pothinus asked. He had been her advisor, her tutor, her administrator, even her nanny at times, and how he had changed!

Pothinus was tall and elegant. His shiny bald pate and piercing kohl-adorned eyes, combined with his crackling voice, gave him a sophisticated appearance. He wore a clean, white shendyt, bronze bracelets, and an elegant gold necklace. *All paid for by me and my father,* Cleopatra mused.

"Why are some Gabiniani in our eastern borders, and extorting grain merchants?"

Pothinus looked confounded. He looked to Achillas, who appeared surprised.

"I have heard no such thing, Your Majesty. Have you, Achillas?"

The general shook his head. "All of them are under my command, Your Majesty. I know of no one conducting mischief in our eastern borders."

She appraised them, saying nothing, letting a suffocating blanket of discomfort descend on them. After almost an agonizing minute, she turned to Apollodorus, a captain of her guards. "They say they know nothing."

Achillas made a subtle show of displeasure.

"I beg your indulgence, Your Majesty, but we have received no such reports," Pothinus said.

"Perhaps you are not paying enough attention," said Cleopatra. "For too long you both have left those dogs without a leash. They do what they want, with no fear of repercussions. How do you expect for us to manage Rome, if we cannot handle gangs of unruly soldiers?"

"We have firm control over them, Your Majesty, and they receive no special patronage," Achillas said indignantly.

Cleopatra walked to Achillas and stood before him. The general bowed and looked at his feet. "Oh, Achillas. You are a brave general. Accomplished, like the great Romans and Seleucids. But sometimes generals behave like kind fathers to their troops, and that has been the case with the Gabiniani. You think you have control over them, for you see them too kindly. It is no fault of yours."

Achillas said nothing.

Cleopatra addressed both. "I have an order for you, to be executed immediately."

The two bowed. "Yes, Your Majesty."

"Both of you shall leave to Pelusium, and then to the borders of Gaza to investigate these reports personally. You will come back in thirty days and give me a detailed account of the state of the border and the extent of truth in this news."

Pothinus looked surprised. "Your Majesty, my place is here, by your side, helping to quell unrest and find a path forward to bring solace to the suffering millions! King Ptolemy needs me by his side."

"I will not ascend to the heavens if you are away for a month, dear Pothinus, for you have trained me well. The Prime Minister, *Dioketes,* and the local administrator, *Hypodioketes,* will assist me in regional affairs, and the Tribune has agreed to protect our interests for now. My brother is away for a few days to rest and will not require your services."

She raised her palm to stop Pothinus from speaking more. A court administrator came forward, holding an order scroll. Cleopatra pointed for the man to give the order to Achillas, who accepted it without comment, and bowed to the queen in acceptance.

"You will leave immediately, and I await your return," she said, and dismissed them.

Pothinus looked unhappy, but Achillas maintained his composure as the two left the chambers.

She turned to Apollodorus. "Make sure to have them followed."

He nodded. Cleopatra asked the rest to leave and addressed Apollodorus. "When is my brother returning?"

"In three days, Your Majesty. He remains at the palace by the sea."

Cleopatra walked towards Apollodorus. He shuffled on his feet when she stood uncomfortably close to him. She smiled and stepped back.

"Why have you not married yet, Apollodorus?" she asked.

Apollodorus stammered, "Your Majesty?"

"Why have you not married? You are a man that many women would desire."

He blushed and looked befuddled. "I am at your service, Your Majesty. I have had no time."

"Perhaps I should like it that way," she said coyly.

It was fun toying with these military men, she thought, now that her father was no longer around to control her. After all, she was the queen, and her brother was an idiot.

Apollodorus mustered his courage. "And I obey," he said, almost allowing a smile rise up behind the dark curls of his beard.

Cleopatra stepped back, becoming serious again. "I want you to keep my brother where he is. Relieve Achillas' guards, place your own, and tell him that it is on my orders, for his safety."

"His Majesty's safety?" Apollodorus asked, confused.

"Yes," she said, smiling. "And don't let him leave."

CHAPTER 14

ALEXANDRIA

CLEOPATRA

Ptolemy looked at her fearfully. The boy's eyes were brimming with tears, but he was trying to project strength.

"You are lying!" he shouted, even as his eyes darted to the slightly ajar door, outside which three gruff soldiers stood.

Cleopatra moved towards him and placed a gentle hand on his cheek. He recoiled but did not walk away.

"It is true. You know our history, brother. Why are you surprised that there was a conspiracy to kill you? That is what the Romans want!" she said, her voice soft, gentle, understanding.

"Where is Achillas? I want him here!"

"Achillas is in Pelusium dealing with pirates. I have had to act quickly to protect you. You are safe here."

"I am a prisoner! You have not let me out in seven days," he complained, even as a few drops spilled from his eyes. His cheeks were red with anger, and he paced around helplessly.

"Do you know what the Romans do to deposed kings?" she asked.

Ptolemy did not answer.

"They parade the kings in their forum and strangle them in front of everyone. They also torture them to break their spirit. I heard that–"

"Enough! Why do they want to kill me, and not you?"

Cleopatra leaned back and sat on a cushion. She played with her diadem and patted her bun. "Oh, my dear brother.

A young king is an easy target. Romans do not fear women. They worry that you will become strong and powerful."

Ptolemy's little chest puffed up. "They should worry about me!"

"Which is why they want to kill you first, before you become a lion. A cub is more vulnerable."

"But I am king now. I can order Achillas to build an army and challenge the Romans."

Cleopatra smiled. She walked towards the boy, who was now sitting on his bed. She sat by his side.

"Oh, my dear brother. Has Theodotus or Pothinus taught you about Roman armies and how their barbarian generals behave?"

Ptolemy shook his head. Cleopatra knew that he had not yet come of age to begin the deep discourse on Romans. Besides, the boy was not the sharpest mind, as she and Arsinoe had both often remarked. While she never stated it publicly, and often felt guilty about feeling it, Cleopatra saw her brother to be like her father—weak, lacking sound decision-making and inner strength. Even though she was young then, she had hated how her father supplicated himself to the wretched Romans when they were in Rome, years ago.

"You will learn soon, and you have much to learn to be prepared. They are strong and vicious, and we must be calm and prepare quietly. Did you know that the Roman consul Scipio destroyed the great city of Carthage and killed everyone? Or that Publius Cornelius boasted last month that Caesar has defeated the Gauls, killing many thousands, and will eventually execute their chief?"

Ptolemy suddenly looked unsure. "Are they so strong? Our forefather was a general of Alexander himself. Why can we not defeat them?"

Cleopatra smiled. "Because of the mistakes of our great-grandfather and grandfather. Father tried very hard to build us, but we are still too weak. We need time. I have to build us," she said, emphasizing the I, "until you are ready."

He looked at her suspiciously. "How did you find out about the conspiracy?"

"Publius Cornelius is on our side. Our hospitality and kindness have allowed me to find out if there are darker forces that we may be unaware of, with his help."

"Why did Pothinus not tell me?"

"Because he is away with Achillas and did not know either. Remember your lessons, my brother—when a conspiracy is afoot, those who are its targets and learn of it must keep their steps as closely guarded as possible. Every word to someone who is not family has a chance to leak like a sieve and reach those who may be plotting. You know this from your lessons."

Ptolemy rubbed his eyes and sniveled. "Yes, I remember. How long do I need to be here?"

"Another fifteen to twenty days, until Achillas and Pothinus return. I want them by your side, protecting you, as I alone cannot do it while managing your kingdom, Your Majesty," she said playfully, bringing a smile to his face.

When he calmed, Cleopatra continued. "For our safety, yours, I will be making some changes. Do I have your support if Pothinus and Achillas object? They are not family, brother."

Ptolemy tried to put on a thoughtful face. He finally agreed.

She knew she needed all the time she could buy before they all turned on her.

CHAPTER 15

ALEXANDRIA

POTHINUS

Pothinus was apoplectic. They had found nothing in Pelusium or in the eastern borders; *nothing*! The entire trip was a miserable waste, away from the affairs of the capital, while Cleopatra hatched her devious plans with them away. Had she lied? Just made it up to take them out of Alexandria?

By the time they returned, Cleopatra, with His Majesty Ptolemy's agreement, had made major changes. Apollodorus the Sicilian, an army officer who had risen through the ranks and proved himself to be a very capable commander, had been appointed the Chief of Royal Guard, overseeing both Cleopatra's and Ptolemy's security. Achillas retained the title of general but no longer had authority over Apollodorus and his legions, which accounted for nearly a third of the army. Metjen, an Egyptian of high status and one of Cleopatra's tutors, had become her principal advisor, with Pothinus retaining his title of chief advisor and officer of Roman affairs.

But the biggest slap? She had ordered that Theodotus and Pothinus continue His Majesty's education, and that Ptolemy would recede from public duty until he came of age.

That conniving harlot!

But Pothinus was no fool.

He gathered his two trusted associates–Achillas and Theodotus–and managed to gain an uninterrupted audience with the Roman Tribune.

"What brings all of you, senior men of the royal house?" Lucius said as he avoided Pothinus' eyes at the mention of *men*. Pothinus knew that the Romans always found the employment of high-ranked eunuchs rather unbecoming, but he cared for none of it. A supercilious Roman's discomfort was the least of his concerns.

"You may have heard of Her Majesty's recent announcement, Magistrate."

"I have. A most unusual move. But Cleopatra assures me it is in the best interests of the people and the interests of Rome," he said as he poured himself some fine wine.

Even the Romans have their fair share of idiots.

"If I may, Tribune, does the Senate not care about the balance of rule and stability in Egypt? Does the great Pompey?"

Lucius raised his eyebrows. "Go on."

"Every move Her Majesty has made so far, and I am not saying that she is not entitled to her authority, but it undermines His Majesty. If she gains absolute power, then you should expect great unrest. Do you not remember the trouble under her sister's time?"

The Roman took another sip. He adjusted his toga and looked at Achillas. "What is your opinion, General?"

"Many in the army and administration do not hold very favorable views of Her Majesty," he said. "His Excellency Pothinus knows the affairs of the state. If Consul Pompey wishes stability, then we will need to act quickly, Magistrate."

The Tribune, an elected magistrate of Rome, had much to worry about. Pothinus knew that Lucius' role was not just one of peaceful transition, but also maintenance of ongoing reparations and uninterrupted trade. If he left Egypt in disarray, he would incur the wrath of powerful men.

The Tribune cleared his throat. "What do you propose?" he finally said, looking at Pothinus.

Pothinus looked to Achillas, who nodded. It was time to make it abundantly clear to the Tribune what should happen.

CHAPTER 16

ALEXANDRIA

CLEOPATRA

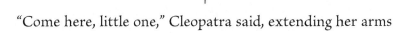

"Come here, little one," Cleopatra said, extending her arms to the toddler who hugged Apollodorus' legs.

Apollodorus gently pried at the child's chubby fingers and cooed at her. "Her Majesty wants you there. It is a blessing. Go, Iras!"

But Iras, with her golden curls and peachy cheeks, had little regard for royalty. She shook her head vigorously and ran behind another shy girl who stood beside Apollodorus.

"What is your name?" Cleopatra asked the girl.

The girl stepped forward and knelt before her. "Charmian, Your Majesty. It is my life's honor to have met you."

"You may rise, Charmian. How do you know Apollodorus?"

"I care for Iras, who is Apollodorus' niece," Charmian said as she gently held Iras' hand and pulled the little girl forward. "Kneel, Iras," she said soothingly.

Cleopatra giggled as Iras knelt, and then promptly settled on all fours to examine the blue and orange patterns on the marble floor. The toddler proceeded to lick the floor, causing Charmian to grab her waist and lift her.

Apollodorus stepped forward. "My brother died in a military campaign two years ago, and his wife had already died in childbirth. Charmian's mother is ill, and her father passed from disease. She cares for Iras, whom I rear as my daughter, Your Majesty."

She nodded. Such tragedies were all too common. Apollodorus was Cleopatra's rock. She depended on him now more than ever. Years ago, he had arrived as part of Gabinius' legion, as a well-trained soldier of Rome, and had settled down in Egypt. His brother too had arrived similarly.

Cleopatra had realized how little she knew about this man who had been by her side loyally for years. She hoped to know him better, even if he was of common blood. And that too a Sicilian, not even Greek or Macedonian.

My forefathers married commoners as well, she thought, and hastily dismissed the wandering muse.

She appraised Charmian. There was devotion in the girl's face. She could not have been more than thirteen or fourteen. If she was trusted by Apollodorus, then Cleopatra could trust her too.

"What do you do well, Charmian?" she asked, even as the girl futilely tried to entice Iras, who was now busy testing the purple cushions by Cleopatra's side.

Charmian gave up on restraining Iras after Cleopatra told her to let the toddler be. "I am well versed in all matters of caring for a child, cooking, and cleaning, Your Majesty. I also oversee slaves and servants at Apollodorus' house and his farm."

Cleopatra smiled at Apollodorus. "I did not imagine you to be a farmer!"

He grinned sheepishly. "My brother, Your Majesty. I tend to it now when I can, for it keeps my mind calmer."

"I hope you won't attack our enemies with radishes and turnips, Apollodorus," she said with mock seriousness, causing Charmian to giggle loudly.

"The cabbages may be more potent, Your Majesty," she said boldly, causing Cleopatra to laugh. *I like her!*

Cleopatra fixed her focus on Charmian. "Well, Charmian, would you be interested in being by my side as one of my maids?"

Charmian stammered and looked helplessly at Apollodorus, who seemed tongue-tied.

Cleopatra continued. "You will be paid well. Iras will receive care along with the others in the royal quarters. You will even get a few hours to learn to read. I am sure the farmer here," she said, grinning, "can find someone else to supervise his crop. Are you paying your taxes, Apollodorus?"

"How can we say no to Her Majesty, divine Isis?" Apollodorus said, almost overcome with emotion. Charmian had tears in her eyes as she accepted the new role. Iras, of course, did not care, for she had proceeded to bang a brass lamp against a pillar until Charmian pulled her away.

They spent some more time with Cleopatra asking them questions on their lives and backgrounds. It was as if the iron shackles of formality had been cut away. This comfortable conversation was such a far departure from the stuffiness of courtrooms and the excesses of royal parties for dignitaries. Charmian was polite, yet witty and intelligent. Cleopatra was enjoying their company when a messenger arrived, bringing news that the Tribune wished for an urgent audience.

What now?

"Bring him in," she said. "Apollodorus, stay with me. Charmian, take Iras with the attendants."

Charmian bowed and left with a howling Iras, who had by then taken a very particular liking to a fluffy cat.

"My apologies about the child, Your Majesty," began Apollodorus. She scolded him and waited for Publius Cornelius to make his appearance.

The Roman arrived, looking healthy but concerned. He bowed to Cleopatra, who took her chair as he stood before her. She decided to skip the small talk and go straight to his urgency.

"What brings you here, Tribune?"

"Certain matters cause concern, Your Majesty. It is my duty to ensure that the affairs of Egypt are resolved amicably," he said, enunciating his Greek slowly, carefully, and very irritatingly. She knew that senior Roman officers struggled with the idea of respecting a foreign ruler, much less a queen, and one only just nearing nineteen at that.

"What affairs, Tribune? We are doing what we must in a drought. We have made our monthly payments, even if with a small shortfall on account of our challenges."

Publius wiped his pate. "It is not so much the question of current payments, Your Majesty, but the ability to continue without interruption."

Pothinus and Achillas must have met with the man.

"And why is that a concern, now that there has been a peaceful transition of power?"

The Tribune looked around for a seat. It was clear that he disliked looking *up* to this girl, but she was in the mood for taking pleasure from his discomfort. "Well, recent developments of your unilaterally announcing changes to the administrative structures and military divisions have created pause."

"As is my right to make those changes, as the older of the co-rulers. My brother does not yet appreciate the complexities I am confronted with. And, it appears, neither does the Tribune."

Publius Cornelius' cheeks reddened at the slight. "The principle of co-rule requires equal voice in major decisions. His Majesty is served by his advisors–"

"He agreed to these changes–"

"Without the presence of his advisors," said Publius, more forcefully this time, cutting her off.

How dare he!

"May you not interrupt Her Majesty, Tribune. This is not the Senate!" Apollodorus raised his voice.

The Tribune gathered his thoughts. He bowed. "I apologize for the breach of protocol, Your Majesty, but it is my duty, on behalf of the people of Rome and your father's will, that His Majesty's interests are protected along with yours. I have conferred with your brother, His Majesty, and it is my decision, and his, that Pothinus is declared regent for the minor and Achillas his protective guard."

Cleopatra was furious. How dare this man decide for *her kingdom*, without her consent, about her brother!

"You may have read Aristotle, Tribune, as have I. Is it not a poet he quotes that *silence is a woman's glory*? That may be so in Rome and Greece. But it has not been the way with the Ptolemies. Our queens have not been silent, and neither will I. My advisors tell me much about not antagonizing Rome, and yet you meddle in our affairs!" She leaned forward and pointed to Publius.

The Tribune was taken aback, but as an experienced politician himself, he did not stutter and run away. Cleopatra knew, after all, that he came with the might of Pompey and Cicero behind him. It is not the python's small head that one must worry about, but its massive and powerful body.

"And you retain that authority, Your Majesty," he said. "But it does not suppose that His Majesty is not entitled to his. And an appropriate balance is maintained by affording him wise regency under Pothinus and General Achillas. I have so reported to the Senate as well."

He was clever. Saying he had already so reported to the Senate meant that going against it would draw ire. She clenched her jaws but bit her tongue. To create greater conflict now, without having assessed her own strength fully and how much of the army and the people were behind her, could be fatally dangerous.

She smiled at the Roman. "I think that arrangement is acceptable. After all, I wish to rule a stable kingdom rather than one that is mired in strife. We are glad you are here, Tribune, for without your will and the support of Rome, we might have devolved into a civil war. Do not interpret my anger as anything more than a new ruler wearing the burdens of a crown."

The Roman smiled. "You are gracious. Pompey Magnus was an admirer of your father, and he wishes nothing more than the stability of this ancient land."

Admirer? More like a pig that wanted to satiate its hunger with our money and grain.

"Of course! And we are indebted to him and deeply appreciative of his support."

They then spent some time on small talk–about her challenges, the situation in the countryside, people's perceptions of the new rulers and so on, until Cleopatra tired of him. Once she dismissed the Tribune, she turned to Apollodorus.

"The gall of the man. Is there nothing we can do to rid ourselves of these wretches?"

"I know little of the politics, Your Majesty. But militarily, they are exceedingly powerful. No amount of diplomacy will keep them away permanently. They are like hungry dogs. There is only so long that they will watch a bone from afar."

She looked at Apollodorus and absent-mindedly played with her hair until she became conscious of her unroyal-like behavior. She brought her mind back to current matters: this man knew about Rome's might—he was one of her soldiers. But how long must she deal with those bastards?

Apollodorus, oblivious to her thoughts, continued. "We cannot hope to beat them easily without training our forces and building an army that is willing to take on Rome."

"Well, then that is what we will do," she said, and smiled at his astonished face.

CHAPTER 17

ALEXANDRIA

POTHINUS

———◇◆◇———

Pothinus' elation at being officially nominated as regent for His Majesty Ptolemy XIII and gaining some control over the direction of Egypt was short-lived. The sands of allegiances had shifted beneath his feet, with some of the powerful administrators and priests having quietly aligned with Cleopatra and rebuffing his attempts to have a say in major decisions.

Cleopatra was unmistakably building *her* portion of the army, against his objections. She had directed precious tax revenue toward expanding Apollodorus' battalions. When he confronted her, she was belligerent, accusing Pothinus of undermining Egypt's security and 'being in Rome's filthy pocket,' and that he and Theodotus were weakening Ptolemy.

The young king, still maturing in his mind—and hopelessly stuck between his manipulative and increasingly powerful sister, and the counsel of the wise and experienced officials like himself—was vacillating in what actions he must take. He had, foolishly and in fear, left his sister to make most of the decisions, which had led to the current travesty of their isolation.

But on this day, Pothinus went with Theodotus to argue about a critically important public relations matter.

The minting of coins.

The need to have both royals on the coin was of paramount importance, for that told the people who the rulers were and that their roles were of equal importance. Every coin sent a message to its holder on who the real ruler was. To every administrator, priest, soldier, farmer, guard, merchant, tradesman, ambassador, dignitary... everyone! And now, this vexatious girl had managed to have the first batch released *without* His Majesty!

"My brother is still not of age! Why are you here to make his case? I am the one ruling the kingdom, and when the time is right, he will be on the coin!" she shouted at him. When angry, which was rare, she squeezed her eyes almost shut and became animated, swinging her arms and sometimes shaking her head in rapid bursts.

"Your Majesty, whether he is of age or not is immaterial. You are co-rulers, and he must find his place on the coin, so people know!" Pothinus implored, trying to control his temper. He was feeling bolder, for the Roman Tribune had told him that what Cleopatra had done was improper, but he was unwilling to talk to the queen about that. *Weasel!*

"You are his regent, Pothinus, not his father. You are burning the mountain of goodwill with me. You were once my tutor, but do not think you can speak to me as an equal," she said haughtily.

Perhaps it was my mistake imbuing you with this spirit and knowledge.

"I meant no disrespect, Your Majesty, but every tip of the scale where one favors the other is a direction towards disaster. My counsel–"

"Your counsel to my father is what led us to this state!" she said, her voice dripping with contempt. "If you were a competent advisor, you would not have allowed him to become a flutist, kissing Roman feet and spending money we did not have."

Pothinus was taken aback. He was aware of Cleopatra's coin reforms. Since the debasement of Ptolemaic currency, she had resorted to minting bronze coins with only a third of silver. While those were needed measures, she had no right to *exclude* a co-ruler. Anyone who looked at past coins would see both the king and queen on them, and she was flouting that precedent.

Pothinus involuntarily stepped forward aggressively, as he sometimes did when the royal children were young pupils in his class. After all, was it not Menander who once said that *He who is not thrashed cannot be educated*, a thought further echoed by their own famous Alexandrian grammarian Apollonius Dyscolus? While Pothinus never laid his hand on the royal children, he had many times disciplined them in other ways.

Cleopatra flinched. Almost as if he were a falcon sweeping from above, Apollodorus rushed forward and gripped Pothinus by the neck. Apollodorus' iron fingers squeezed his neck, and floating figures swam in Pothinus' eyes. Unable to speak, he tried to remove Apollodorus' hand. His ears began to ring, and he heard some shouting and yelling, and the bastard finally let him go.

Pothinus sunk to his knees, wheezing, nursing his throat. Cleopatra yelled, "Apollodorus, what is wrong with you? Stay back. Get up, Pothinus!"

Pothinus rose to his feet. A rage developed in him, but this was not the time or place to display the cauldron in his chest. "I intended no harm, Your Majesty," he rasped, "I was only overcome by the passion of my arguments, as I sometimes was when I taught you."

As he gathered his breath, she addressed him, her eyes blazing with icy fire. "You are no longer my tutor, Pothinus, and you shall treat me as your queen. Nothing less. And you as well, Theodotus."

She leaned back on her chair and adjusted a bracelet. "What else do you wish to talk about?"

Pothinus bowed and looked at Theodotus, who looked too frightened to speak. *Coward. A big mouth at other times—rhetorician, indeed!*

"Your Majesty, you know that His Majesty King Ptolemy will not be pleased with this development. I will have to unhappily report this to him, considering that you two are no longer on speaking terms," Pothinus said.

After Ptolemy had left his unofficial house arrest, Pothinus and Achillas had taken pains to explain to the young king that he had been confined and scared so that his sister could make independent decisions. It had still taken much time and persuasion to slowly change his mind. And then the relationship had deteriorated to such an extent that the siblings no longer saw each other.

"Be his tutors and let him study. He is too young to rule, and his time will come. Now leave," she said, dismissing them. Apollodorus and his guards moved forward menacingly.

Pothinus retreated along with Theodotus. He fumed on his way back.

Fucking bitch.

"How dare she leave me out of the coins? How dare she!" Ptolemy yelled. Pothinus had managed to rile up the young king, and he now paced in his throne room, shouting at the cowering officials, some of whom were from the treasury.

"Why did you agree to mint them without me? It is treason! Have they not told you?" he shouted at one of the men, a senior official in the treasury. Once close to Pothinus, and a merry fellow in bribery and pilferage schemes, he found himself on the wrong side, having gone with Cleopatra behind Pothinus' back. And he still stood there, unrepentant.

"His Majesty asks you a question!" Pothinus added, and the man looked at him with disdain, even as he kept his head low while looking at Ptolemy.

"I did not go against Your Majesty. I was told by Her Majesty that this was the arrangement–"

"And I had told you not to accept unilateral directives without telling us first!" Pothinus shouted.

By then, Ptolemy had worked himself up to a fine rage, screaming about his sister attempting to dethrone him, about officials being guilty of treasonous conduct, and about how they thought he was stupid when he was the brightest king of his age anywhere in the world.

"I want you to halt all further minting, and no more coins without me on them!" he said, pointing to the man.

The official looked confused. "Your Majesty, my orders are to mint them without delay to help the traders and merchants. I cannot stop."

"You were with us!" Pothinus piled on. "You suckled on my tit like a hungry calf for years, building your estates, and now you dare defy our request?"

The man turned his beady eyes on Pothinus. "And you benefited from that arrangement for your own purposes!" he shouted. "I bow to His Majesty, but it is Her Majesty that makes decisions–"

At that, Ptolemy erupted. Spittle flying from his mouth, he accused the defiant official of treason and insubordination. Pothinus hoped that the message was clear, and they would be more careful next time, even if it was too late now. But the man's last sentence had a terrible effect.

Suddenly, Ptolemy stopped. The boy panted and caught his breath. He turned to the royal guard.

"Execute him!"

"Your Majesty! I had nothing–" The man looked at Pothinus frantically.

A guard moved behind the man to arrest him. Pothinus considered his response and decided to leave it be.

Messages had to be sent, and he could absolve himself of this.

As the man struggled and implored, the guards began to drag him away, but Ptolemy, his veins pulsing, shouted after them. "No, here!" he screamed, his childish voice shrill in the hall.

The guards looked befuddled. But the king kept shouting, "Here, here!"

Pothinus was about to intervene but thought the better of it. One of the guards had a metal wire in his belt. He pulled it out and began to garrote the man, who began to struggle and gasp, his eyes bulging from his sockets, and he soiled himself. The wire, instead of just choking him, began to cut into his neck, streaming blood down his body and causing him to gurgle and rasp.

Young Majesty Ptolemy, who had never actually *witnessed* an execution, was horrified. He suddenly shouted, "Stop! Stop!" confusing the guard, who slackened his hold, causing the man's half-severed head to droop down grotesquely. Ptolemy turned to the other side and began to retch, which brought his attendants running.

Pothinus looked at the guard and gestured to continue. The terrible scene continued a bit longer until the man was dead. Ptolemy, still heaving with his face deathly white, had left the chamber with his attendants. Theodotus looked at Pothinus and grinned. This message might send a warning to Cleopatra.

CHAPTER 18

NEAR MEMPHIS

CLEOPATRA

———◇———

Cleopatra recognized that broken communication between her and her brother was causing stress and confusion among the officials and the army. Conflicting orders had to be resolved through a painful and frustrating process of employing intermediaries when neither royal was willing to speak directly to the other. In some documents, Ptolemy's name appeared before hers, a marked departure from the past where she appeared exclusively on all official communications, having excluded Ptolemy.

She had not stopped building her army, and Ptolemy was interfering with the minting of additional coins. Food riots in different parts of the country were being handled in mixed ways; Cleopatra preferred exemptions and pardons, while Ptolemy often resorted to penalties and sound beatings. Pothinus and Theodotus had stopped meeting her, and Achillas was spending more time than necessary with the Tribune, who, she knew, was desperate to return to Rome.

What was more concerning was that several Gabiniani had defected from Apollodorus' legions and joined Achillas, and they were unwilling to reconsider their position. She was sure that Pothinus was behind all this, with Achillas' support. Her brother, lacking hers or Arsinoe's intelligence, was becoming a menace with his temper and willingness to be molded like clay by his conniving advisors.

Sensing loss of leverage and realizing that the continuation of this impasse would alienate her bureaucracy and lead to a civil war, as an act of reconciliation, she suggested a joint celebration with her brother. The royals would go together in carriages, accompanied by senior officials, and show themselves in harmony. They would travel south to the great temple of Amun and Isis in Memphis, offer prayers, and return on a royal barge.

After several days, a response arrived from Ptolemy's side: acceptance. She sighed with relief, hoping that with her persuasive skills and sisterly approach, she could entice her brother back to her camp again. If she could get rid of Pothinus and Achillas, she would regain the upper hand. The only condition was that both parties would not travel with large military contingents. Only a light guard would accompany the trip. The reasons were multi-fold: at times of unrest, traveling with an army would send a terrible message and further alienate the people. The chances of conflict and accident were high, since the two royals had not yet reconciled.

The procession began from the palace, going through the winding roads until it hit the Nile. Then, they traveled by separate barges down the river, followed by their attendants, slaves, advisors, musicians, actors, dancers, and singers. They met adoring and worshipping throngs along the way. At various times, she and her brother managed to make small talk, but with Pothinus and Theodotus hanging around him like vultures it was impossible to have meaningful conversations. She hoped the time would arrive.

On the sixth day of processions, they finally shifted to a land caravan, with Cleopatra and Ptolemy each on their slave-carried litters. She was attended by Charmian, who by now had become her favorite attendant and responsible for all her needs except food tasting. Apollodorus led her royal guard. Achillas was not in attendance (much to her discomfort; could the general be scheming in Alexandria?), but one of his lieutenants led Ptolemy's contingent.

She sighed with relief as the caravan entered a low gorge. The shade combined with cooler wind flowing from the riverside lessened the burden of traveling in the heat. Apollodorus had dismounted from his horse and walked alongside the litter. The area was desolate, with no hint of civilization–a welcome respite and departure from the madness of Alexandria and the continuous din of chants and bells in the temples.

Ptolemy pulled alongside in his litter. He looked at her and smiled. Her brother rarely smiled. Pothinus, who was walking beside Ptolemy, bowed to her.

"Does this travel please you, brother?" she shouted, trying to be heard over the chatter of the walking many and the sounds of nature.

"It does," he said, almost with glee. "The people love me!"

"They are pleased to see their king," she said.

He nodded and looked ahead. "My descent is like nightfall," he said, grinning.

"What?"

Then it flashed to her. He was quoting Homer, except that Homer had said *His descent*, referring to Apollo coming down from Olympus. The boy had learned to quote the great poet.

But why did he say that?

A strange fear gripped her heart. She had heard Theodotus use that phrase whenever he referred to any event that occurred suddenly and furiously. Or when an angry god, or a king with purpose, came down to lay his might on someone.

Cleopatra turned to Apollodorus, who was squinting at something at a distance.

"Apollodorus!"

He did not hear her in the noise of the march. She shouted at him again: "Apollodorus!"

He turned to her. He looked concerned.

"I suspect something untoward might happen. My brother–"

Anxiety rose in her rapidly like water gushing from a broken levee. She broke off mid-sentence and noticed Ptolemy's litter suddenly pulling away from hers, almost trotting.

Apollodorus hastily mounted his horse and shouted for the royal guard to surround Cleopatra's litter.

Suddenly, there was a loud commotion from ahead, and a stone the size of a fist came flying from the side and just missed them.

"Ambush!" Apollodorus screamed.

CHAPTER 19

NORTHERN ITALY - TWO MONTHS EARLIER

JULIUS CAESAR

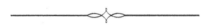

It had been a long march, and he was preoccupied with various thoughts. Caesar wiped his balding pate with a fresh napkin and peeked out of the carriage. It would be dark soon, and the countryside was quiet. Legion XIII, his powerful and feared force that had brought him many victories in Gaul, marched in front and behind. The disciplined and proud unit of 4,500 battle-hardened men would be pressed to service many more times, he thought.

He parted the curtain. "Where are we?" he asked the Centurion walking beside his carriage. The glowing orb was close to setting in the far west, and the sky was suffused with deep blues and blacks that morphed into a glowing orange near the horizon.

The Centurion, dressed in his red-feathered plumes and polished helmet, shouted some questions to the men ahead. "I will report back soon, sir," he said.

Caesar leaned on his cushion. It was as if a thick rope was being tightened around his stomach. Fighting foreign tribes and rebelling populations was entirely different from conflict with his own people and other powerful men of Rome. Pompey, once his father-in-law, had stood against him. The Senate was asking him to disband his army, but not forcing Pompey to do the same, all under the guise of legitimacy.

How grossly unfair!

If he disbanded his army, no doubt the poisonous snakes in the Senate would have him arrested and executed for the various crimes they said he had committed. It was time to stand up for what was his, and to bring Rome under the control of righteous men. He did not know yet if the army had already crossed the Italian border, violating Roman law.

The curtain parted again, and the Centurion stuck his head in even as he kept pace. "We are near the river Rubicon, sir," he said. "Some cohorts have crossed the river–it is shallow. The town of Ariminum is near, about ten miles."

We have crossed the border, he thought as he smoothed his toga. The breeze was pleasant. To the south, he noticed the faint yellow tinge of the town's nightlights.

"Halt!" Caesar ordered the coachman. He stepped out of the carriage and stepped on to the gravelly path. Inhaling deeply, he walked towards the clear stream of the little river.

Caesar shivered in the cold, but he was invigorated. He pulled up his toga and washed his feet. He then stooped to wash his face in the chilly water.

"We are in Italy, then?"

"Yes, sir."

He looked towards the darkening south, his mind experiencing rapid waves of resolve and doubt. His army, most of it ahead of him, had already crossed the river and were slowly marching forward–disciplined and proud.

Rome was in disarray. The eastern provinces were making noises of discontent. He had also heard of some trouble with the brother and sister ruling Egypt, though he cared little for them, as he had greater challenges to confront—Pompey Magnus being the biggest. Going up against that formidable and revered general meant gambling with life and death.

But Caesar was now fifty-one years of age. A veteran of politics and conflict. A man who had subdued the Gauls and expanded Rome's reach as no one else had. A man hailed as a brilliant general. A renowned lover. A hero to the people of Rome.

He slapped the Centurion on his shoulder. "Well, the die is cast. Tell the men we will rest when we reach Ariminum," he said, and tapped the soldier's chest armor.

He would take the fight to the heart of the Republic.

CHAPTER 20

NEAR MEMPHIS

CLEOPATRA

The slaves hurriedly lowered the platform to the ground. Soldiers surrounded the litter and immediately provided a cover over her head, creating a leather-bound, wood-shield based roof.

Blood rushed to Cleopatra's ears as the shields pressed down on her. The light vanished, with only slivers of the sun coming through the interlocked shields. She lay flat and reached down to a ceremonial dagger on her waist. That was when she heard multiple *thuds* on the shields.

Rocks?

She flinched every time a heavy object impacted the shields. The cacophony was muffled–hooves, shouts, screams, and neighs filled the air. Suddenly, the fear vanished, and fury rose.

How dare they attack their Queen? How dare they attempt to take the life of Isis herself?

She tried to push herself up, but was pinned down by the shields. She banged on some and shouted, "Let me up! Now!"

But no one could hear her. She flailed about until she found purchase in a crack between two shields. She pried them apart as hard as she could. And before the surprised soldiers could decide what to do, she was out, exploding from between the shields.

What she saw chilled her, even in the afternoon heat of the desert sun. In the hellish dust that surrounded them, her men fought shrouded invaders with swords and axes. Many lay dead on the ground, friend and foe, and there was no sign of her brother's entourage. She stood, and two of her guards ran around to cover her. "Your Majesty, lie down! Lie down!"

She ignored them and tried to charge towards one of the shrouded men battling with one of her guards. The man was distracted for a moment, a chance that her guard took to strike him down. Strong hands grabbed her waist, pulling her back, and pushed her again into a ring of guards.

Apollodorus.

His teeth bared in a snarl, he shouted at her, "Stay where you are, Your Majesty, do not put yourself at risk!"

She was shocked at the admonition, but before she could say anything, she was tightly barricaded again by heavily armed guards. They would not let her go, even as she yelled and pushed. She calmed down quickly, and that was when a projectile–a chipped stone—came flying through a gap and struck her on the collar bone. She screamed with pain. The guard ring around her began to move, and a soldier turned to her. "Your Majesty, please move with us. Keep moving! Move!"

They held their shields up and fought their way through the melee. She stumbled in a red haze of pain and had to be picked up more than once as she tripped on moving feet.

Cleopatra prayed to the ancient Egyptian and Greek gods to spare her. Just then, she heard a great commotion, and one of her protectors shouted, "Achillas' men!"

Were Achillas' men attacking her? She had survived a projectile during the riots in Alexandria. Had fate ordained that she would die from flying stones?

But there were whoops of joy. She shouted in rage, unable to see anything. She punched one of the burly men and yelled, "Let me out!"

The man, no doubt mortified being punched by her, finally turned and knelt by her. "You are safe now, Your Majesty."

They had moved her to the edge of a bluff below an overhang, protecting her from any projectiles. In front, in the middle of all the rising dust and madness, there was slaughter. Her guards, along with her brother's, were butchering the shrouded men. She wanted to run down, fight with them, act like a general. But the men firmly held their ground, not allowing her any movements except to peek between their shoulders.

A deep sense of doubt nagged at her. She turned to one of the guards. "Tell them not to kill everyone! Tell them to capture some of them! Find Apollodorus!"

The man ran down an incline and vanished into the fighting crowds. But to anyone who saw, the vicious culling of the ambushers was evident–now outnumbered, they fell like flies, their heads flying and their torsos impaled.

Something wet snaked down her cheeks, and Cleopatra tasted a drop of metallic saltiness. She *hated* the smell and feeling of running blood. She tried to lift her hand and grunted with the sharp pain that rose from her shoulders.

Suddenly, the world began to swim.

The blue skies darkened.

Was the weather–

She was on her litter. Two bandaged slaves fanned her. There was a tent shade over her head. Her head still swam, and when she tried to rise, she felt Charmian's palms on the nape of her neck, steadying her. Apollodorus was talking to officers nearby. She could hear the gentle flowing sound of the river.

"Do you feel comfortable, Your Majesty?" Charmian asked. She too was bandaged on her head and arms. Streaks of blood were visible down her neck.

Cleopatra nodded. Her mind was clear and her body energized after water, bread, and several spoons of honey. She was pleased to see Charmian in good spirits. Two of her slave girls had died under a hail of projectiles, and so had several litter-carriers. But they were slaves anyway.

It took some time, but the cooling evening breeze brought life back to her, including anger.

"What happened? Tell me everything!" she demanded of Apollodorus. "Where is my brother? Did they have anything to do with this? That bastard eunuch, he was the one behind all this. Tell me!"

Apollodorus let her calm down. She realized that she was shaking; how unbecoming of a Queen, a Pharaoh, and an embodiment of a goddess! She suppressed the rage and let her mind rest. And finally, as dusk made its presence and the lamps flickered in that makeshift tent, Cleopatra engaged Apollodorus in a calm conversation.

He is fine. Hurt. But Apollodorus is fine.

He explained that the low hills in that desolate stretch afforded easy planning for an attack, and that the attackers knew beforehand the path of the caravan, which was supposed to be a closely guarded secret. The men appeared to be mostly local, though investigations would reveal if this were the result of some fool's idea of a rebellion against the throne, or a more treacherous plot. The problem was that barring two completely clueless men, the rest of the attackers had been butchered in the fight. He said that while her royal guard was handling the skirmish quite well, it had become an utter rout when Ptolemy's men joined, and together they had put every ambusher to sword and spear.

She could see Apollodorus' worries and doubts as he explained. But she had to ask.

"Did you know that my brother's litter pulled off from me just prior to the commotion?"

"I thought I noticed it, Your Majesty, but I was distracted by the flashes in the front. Mirror signals."

"Why did my brother's forces not join you in the initial stages? Where were they?"

Apollodorus looked concerned. He nursed his forearm and looked outside at the flowing water. "It was puzzling, Your Majesty. The attack came only in our direction, on our segment of the caravan. Why did they take so long to come to our aid?"

"Where are they?"

"Camped about a mile upstream. They lost some men, though not as many as ours."

"My brother?"

"He is fine. They have sent word that they wish to speak."

Another trap? Or was it genuine?

"Tell them to leave all their guards behind. Only my brother and Pothinus. On flat, neutral ground. Scout the location. You should have checked before, Apollodorus!"

He seemed offended at the chastisement. "I had not one inkling of this, Your Majesty. I would never put your safety–"

"And yet here I am, with a possibly broken collarbone and bruised neck!" she yelled.

His face fell. Apollodorus bowed to her. "I apologize deeply, Your Divine Majesty, I have failed. It was never my intention. I have failed."

A sense of guilt hugged her gently and squeezed her chest. Apollodorus had saved her. But he had also failed to protect her adequately. But for now, any penalty had to wait.

"We will speak of it later, Apollodorus. Send word back to my brother, and we will hear their story tomorrow."

But Apollodorus was not finished. "This is the second time you have exposed yourself to a dangerous situation, Your Majesty. You should let us soldiers handle conflict."

She stared at him. And then she said, "You do know that Alexander was king at sixteen?"

"Yes, Your Majesty."

"Did his advisors tell him to sit in a tent and watch battles?"

"No, Your Majesty."

"Did he stand far behind eating grapes while his army fought Darius?"

"No, Your Majesty."

"Do kings typically relax with some women when their armies fight?"

"No, Your Majesty."

"Then why am I not allowed to lead from the front? Because I am a woman?"

Apollodorus looked like he would say *yes*, but checked his tongue. "I understand, Your Majesty. It is only my concern for you, and may you punish me for saying this, but it is not because you are a woman. It is because you have not been trained in battle."

She was annoyed, but also secretly pleased that he'd held his ground. He had a point. She relented somewhat. "That may be so," she said. "But I will do it when I see fit."

He nodded in agreement.

"Well, let us see what my idiot brother has to say tomorrow," she said finally, nursing her pulsating shoulder.

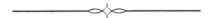

The two parties convened before the day's heat began. Cleopatra walked with Apollodorus, and Ptolemy arrived with Pothinus, with the rest of their mutual guard standing at a significant distance and waiting. They were accompanied by two slaves, carrying basic necessities, should the parley take longer than anticipated.

The air was still cool and calm, hiding the storm in her mind.

Her brother looked small in his bright white linen gown with oversized gold bracelets on his thin wrists. His freckles looked even more prominent today. She thought he looked like a rat when he pouted in concentration. Her neck and shoulder still hurt. The royal physician had assured her that nothing was broken, but the bruise had turned the skin purple. Movements of her neck and left arm still generated waves of pain.

They faced each other and sat on simple stools set by the slaves, beneath a basic canopy that provided some shade from the still young and rising sun. Pothinus inquired after her well-being while her brother sat quietly, saying nothing.

Cleopatra waited for them to explain their story. After all, it was *she* who had been attacked. Finally, after minutes of uncomfortable silence, Pothinus spoke. "His Majesty wishes to convey that my words are his."

She looked at him. This sniveling, oily eunuch had firmly entrenched himself in her brother's orbit. What a transformation from a tutor and guide, to one who was now plotting against her!

"Perhaps His Majesty would like to know if his sister and Queen is well," she said testily.

Ptolemy fidgeted but did not respond. Pothinus, standing beside her brother and looking down, finally spoke. "His Majesty has a concern he wishes to express."

She looked at Pothinus and then her brother, who was avoiding her eyes and acting nervous.

"What is it, my brother?" she said a little more gently. She had to mellow him before accusing them of having planned this. She was certain.

He did not open his mouth but instead began to chew on his lips and rub his palms. Pothinus looked irritated. He cleared his throat and said again, "Does His Majesty have something to convey?" more firmly this time.

Ptolemy nodded.

Pothinus has this little runt under his thumb. What a shame!

She was getting impatient. Perhaps it was time to open the conversation herself.

Suddenly, Ptolemy stood.

He pointed to her and shouted in a shrill voice, "You organized this attack! You are trying to kill me!"

Pothinus watched with no uncertain pleasure Her Majesty's shock at His Majesty's accusation. She almost jumped from her chair and struck her brother, but had to be controlled by Apollodorus, that low-born who had somehow wormed his way up to be her chief protector.

"How dare you accuse *me* of trying to kill you, you rat! It was you who tried to assassinate me. You ran away before the attack began!"

Ptolemy began to shout. His young voice had still not broken to that of a man's, and it was still like a girl's–high-pitched, petulant. "I did not run! I did not run anywhere! It was my guards who came to your rescue, even though you had something to do with it. Tell her, Pothinus!"

The two screamed recriminations at each other—of deceit, dishonesty, and that she had lured them here on the pretext of rapprochement while trying to usurp the throne, and so on.

Pothinus and Apollodorus waited quietly for them to calm down. Any orders during the shouting match were promptly ignored and forgotten. Pothinus finally spoke. "Your Majesties, Egypt requires that the two of you rule harmoniously. We know that the countryside is experiencing unrest, and this is probably nothing more than a local fool taking advantage of this lightly-guarded caravan."

"How did a local fool know of your route, then?" she asked sharply.

Pothinus dropped his voice, like a tutor schooling his children. "Your Majesty, you have seen this land. Men hear of royal trips and transmit them quickly. The ground is often flat, and one can see for miles. It does not take much for one to muster their idiot-gang and mount an attack after stalking their prey. It is trivial, really."

She stared at him but did not respond to the condescension. "Tell that to my brother, who dared to accuse me! Why would I ask those trying to kill him to attack me instead, and break my shoulder?"

Pothinus prevented this from becoming another shouting round by quickly saying that there was no evidence that either sibling tried to kill the other, and that this must be an external conspiracy or foolhardy attempt, and that further investigations would reveal the truth.

But the damage was done. Any hope for reconciliation was dead.

"I will stay in my half of the palace, and we will use intermediaries for joint ruling," Cleopatra finally said.

"I will be ruling, and I don't need your permission. We should divide the regions!" Ptolemy said, using some of the ideas Pothinus had drilled in him.

"Not a chance. I will–"

Pothinus cut her off. "Your Majesty, two additional units from Apollodorus' forces have defected to Achillas. Your army is outnumbered, and more tax administrators and junior *Dioketes* have sworn allegiance to His Majesty. I suggest a truce until we have clarity for the future."

Cleopatra appeared horrified. She looked at Apollodorus, who seemed equally clueless of these developments. "You are conspiring behind my back, treasonous scoundrel!" she screamed. Her reddish-brown hair was disheveled, and she seemed to bite her lip to suppress a sob.

Pothinus had never enjoyed an encounter with her more than today's. But with Ptolemy fully behind him, he continued. "Your Majesty, I follow orders from His Majesty and serve him as his regent. I have done nothing conspiratorial–the people are getting tired and worried about the royal squabbles. They seek peace. I beseech you to maintain balance for some time when tempers are high."

She was breathing heavily. And then, after a bit, she lowered her head and calmed down. "Is there a danger to my life, brother?" she asked directly.

The idiot little Majesty, instead of answering confidently, looked at Pothinus as if he had to respond to that stark question. Pothinus almost stammered before gathering his wits. "Of course not, Your Majesty!" he said, putting on the most outraged voice. "You and Princess Arsinoe are safe. Everyone desires a return to ways of the royal houses, with the king as ruler," he said, emphasizing the *king*.

Cleopatra stared at Pothinus and spoke nothing. Her cheeks were red, and her light-gray eyes were wet but defiant. She stood and grimaced, perhaps due to her injury. "Very well. That is the way it shall be, then. I will appoint new intermediaries who will speak to *His Majesty*," she said, mocking the last few words and swaying her hips in a way she did when she was younger and making fun of her brother.

Ptolemy, still with one foot in his childhood, yelled, "Don't tease me!"

Pothinus controlled the urge to spank him. He bowed to Cleopatra, who stormed out of the tent with Apollodorus and her slaves in tow.

I am dealing with petulant children!

The balance had shifted in their favor.

The trap may have failed this time, but I will make sure the next one doesn't, he thought gleefully. But he was still frustrated over how she or Apollodorus had seen the danger and reacted quickly, so that the full power of the ambush was dulled, leading to its failure.

The idiot little Majesty had no clue at all.

He would need to speak to Achillas and Theodotus on what to do next. She had to go, one way or the other.

CHAPTER 21

ALEXANDRIA

CLEOPATRA

———————◇◆◇———————

An uneasy stalemate prevailed in Alexandria after their return. Once again, laboriously negotiated rules of engagement, ownership, privilege, tax rights and disbursement, jurisdiction, and ceremonial grants governed how officials would act on various occasions. What had become clear to Cleopatra was that she was slowly losing her foothold. More officials defected to the 'Ptolemy camp,' now firmly managed by Pothinus and Achillas with Theodotus following them around. Arsinoe had been subdued for months–now staying quietly with Cleopatra after she'd told her younger sister that she would be in danger otherwise.

Publius Cornelius, the impotent Tribune, had done little to help her. He was all too happy for anyone to take charge, and better if it were not a woman. She had strengthened Apollodorus' forces, made sure to have her representatives in trading posts, and placed soldiers along merchant routes to protect her revenues. She still officiated many ceremonies, and went out when she could, to be seen by the Alexandrians. She still received her subjects, though the frequency had reduced, what with his idiot little Majesty sitting on the throne and dispensing dumb justice with the help of Pothinus the rat and Theodotus the dog.

On this day, she decided to put some of those anxieties out of her mind and instead summoned an artist to do a portrait, to be used as a template for new coins and statues. The man sat in front of a five-by-six-foot clay wall, surrounded by various dyes and pigments. He was talented, no doubt, but he lacked the subtle understanding of how a royal portrait must be made, especially one of a queen. She was getting impatient, and he was strangely argumentative, even if in the politest of manners. Arsinoe being an insufferable twat and Charmian giggling like an idiot next to her did not help. She had asked them to join her, for they were an oasis of casual happiness, away from the stuffy formality everywhere else.

"My nose is too straight. You have to bend it more, so I look more severe," she told him.

"Yes, make it look like a hook. Like an angry crow's beak would be even better," offered Arsinoe very helpfully.

The man—Agoras, he called himself—was at a loss on how to handle them. "If I may say so, Your Majesty, the portrait will do no justice to your beauty–"

"Are you attempting to entice the Queen?" Charmian asked. "How dare you!"

Agoras stammered. "No, no, I was just suggesting…"

"My sister will make a terrible wife," Arsinoe said, almost causing Cleopatra to laugh out loud. The man put his head between his palms.

"Both of you, quiet, or I will have you whipped," she said to them. Charmian obediently shut her mouth, but Arsinoe, of course, would not listen. That was the penalty for bringing her here.

"Agoras, did you not say you came from a long lineage of royal artists?" Cleopatra asked him.

He bowed. "I did, Your Majesty. I maybe new, but I am sure I will satisfy–"

"Look, he used the word *satisfy*. The cheeky bastard!" Arsinoe exclaimed. "We should have his head!"

Agoras looked mortified. "No, Your Majesties, that was not–"

Cleopatra raised her palm to shut him. She turned to Arsinoe, who was grinning, and Charmian had her palm across her lips.

"Guards!" she yelled. "Take these two away. Don't let them in," she ordered. And with much protest, Arsinoe left, but not before telling Agoras that he was welcome to do her portrait anytime, as long as he was naked.

It took several moments for the poor man to compose himself.

"No one will have your head, Agoras. My sister and attendant think they are funny. Let us return to the task at hand."

Agoras looked immensely relieved. He was quite young, maybe only a few years older than her. He was a good-looking man. Perhaps Charmian, who had much interest in painting and statues, might find good companionship. He did not have the rough, soldier-like handsomeness of Apollodorus–

She dismissed the thoughts and turned to him. "Has your father not taught you about the rules of portraying Ptolemaic queens? Have you not seen them?"

"I have seen past portraits, Your Majesty. They do no justice."

She shook her head. "This is not about justice to one's true form, Agoras. The people like to see their royals as men. I must be portrayed with a likeness to my father and forefathers–and that means a more severe look. Do not make me explain this again," she said, sternly this time.

So, the man returned to his craft. He dabbed with his fine brush as she sat quietly, in an elegant gown and diadem, her hair bunched in a bun.

Then he slightly bent her mostly straight and rather long nose (which she hated).

Then he protruded her chin.

Then he made her rounded cheeks more sullen.

Then he thinned her fuller lips.

She knew that she was not as conventionally beautiful as her sister, but she certainly did not look much like the woman in the portrait, who now looked like her grandfather in a woman's wig.

Agoras looked unhappy, making his displeasure known by often looking at her, and at his portrait, and subtly shaking his head. She was amused by this but said nothing.

"Excellent!" she said. "This is the type of portrait that is suitable for the people, Agoras. I will have you back when I wish to have one that actually looks like me."

Agoras bowed to her. "It is my honor and privilege, Your Majesty, to serve the royal house."

She wanted to ask him a few questions, but a messenger walked in urgently. "Your Majesty, the Tribune requests your immediate presence."

What was it this time?

"Why?"

"He says there is urgent news from Rome."

CHAPTER 22

ALEXANDRIA

CLEOPATRA

Cleopatra's brother and his men were already in the meeting hall by the time she arrived. So was the Tribune, along with another Roman, presumably the messenger. Pothinus and Achillas looked at her and bowed, while her brother scowled and said nothing.

Apollodorus stood behind her. Metjen took a chair by her side.

Once they were all seated, Publius Cornelius took center stage. "Your Majesties, much has happened in Rome. You should know of these developments, for they have an impact on your kingdom."

From the looks of it, no one knew *exactly* what the message was. It was clear that the Romans had kept it a secret, which pleased her slightly, for that meant the Tribune had not become entirely partial to Ptolemy.

Pothinus had put on some weight. His once-taut belly had begun to sag, and the kohl under his eyes struggled to conceal the lines. Achillas looked smug as ever.

Publius continued, now with all eyes on him.

"You should know that Julius Caesar, general of the Gaelic expedition, crossed into Italy with a single legion, three months ago."

There were murmurs in the room. Metjen leaned to Cleopatra and whispered, "A returning general is required to disband his army before entering Italy. To not comply is against Roman law and punishable by death."

Cleopatra was aware of the rules of *Imperium*, but not with sufficient clarity.

"Fearing that civil war that might endanger the citizens, Pompey Magnus and his close confidants have left Rome, and are now gathering in Greece to prepare for battle with Caesar and end his criminal conquests."

Publius studied the faces of his audience. Cleopatra chose to be quiet. She wanted to hear the message first before offering commentary. Besides, in her precarious position, she had to choose her words carefully.

"Caesar's criminal acts will be punished. The great Pompey is building his forces…"

"You told us that already, Tribune. What must we make of this fight in Rome?" she asked. "We will seek cordial relations with whoever prevails in the end. What happens in Rome is of little concern to us."

Publius made a show of moving around. "Egypt owes Rome seventeen million and five hundred thousand denarii, Your Majesties. The repayments have been slow. It is understandable, given the challenges, but now is the time for Egypt to repay a small portion in favor of the winning alliance."

"That is just over five thousand talents. Tribune, you know that we are nowhere near capable of paying such large sums when our people are starving," she said. Perhaps the Tribune knew that she was not entirely truthful, for the kingdom had much more than three thousand talents. But why should they part with it for two squabblers?

"No, Your Majesty," Publius said. "Pompey does not seek payment in full. But he asks for a hundred ships and a thousand soldiers."

"Then he shall have it, by our generosity!" proclaimed Ptolemy, much to everyone's surprise. He looked proud and commanding, or so he thought. Pothinus leaned and whispered something in his little idiot Majesty's ears, while Cleopatra had to think quickly how to walk back.

"My brother is a co-ruler, and we will come to a joint decision. Why must we favor Pompey alone, Tribune? We wish to stay neutral in this conflict. If those are his terms, then whatever we agree, we must divide it between the two parties. What happens if Pompey loses?"

Meanwhile, whatever Pothinus whispered had worked. Ptolemy's high-pitched voice came through again. "When I said he shall have our generosity, I did not mean we will give what he wants, but that we will provide some manner of assistance."

Publius almost ignored Ptolemy and turned his eyes to Cleopatra. "Pompey will win. He has the support of the people, many generals, and senators. He is an accomplished general–"

"Then why did he abandon Rome?" she asked sharply.

Publius stammered, "Caesar did what he was never expected to do, in violation of all rules. Pompey, the honorable man that he is, never expected his son-in-law to behave as he did. His evacuation of Rome had nothing to do with his prowess, Your Majesty. It was simply a prudent step to ensure preparation and spare Rome from violence."

That dirty city might as well be burned down and rebuilt, she thought.

"I have heard much of this man, Caesar, but Pompey was my father's patron. So perhaps it is just that we support him in the hour of his need. I am sure that Caesar is a reasonable man who would know why we supported his rival, should he ever–"

"Pompey will win, Your Majesty. That is certain."

Cleopatra leaned forward slightly. "You are in my court, Tribune. You may be from Rome, but you will respect this throne. Do not interrupt me when I am speaking. That is the second time."

Publius Cornelius stepped back and apologized.

Cleopatra continued. "There are no certainties on who wins and who loses, Tribune, and you know that. The Persians conquered the great Pharaohs of this land. Then Alexander conquered the Persians. Then god conquered Alexander before he saw the age of thirty-five. The great Hannibal massacred Romans at Cannae. And then Scipio conquered Hannibal. My own sister thought she was invincible. So do not tell me to be certain of anything. Pompey has asked for help, and we will extend our generosity, as His Majesty, my brother Ptolemy, said himself," she said, looking at the young Ptolemy, who looked mighty pleased by her acknowledgment.

The Tribune appraised her. "That may be true, Your Majesty. And I say this with much humility and respect that it is rare for us to see women of your knowledge of history and administration back home. But I must resist; it is Pompey who seeks your support, and not Caesar. The people of Rome, who are guarantors to your rule," he said pointedly, "are behind Pompey. You may see neutrality by supporting both, but Rome will see that as betrayal."

As much as she despised the Romans and the current situation, she could not help but admire the Tribune for standing his ground. The reality, she knew, was that there was no way Egypt could refuse. What was worse was that her country's forces were now divided in two, between her brother and herself, which meant there was absolutely no question of taking on Rome in any capacity.

"Fine. Let us speak of the request. A hundred new ships and a thousand soldiers is far beyond our ability on such short notice. We cannot send away what we have and expose our naval trade routes to piracy," she said.

Finally, Pothinus spoke. "Her Majesty speaks for us. Our fleet is spread over a long shoreline, and our building capacity is hindered by unrest. The request is too high. We could perhaps send a hundred soldiers and ten ships immediately. Surely that is meaningful?"

Publius smiled. "You take me for a fool, Chief Advisor Pothinus," he said. "What is worse, you think such an offer would be seen kindly by the receiver."

Pothinus smiled, and Cleopatra knew that this was simply a time-honored tactic of negotiations: begin at a senselessly low number to reach one that was acceptable to both parties.

Cleopatra leaned back on her chair. She adjusted her thin gold necklace and played with her bracelets. She whispered to Metjen, "What can we provide, and how much of the debt should we ask him to clear?"

They conferred a bit. Metjen was a smart man—astute with logistics and currency. Meanwhile, Pothinus and Publius traded polite insults and danced around numbers.

Finally, Cleopatra raised her palm, and the chatter died. "We have a number that might be mutually agreeable, assuming His Majesty approves as well, of course."

Ptolemy, already pleased once by her acknowledgment, sat straight. The boy, still only thirteen, was desperate for validation, and she was giving it to him in a powerful forum. His crown was too big for his head, and she knew that Pothinus and Theodotus probably filled that head with much fear of her.

"You may go ahead, sister," he said, raising his hand and lazily dropping it on his lap.

"This is our firm proposal, Tribune. Five hundred soldiers. That is almost a tenth of a full Roman legion, if I know my lessons."

He smiled. "You are taught well, Your Majesty."

She continued, "The unit will include some Gabiniani who have expressed their desire to return to Roman folds. As you know, these men are hardened veterans of Rome and will require little to no training in your methods. Also, sixty ships, ready to leave. Well-built and capable of carrying both men and weapons, and armed with grapple hooks and other implements. They are amongst the best you will find anywhere in the world, now pressed to service on behalf of our friend Pompey Magnus."

She looked at Pothinus and Achillas. They nodded.

Ptolemy listened to their whispers and nodded his head as well. "I concur," he said.

The Tribune whispered to his man. And after several tense moments, he addressed them. "Your Majesties have been generous," he said, and made a dramatic show of deference by bowing low and then expanding his arms wide. "We humbly accept the offer."

It was then time to haggle on the quantum of debt repayment this offer constituted, and that went through several rounds of shouting, cajoling, discussing, and arguing until a suitable number was arrived at. Eventually, hours after they began, when everyone was tired, the agreement ended.

When they finally signed a joint decree of support, Cleopatra wondered whether this would ever help her at all.

But more importantly, why was it that her brother and his advisors were so amenable?

CHAPTER 23

ALEXANDRIA

POTHINUS

Young King Ptolemy was quite pleased as they returned to their section of the palace. Pothinus walked with him, with Theodotus in tow. The long corridor ran parallel to the northern boundary of the palace, with the deep blue sea on one side. It was designed for long walks and rich conversation. Lined with granite statues of lions and intermittently sprinkled with lovely marble sculptures of maidens holding pots and warriors with bows raised towards the skies over the sea, the pathway also afforded clear views of the awe-inspiring lighthouse on the west. A cool breeze flowed, and seagulls soared in the sky. Pothinus wore a fine linen shendyt, but was otherwise naked from the waist up, which made the walk comfortable.

Let me take advantage of this good mood and fine air, Pothinus thought.

"That was an acceptable agreement, Your Majesty, though Rome is a hungry, greedy pig. The more you offer, the more it will want," Pothinus said.

Ptolemy clucked. "We will handle Rome. But did you see my scared sister? She wanted my approval. We have finally beaten her!"

Pothinus looked down at the bobbing head, with its curly dark hair and unsightly Uraeus crown. *Oh, child.*

"If I may, Your Majesty, without angering you, of course?"

Ptolemy turned to him. "Go ahead. Are you going to lecture me about something again?"

Pothinus smiled. His Majesty was beginning to show signs of maturity. He'd probably guessed what Pothinus was about to say.

"Your sister did that only to put you at ease. It is a common ruling tactic–" he said, trying to sound nonchalant.

"Yes, yes. It's political theater. Made to make an enemy comfortable until..." He made slashing sign across the neck. "And so on, blah blah blah. I know, Pothinus."

Pothinus was surprised at how His Majesty took the insinuation in his stride. "You are astute, Your Majesty. I know of a certain poison that, when laced with honey, tastes sweet and gives a heady sensation until it shuts down the heart," he said, and cracked his knuckles.

"So, what are you suggesting? And stop cracking your knuckles. Your fingers will break."

"I apologize, Your Majesty," Pothinus said, smiling. He looked at Theodotus, who took the lead this time. Pothinus had admonished the rhetorician that there were times when Theodotus was expected to lead and stick his neck out with dangerous ideas, rather than leave it all to Pothinus. *Stop being a coward who soars on a stage but weeps on the ground,* he had shamed Theodotus.

Theodotus stepped forward alongside His Majesty. "You strike when the iron is hot, Your Majesty. Your father, may the heavens bless him for eternity, waited too long, until your sister was heady with power. You know from the works of Aristotle and Plato that men by nature are superior, and women, who take upon the task of educating themselves, seek to find equality when the world and the gods see none."

Ptolemy nodded thoughtfully. "My sister takes an undue interest in education."

Pothinus felt a tinge of regret speaking ill of Cleopatra. She was the brightest of the children, and the first to command the many languages of the region. As a native Egyptian who resented the Royal House's reluctance to learn the language of the land, Pothinus appreciated Cleopatra's efforts on not just adopting the local cultural elements, but also learning the language. But such thoughts had to be put aside now.

Theodotus bowed. "And so did your elder sister Berenice, who you were not acquainted with on account of your age difference. It took your great father considerable effort to get rid of her, which in turn put us in the debt of Rome."

Ptolemy bobbed his head up and down. "That is very true," he said as he rubbed his hairless chin and looked at the seagulls.

Theodotus continued. "Her Highness Cleopatra, while I seek not to interpret the royals' thoughts as they are above my station, did keep you confined. Your bright mind, Your Majesty, surely sees the dangers to this kingdom if its governance were handed to a woman. You know from the lessons of your illustrious ancestors, Your Majesty, that there can only be one lion on the perch."

Ptolemy adjusted his crown, and after some fight, removed it and handed it to Pothinus. He wiped his sweaty hair and rubbed his flat cheeks. "We cannot let her become too powerful."

Pothinus took over the conversation. "The affairs in Rome will come to a head soon. It will be Caesar or Pompey. And no matter who it is, that scoundrel will turn his attention to us. Do we really want ambitious, learned Roman generals, who share none of our relaxed attitudes towards women, to come here and see that a woman rules alongside a man? What signals would we send to them?"

"One of weakness," Ptolemy declared emphatically.

His Little Majesty is seeing our ways.

"His Majesty certainly remembers the events not too long ago, with the mint and the decrees."

"She tried to sideline me completely. Thought she could make me vanish," he said bitterly. "Do you think we can ask Achillas to march on her? She has considerable support still amongst people, priests, and various administrators."

Pothinus was surprised at the bold turn of the dialogue. He knew that royals were fickle, and sometimes men lost their heads for uttering the wrong word or suggesting the wrong idea. But they had covered much ground, and after months of steady drips into Little Majesty's head, the slow ships of destiny were turning.

"A military adventure could be terribly risky, Your Majesty," Pothinus said, rubbing his elegant and wiry hands.

"What about assassinating her?"

Pothinus was shocked. But he had to tread carefully and not look too eager. Theodotus looked mighty pleased behind his thick and unruly beard and bushy eyebrows.

"No, Your Majesty," Pothinus said softly. "The events near Memphis have led to considerably tighter security, and the most important thing is that any action to put you in a position of strength cannot be seen in the context of you seeking to cause direct harm to your sister. You must be above suspicion. It cannot be the military. It cannot be official assassins."

"What can we do, then?"

Pothinus smiled gently, like a concerned uncle imparting wisdom to his nephew. "This is Alexandria, Your Majesty," he said, to a puzzled little freckled face.

CHAPTER 24

ALEXANDRIA

———◇———

The hooded men all sat in a circle. He had called for an urgent conference–sending his messengers into the dark underbelly of Alexandria.

There were seven, not all known to each other, but aligned around a common cause. He knew who they were and their unsavory reputations. Smugglers, bandits, rabble-rousers, extortionists, corrupt tax and union officials, a combination of more than one such trait–such were their backgrounds. They each had significant followings and influence.

"This state of unrest and confusion must end," he said forcefully. "There is only so long we can manage the current situation. One royal must rule."

There were many exclamations of agreement. One of the men, a Macedonian by his accent, spoke through his muffled cloth. "We prefer to run our business in a state of calm. All this nonsense is forcing us to watch our backs all the time. This climate is no good for us."

Business, he thought, and smiled inwardly. These scoundrels did not engage in an honest day's work. Unfortunately, he needed them for now. "Well, I have a proposal."

They listened to him intently. Apart from a few questions, there was no real opposition, even though they knew that what he was proposing, should it leak, would lead to all their heads paraded on spikes.

A burly man spoke. "Will the military stay away? We do not want a cavalry charging down on us."

"They will. A joint exercise of commands has been called, and all the major units, including the bulk of the Gabiniani, are already away."

"What about the mercenaries–the Thracians, for example?"

"You should expect some intervention! Surely you do not think that the palace will be left open like a whorehouse for anyone to do what they please."

The men murmured and discussed amongst themselves. "That is fine, so long as we do not have a major armed conflict."

"There won't be," he said, more forcefully this time. "But can you gather your men and get ready?"

"How much time do we have?" another man asked. His voice was soft and whispery, but he had built a reputation for brutality and troublemaking. No shopkeeper in the south-western block near the lake escaped from paying his 'dues', failing which they might find themselves short of a limb or an ear.

"In two days. I have heard of some royal trips, and this needs to happen before then."

They discussed compensation, rule changes after their plan was implemented, territory assignments (*you will need to arrest and get rid of so-and-so, officially*), roles in the court and palace, and so on. After all, if one of the co-rulers was dead, the other one could issue decrees without restraint.

"We will do as you said and see if we can force an exile, just like their father," one of the men sniggered. The famous Alexandrian riots were potent and capable of running out even royals. "What if we run into problems?"

He knew what the man insinuated.

"If it comes to it, death should be quick. Do not make a display of it," he said, and the men nodded.

But throughout the conversation, he noticed that two men were uncharacteristically quiet. They said little, which was unlike their garrulous style. And they were overly enthusiastic about every proposal. The only time they objected was on the timeline. They wanted four more days, apparently just to gather their men. *Not like they need to build an army*, he thought. And they both were rather consistent with their thoughts, considering each man had said he did not know the others. He had also caught them exchanging glances from time to time.

When the group finally stood, affirmed the plan and made a hasty departure, lest they were seen together, the two men hesitated and lingered. He finally decided to talk to them. They joined him and his two bodyguards in a darkened corner and huddled.

"I know who you are, but you have no danger from us, Apollodorus," one of the men said, surprising him. "But you must know something…"

Apollodorus quickly dropped the idea of protesting his identity. But did anyone else know who he was? He had shaved off his facial hair, worn a crude wig, and adorned himself with hideous, washable tattoos of Greek gods to conceal himself.

"You know that I require utmost secrecy," he whispered, worried. Her Majesty had insisted that he conduct this conversation personally, which was an indication of trust, but it had created its own risks.

"It is not us you must worry about, Apollodorus," said the other man. He placed a firm and friendly hand on his shoulder. "But we have heard rumors of a larger, similar plan afoot—and not in your favor."

CHAPTER 25

ALEXANDRIA

CLEOPATRA

———◇———

She was in the bath with her sister when Charmian burst in breathlessly. "Your Majesty, Apollodorus is here. He is demanding to see you immediately!"

Cleopatra was annoyed. She did not mind seeing the man, but she was in the middle of a bath, naked, blissfully happy—which was rare these days—and he comes running to ruin it!

"Can he not wait?" she asked, though in her heart she was anxious to hear the news of her plan.

"He says immediately. I had to stop him from rushing in here," Charmian said nervously.

Cleopatra slapped the hand of a maid who was applying a perfumed liquid to her back. "Pour some water on my shoulders. I need to get out," she said. "Tell him I will be out very shortly."

They quickly poured some water on her and draped a comfortable green gown on. She left her curly hair loose and stepped out of the bath chamber. Apollodorus stood near the waiting area and bowed to her.

"Your Majesty, I could not wait," he whispered urgently.

She gestured for him to walk with her to an adjoining room. "What is it? Is this about our plan?"

He nodded in the affirmative. "I fear that Pothinus has hatched a similar one against us, or found out when we reached out to those men."

Her heart sank. "How do you know?"

Apollodorus quickly narrated his meeting with the gang leaders and the revelation by the two men in the end.

Her heart beat wildly. Her brother's bastards were a step ahead of her again. "What does that mean?"

"We may have acted too slow, Your Majesty. We do not have enough time to recall my legions, and there are rumors swirling about large mobs on the way to the palace."

Cleopatra rapped Apollodorus' arm with her knuckles. "What does that mean, Apollodorus? What are you proposing?"

He looked uncomfortable, and then the big man finally spoke. "We must get out, quickly. I will summon the royal guard, secure some of your coin, and prepare a travel caravan. Her Highness Arsinoe must join you."

Cleopatra was stunned. The water drops cooled on her face. Absentmindedly she smoothed her hair, paralyzed by the inability to decide. Apollodorus' expression changed from a gentle servant of Her Majesty to that of a commanding general.

His hands shot up on both sides and gripped her by the shoulders, shocking her back to senses. It was an entirely inappropriate gesture, but she found herself strangely comforted.

"You must get ready to leave, Your Majesty. Now! My men will provide instructions."

She stuttered. "Leave? Leave to where? When are we returning?"

He looked stern but resolute. "We must leave Egypt, Your Majesty, unless you wish to be hung on a post and displayed."

CHAPTER 26

ALEXANDRIA

The frantic activity in the eastern section of the vast palace complex was a gentle calm compared to the madness at the center. Two Alexandrian mobs, armed with machetes, knives, stones, swords, spears, torches, hammers, and spikes, descended on the hapless guards. They converged in a frothing ocean of mob madness—screaming, shouting, setting fire to what they could, and went at each other, hacking and chopping. The pro-Cleopatra gang was smaller compared to the pro-Ptolemy crowd, which was not only better armed, but Achillas had clandestinely managed to keep some reserves who came to the aid of the pro-Ptolemy gang.

The pro-Cleopatra crowd gave up quickly and ran for their lives, and some conveniently switched, no doubt interested in whatever bounty and loot they could gather. As the mass congregated outside, shouting and baying for blood, with various slogans for peace and prosperity, a small group of determined men barged into the palace, unopposed due to Achillas' guards' support, and made their way to the eastern quarters where Her Majesty Cleopatra and Arsinoe lived.

Their instructions were clear.

"You have to leave with us, Arsinoe. This is no time to argue!" Cleopatra yelled at her belligerent sister, who refused to evacuate. The diminutive bundle of fire, wearing a matching purple *peplos*, was arguing about how the riots were Cleopatra's fault and that she was safe.

Having no time to argue, Cleopatra ordered the guards to restrain her sister and drag her into a waiting carriage.

"You can't do that, you bitch. You can't have me arrested! I won't go!" she screamed, and then heaped many other expletives she had learned from her maids. Arsinoe's face was red, her hair flew everywhere, and she balled her fists and screamed some more. When that was ignored by a harried Cleopatra who was busy issuing orders, Arsinoe made every threat to the guards. "I will have you hanged if you touch me, you oaf! I will have your head paraded in your village! I swear I will have your balls served to dogs!"

She fought every step of the way and kicked like a toddler throwing tantrums until the burly guards, who only reported to Cleopatra, wrapped a silk kerchief over her mouth and tied her hands. Finally, once she calmed, she began to sob and chose the maids she wanted to wait on her, and some valuables and personal possessions she would like to take.

Apollodorus had planned well. He had secured a not insignificant amount of coin, gold, silver, and keys to treasuries in secret locations. He had also sent messengers in advance to the eastern corners to secure support for safe passage, along with asking the remote units to join them. He knew that Pothinus and the Ptolemy cabal would be implementing similar measures to prevent them from leaving. It was a matter of time as to who would make it out quickly.

As the noises became louder, Apollodorus dispatched a small unit of his highly trained men to kill any intruders to the royal quarters, while he ushered Cleopatra, Charmian, Iras, and a few others to the waiting carriages.

Cleopatra looked at her familiar spaces with teary eyes. The silk-draped couches, the dyed marble columns, the dispassionate sphinxes, the rose and lotus garden, papyrus frond-topped columns, judgmental Pharaoh statues... She remembered the events when she was just eleven, when her father had been chased out of the palace and sought refuge in Rome. The terrible memories lingered. She had been wrenched from the safety of her palace and taken away to a depressing foreign land.

The events became a blur, and when she finally heard the sound of metal on metal clanging through the soaring halls and reflecting off the marble columns, she knew it was time.

Cleopatra, Charmian, and Iras were put in a fast horse-driven carriage that was indistinguishable from thirteen others. Arsinoe, with her tutor and advisor Ganymedes, was in a different vehicle. With a solid protective cover around them, and led by Apollodorus himself, they exited from a secret gate on the north-eastern end, driving through a thickly wooded path that led to the marshes where it was impossible for large crowds to pursue. She could see some fires at a distance and large plumes of dust, but the musky odor of the reedy marshes in the late afternoon sun was still a welcome sensation.

As she watched her palace recede, Cleopatra was filled with anger and a strange sensation. How quickly things changed, and how her dithering and not striking first had possibly cost her throne and her future. Did she now have to beg someone, just like her father did?

Even as the dust obscured the rapidly receding scenery, she resolved never to put herself in such a vulnerable situation again, and prayed to her many gods, from Dionysos to Isis, to put her back on the throne.

The throne of Egypt belonged to her, and her alone.

PART II

Google Maps (c) 2021

CHAPTER 27

ALEXANDRIA

POTHINUS

Pothinus waited for His Majesty to arrive at the throne room. Achillas and Theodotus waited, along with a few other officers and administrators. It had been a tumultuous but exciting hundred days. There was, of course, a minor sense of sadness that his brightest pupil had to be chased out of her home—but she had become dangerous. And worse, she threatened his power and his ability to guide the new king. Pothinus would shape Egypt's destiny with Ptolemy as his cover. The boy, now fourteen, was malleable as clay, his maturing mind molded by shapes that Pothinus conjured.

In just these days, they had stabilized the riots, sent messages to Rome pledging continued friendship, dismissed officials close to Cleopatra, even murdered some of her close circle, and established a pliant bureaucracy that swore loyalty to Ptolemy.

Achillas had spent time building the army and supplying it, and Theodotus schooled the young boy to be more precise, confident, and soaring in his rhetoric, something Ptolemy had severely lacked compared to his sisters. No matter how many times he was told, the young Majesty got excited too quickly and would begin to screech like an angry parrot. But minor were such difficulties. There were times he was sorry for the boy—he had lost his mother early, his sisters were never too kind to him, and he had stepped into a role of responsibility with almost no training and no parental supervision. But wasn't Pothinus someone who bore pain and responsibility at a young age too? Did the gods make it easier for him? The world was a difficult place, and the royals had a far better life than most others. He dismissed his thoughts–he had an idea what His Majesty would scream about now.

Ptolemy rushed into the room, already red in the face, clearly worked up before even discussing anything. His cream chlamys was spotted with juice, and his harried attendant ran behind him, trying to adjust the robes. "Leave me, leave me," he yelled at her, and then turned to Pothinus. "Where is Achillas?"

"He is away in training, Your Majesty," Pothinus said.

"I told him to be here! Is he defying my orders?"

I must arrange someone to re-teach mathematics to this boy.

"He is two days away, Your Majesty. He could not be here on short notice."

"Fine. Fine. You know why I wanted you here."

"I prefer not to guess His Majesty's mind," he said, bowing deferentially.

Ptolemy sat on his chair with his legs still dangling from it. He looked upset.

"What worries you, Your Majesty? How can I help assuage your pressures?"

The boy fixed his glassy gray eyes on him and adjusted his silver necklace. "I heard about Cleopatra."

Of course.

"Indeed, Your Majesty."

"How did she escape? Why did we not catch her?"

Pothinus had to face this question every so often, and it was almost as if His Majesty forgot the answer as soon as he heard it.

"She has her own network, Your Majesty. After all, she was queen. They gave her safe harbor in Thebes until she was able to escape. We are stretched too thin to pursue her across the country."

After their escape from Alexandria, Cleopatra and Arsinoe had traveled south to Thebes, well ahead of the pursuing parties. Outposts and spies had reported caravans that were most certainly Cleopatra's, but there was little anyone could do, as it appeared she had several military units that joined her at various stages, creating a force large enough that they could not be stopped without significant military intervention.

But pursuing her with an army made no sense. The primary idea was to dislodge and exile her, and they had completed that mission. Besides, Pothinus did not have to carry the regret of spilling her blood.

Ptolemy looked frustrated, chewing on his lips. "But still, how could we not assassinate her?"

Pothinus put on a pained expression. "We would, Your Majesty, if we could find her definitive whereabouts. Achillas apologizes for his failure, but we are trying," he said, deftly blaming the man who was not here to defend himself.

"Tell him his time is running out. I will have his head!"

"I will, Your Majesty. But right now, we must watch the happenings in Rome to make sure we are unaffected."

"Of course. You've told me that many times. Caesar and Pompey are at each other's throats. We do not know the outcome yet."

"We do not. But we hope that they will stay away."

Ptolemy rubbed his chin and itched his elbow. Both Arsinoe and Ptolemy suffered from a condition of the skin that created itchy spots near the elbows and palms, and needed much treatment to keep in control. Even the kings and queens sometimes suffered the same fate as common blood.

"So, what are they doing there?"

"Who, and where, Your Majesty?"

"My sisters. In Syria. What are they doing there?"

CHAPTER 28

SYRIA

CLEOPATRA

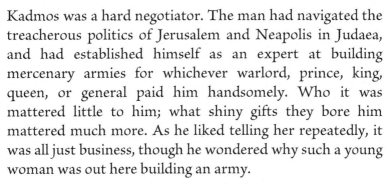

Kadmos was a hard negotiator. The man had navigated the treacherous politics of Jerusalem and Neapolis in Judaea, and had established himself as an expert at building mercenary armies for whichever warlord, prince, king, queen, or general paid him handsomely. Who it was mattered little to him; what shiny gifts they bore him mattered much more. As he liked telling her repeatedly, it was all just business, though he wondered why such a young woman was out here building an army.

Why not just reconcile with your brother, Your Majesty, and retire to a comfortable life? the idiot had said, and barely escaped without his head parting from his neck. But Kadmos knew he could get away with his insolence because she needed him.

Needed him desperately.

She had five thousand men with her, of which two thousand had traveled the challenging roads from Thebes to Pelusium to Gaza to Neapolis to Paneas to Damascus. The remaining had dispersed at various points, ready and willing to be by her side should the need arise. They had camped on the southern outskirts of Damascus, away from well-traveled routes, on higher ground and with a well-designed temporary 'fortress' made of stones and clay. It was an arid area, with nothing but gray rock and bushes for company. Several chieftains along the way had pledged support, but it was evident that while few were hostile, most were non-committal, unsure who would eventually prevail. Most of the areas were under Rome's sphere of influence, and that meant Cleopatra was forced to cobble her army not through the help of regional satraps with their established machinery, but through bribery and enticements.

"I need ten thousand good men, Kadmos. Achillas has over twenty now, and no doubt is building his forces," she said as two maids fanned her in the sweltering heat of the tent. Syria offered no respite, and there was no sea nearby to enjoy the breeze. Sweat, grime, dirt, thorns, and rocks; that was what she had for company. Apart from her incessantly complaining sister, of course. Not that Cleopatra was entirely wanting for comforts, after all; as queen and the incarnation of Isis herself, she had managed to hire and bring with her food tasters, handmaidens, and masseurs. But still, this place was no Alexandria.

Kadmos was an imposing man. At over six feet, he towered over the others, and his dark mustache and beard made him both threatening and credible for his trade. He was an ex-Centurion from a Roman legion, making his skills highly coveted and credible.

He was tattooed in very many places with menacing depictions of monsters and gods. One depicted a naked woman embraced by a four-headed, lion-faced being. In another, a naked woman sat on a beast with the face of a leopard but the body of a horse. In another, a naked woman— there were just many naked women. He called himself a Roman Greek from Syria, whatever that meant, and spoke Greek and Latin fluently. Whether on purpose or such was his style, he came to her tent each morning, sweaty, almost naked except for a flimsy kilt, but with a Roman Centurion's hat, ready to argue this term or that with Apollodorus. He would futilely try to engage with her but was regularly thwarted in his attempts. But on this occasion, Apollodorus was away, supervising security and securing supplies for the group—and for only the second time, Cleopatra was with the man without her general or her advisor. Metjen, her political advisor, had remained in Thebes, awaiting her orders.

But this day's circumstances were intentional. She had sent Apollodorus away, frustrated with the lack of concrete progress, and instead summoned Kadmos herself.

"It appears General Apollodorus is not here to haggle with me today," he said, grinning. He sat in front of her on a low reed stool, and his eyes were at her level even with her sitting on a high chair. The Centurion's helmet shone and the red plumes shook as he looked around the tent.

"He won't be. He has matters to attend to," she said. "But we need to conclude these negotiations, for I must return."

"What is the hurry? It will get nice and cool here, Your Majesty; enjoy our hospitality! We are blessed by your beautiful presence," he said, bowing theatrically.

She knew she would have to suffer his clumsy flirtation, or perhaps take advantage of it depending on how the conversation went. "I would love nothing more than to spend it in your rugged presence, Kadmos. But I have a kingdom to rule," she said, smiling.

Kadmos was pleased with her (finally) friendly demeanor. "Of course. What man could resist you by his side? I could–"

The man smelled like a pig even from this distance. She leaned forward and briefly touched his wrist, and smiled even as she held her breath to prevent inhaling his foul odors. Intentionally, she had dressed in a sheer silk fabric and wore the traditional Egyptian crown of sun and cow horns. She knew that her bearing had a mesmerizing effect on any onlooker. She could see his arousal. No doubt he imagined things he could do to a *queen*! For these men, it was not the sexual conquest of a reasonably good-looking, wealthy woman, but the thrill that the woman was none other than a queen. A real queen.

Kadmos checked his impulses as his eyes darted to the stern guards, not much less imposing than he was. He tried to continue when she clapped suddenly, breaking whatever fantasy was floating in his head.

"Perhaps you will have earned the right to visit me and enjoy our hospitality when I am on the throne. As they say in Alexandria, our treatment of handsome men is like nothing you have ever known," she said, curling her lips in a wicked grin.

Kadmos looked very motivated to complete the negotiations. She knew that he had not been particularly happy having had to engage with Apollodorus and other senior officers, with very little opportunity to speak directly to her. Most of those details were tedious, but they had to finalize numbers for what Cleopatra was willing, and could afford, to pay.

"That would be most appreciated, Your Highness," he said, trying to reach out and grab her hand to kiss. She pulled back and glared at him. The giant shrunk.

"First, the business at hand. Have you finalized the numbers? We have had enough discussions already," she said, brusquely. Kadmos was deflated.

"We can get you ten thousand, Your Majesty. A good mix of Thracians, Macedonians, Romans, Syrians, Medians. All eager to start."

"What does 'good mix' mean? How many have fought wars on behalf of Rome? Are you asking us to pay the same for all?"

Kadmos was taken aback by the questions. He hemmed and hawed, and finally went out to get one of his accountants—Fabricius, a pleasant-looking Roman who looked very knowledgeable and suitably impressed by her acuity.

The accountant continued. "Well, the majority are mercenaries who have fought somewhere or the other, Your Majesty, but about a twentieth were trained by Rome. A tenth, good Parthian soldiers. About a third are new recruits, boys of the finest stock of Parthians and Scythians."

Using fractions and throwing numbers around was a favorite tactic of accountants who preyed on a ruler's insufficient understanding of mathematics.

She leaned back and appraised them. "I did not come all this way to be swindled," she said. Kadmos looked offended, and the accountant showed no expression. *Of course, he knew what they were doing.*

"I take great offense to that, Your Majesty!" Kadmos said, throwing his arms around and adjusting his helmet.

"Oh, enough with the dramatics, Kadmos! A twentieth? That is five hundred soldiers. I want more soldiers trained by Roman generals. More than half are new recruits and barely experienced? I want hard men, not poets and farmers. You are charging me full rates while getting me men who are not worth half of it! And five hundred Parthian? Surely there are more!"

The unflappable Fabricius smiled. "Her Majesty knows her numbers."

"Then speak not to me like I am a maid."

The accountant turned to Kadmos, and then sought her permission to confer outside.

Once they left, Charmian whispered in her ears. "He needed his accountant because all his blood flowed south, and he couldn't think," she said, and they both laughed.

Charmian was allowed the latitude to say the most outrageous things. She was Cleopatra's confidante and had stuck by her side. She was also smart, spending time every day studying and learning new things. Cleopatra had entrusted the administration of the baggage trains and logistics to her, and she had excelled. "It is both disappointing and at the same time favorable that we can entice them if not with words, then with our nipples," she said.

Even little Iras, now only four, lent a helping hand. Her duties were to polish the bronze vessels, wipe cushions, and apply perfume to Cleopatra's neck. It took some training, but she was a dutiful worker now, and a source of much amusement. Every morning, any order was met with a resolute 'no' before a candy or the 'flying game' was offered as reward. The 'flying game' was one of the burly guards picking her up like a projectile and whooping her through the air as if she were a falcon. At the moment, Iras sat examining a wooden wolf toy that opened its mouth when controlled by a string.

They waited for Kadmos and his accountant to return. When they came back, they said they were ready to finalize the agreements. Kadmos wisely let his accountant speak, while he hungrily eyed Cleopatra and Charmian.

"We have considered every avenue, Your Majesty. All of them. We have to, after all, pay our masters, but we recognize that a glorious queen such as yourself will no doubt get her rightful throne back. And we have erred in not factoring the benefits of such a relationship," said the accountant, sounding as sincere as he possibly could, bowing low and shaking his ring-haired head vigorously.

Cleopatra placed her palms on her thighs. "What is your final offer? I wish to conclude this affair with you, Kadmos," she said, turning her attention to Kadmos, slightly playing with the double-entendre. "Having you in my court might put some fear into my enemies."

Kadmos looked mighty pleased, but he was no fool. He made no hasty commitment but let his accountant talk. Wise-head continued. "You know that Rome is busy with its wars, and Caesar and Pompey are raising and building armies. That makes any solider with experience in Roman warfare very expensive. But some do not want to go back to Rome, some have run afoul of Roman laws, and others are greatly enamored by you, Your Majesty."

"And?"

"Here is what we can do. Double the original Roman soldiers. Half of the Parthian and Scythian recruits will instead be experienced soldiers, fantastic with the bow and horse. But for the rest, Your Majesty, you will have to make do with new recruits—some who have battle experience, but certainly need to be trained further."

Cleopatra leaned back and computed the composition. "So, of my ten thousand, I have a thousand soldiers with Roman training, and a thousand-five-hundred experienced Parthian soldiers, and the rest are a mix."

The accountant bowed. "That would be accurate, Your Majesty."

She considered the situation. Every day she spent here, six months since her escape, was a day that Ptolemy's cabal had a chance to strengthen itself. She had to take her army and return.

"Just one more condition," she said.

Kadmos and his accountant looked at each other in puzzlement.

"Kadmos leads the Roman legionaries and joins my army."

CHAPTER 29

SYRIA

CLEOPATRA

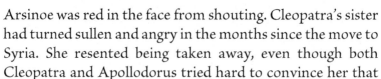

Arsinoe was red in the face from shouting. Cleopatra's sister had turned sullen and angry in the months since the move to Syria. She resented being taken away, even though both Cleopatra and Apollodorus tried hard to convince her that it was for saving her own life.

Arsinoe, having lived a life of luxury, had adjusted poorly to the rigors of the Syrian desert with only a fractional availability of comforts. She hated the stifling heat, the coarse bread, the crude toilet pits, the unctuous Idumeans and Jews, the hard beds, the two-course meals, the warm *sherbets*, and even the way the sun and moon looked in this arid landscape. She hated everything, and soon, everyone. While she had initially accepted the theory that she would be in danger if she stayed back, she had eventually created her own world of conspiracies, and even her eunuch tutor Ganymedes was unable to convince her otherwise.

Arsinoe had recently begun to blame Cleopatra for all her miseries and the root cause for the woes that had descended upon her. She sulked in her tent for hours, refusing to engage with anyone. She mistreated her maids and slaves. She spent hours complaining to Ganymedes about her wretched situation and how it was all Cleopatra's fault, and how her chance to be queen was being subverted.

Have I made a mistake by forcing Arsinoe to come with me? Cleopatra wondered.

Cleopatra had sent her maids and guards away to try to calm her sister, but it was a struggle.

"Why can we not discuss this once we return, Arsinoe? We will leave Syria in a fortnight and prepare to fight our brother. Be by my side, and we can decide what next after we win," she implored, while trying to hold her belligerent seventeen-year-old sister.

"No! Stop trying to hold me. Stay back! You want to be queen yourself, and you will try to kill me."

"If I wanted to kill you, I could have left you alone for the rioters, or I could have you gutted here in this wasteland and make you vanish. Which of that has happened?" Cleopatra shouted back.

Arsinoe crossed her arms and sat on a chair. She rocked back and forth until she calmed. Cleopatra waited.

"Why should I not be queen?"

"Someday, you will be. Neither of us is right now. You could be married to a suitable king–"

"I don't want to leave home. I am not going to some barbarian Italian province or eastern satrapy, or the arid deserts of Libya."

"There are no kings in Italy, didn't Ganymedes teach you? The Parthians are doing quite well in the east. I heard that the lands are beautiful, just like you."

Arsinoe pouted. She scratched her scalp and examined her nails. "Don't flatter me. Why can we not divide the Upper and Lower kingdoms? You be queen of Lower and Alexandria, but I will rule from Thebes."

What is wrong with this girl?

"Thebes? Not much is left there."

"It doesn't matter." Arsinoe leaned forward and yelled, "I want to be queen there. I deserve to be the Queen of Egypt, but you won't let me."

"Arsinoe, do you realize how complicated that would be? Why are you obsessed with this idea? Are you–"

Arsinoe's lips curled up in a sarcastic smile. She had a particular gesture, putting her knuckles beneath her chin and smiling crookedly, when she thought she had a very pertinent point to make. "Obsessed? Dear sister, you are here, raising an army to march against our brother, so you could be Queen! And I am the one who is obsessed?"

Arsinoe had a point. After all, if Cleopatra wanted, she could seek the hands of the many kings in Judaea, Parthia, or even the distant India, and live a life of peace and luxury.

"I am raising an army because otherwise we will be hunted down like dogs and killed—unless that is how you see your glorious end," Cleopatra retorted.

Arsinoe played with her hair and seemed deep in thought. "You are still convinced that they will kill me? I am not. Maybe if you had let me stay behind, I could have married my brother and become queen."

Cleopatra let out a sigh. "Maybe. Or maybe you would be strung up a post, naked for all to see. Or maybe you would disappear in the marshes. Or maybe your head would be paraded–"

"I get it! Enough. I suppose I should thank you for saving me," she said, still cross, but less vehement.

"Or stop fighting me, at least, Arsinoe. We have enough to manage here. Do you want to, with Ganymedes' help, lead two thousand men on the way back?"

Arsinoe's eyes lit up at the mention of heading an army. "Like, a general?"

"More like a queen. But you will consult Ganymedes and follow tactical instructions from Apollodorus. Remember, I own the army. I paid for it. I am their queen."

"Fine, whatever you say, *Your Majesty*," she mocked, but her expressions indicated otherwise. She was thrilled. The question, Cleopatra thought, was how to keep that immature power under control. Unlike her, Arsinoe had no real experience as an administrator. Her perceptions of power were based on what she saw and heard, rather than what she'd experienced and exercised herself.

And some took to power very poorly, abusing it and causing great harm.

Arsinoe left the tent, mollified. But she still worried Cleopatra greatly. Somehow, even after all these months, her sister still doubted Cleopatra's intentions.

And unlike her brother, Arsinoe was bright and dangerous.

Perhaps Arsinoe was going to be a threat to her throne.

CHAPTER 30

SYRIA

CLEOPATRA

It was summer by the time Cleopatra secured her army and began the march to Egypt. The progress would be slow and careful, with time left for periodic updates from the borders to ensure they were not walking into an ambush. All recruits were pledged to the utmost secrecy, and chiefs along the way were told to give a pass to her army, which was split two ways on its march to Egypt. Apollodorus led one contingent with eight thousand, and Kadmos led the rest. Arsinoe accompanied Kadmos' group, a clever move from Cleopatra to ensure that her hot-tempered sister found her match with the intransigent ass who would ensure that the march stayed its course. Fabricius had decided to accompany Kadmos. Cleopatra realized that the true mind behind the operations was Fabricius–the wily Roman knew every which way to enrich and ingratiate himself. He also knew how to keep Kadmos under control. Cleopatra wondered if Fabricius had something on Kadmos that made the burly Centurion listen to him meekly.

The carriage shook on the rocky path, which was surrounded by imposing orange-yellow canyons. It reminded Cleopatra of an interesting gold-leaf bundle she had read from her forefather Ptolemy Soter's library. The founder of her dynasty maintained an exquisite library with his most valued tomes, and the gold-leaf document spoke of an ancient civilization that vanished, presumably by the wrath of god, but apparently left a hidden secret enclave somewhere in the canyons and mountains around her. Could that help her? It was a fleeting thought that she dismissed… there were so many fascinating papyri and scrolls in the palace libraries.

She had asked Apollodorus to join her in the carriage, with Charmian by her side. Her general had worked tirelessly for all these months, not only having saved her, but now trying to get the throne back for her. He was a rare case of a man rising from common blood and proving his value. Tired of the scheming and planning and arguing, she was looking forward to a quiet journey and perhaps knowing a little about the people she most trusted. She would need to know them much more.

Apollodorus sat uncomfortably opposite her on a narrow cushion seat, his knees almost touching hers. She enjoyed toying with him. Charmian sat by her side as they all chatted about nothing important—a welcome departure.

"The rocks are definitely more orange and deeper than back home," Charmian said.

"You should visit western Egypt, Charmian, where the beauty rivals these lands," she said. "The desert is so vast, its colors deep and beautiful, but also frightening in its desolation. My father took me to the temple of the Oracle of Ammon, using the same route the great Alexander took!"

"If you ever go there again, Your Majesty, take me along!" Charmian said. "I have never been anywhere west of Alexandria. Is it a grand temple like the one at Taposiris Magna?"

"No, it is much simpler. It has none of the grand ornamentation. But they say there was an oracle there that foretold great happenings in the world, and that even Greeks listened to it. Did you know, five hundred years ago, that when the Persian king Cambyses sent an army to destroy the oracle, it buried the entire army in the sand?"

Charmian was fascinated. Apollodorus too got curious. "An entire Persian army? In the sand?"

"Yes! Fifty thousand buried somewhere in the desert. My forefather wrote about it and said that he'd found this army, but never divulged where."

They all looked out, wondering what hidden discoveries lay beneath the sands, under the rocks, on the seabed, in the crevasses of this earth.

Cleopatra turned to Apollodorus. "What about you, Apollodorus the Sicilian, where did you grow up? Sicily? I have heard it is a very hilly country."

Apollodorus, his face sweaty and his brown-black beard coated with fine Judaean dust, wiped his face apologetically. "Yes, Sicily, Your Majesty. I spent my first twelve years there before I went off to join the Roman legions. It is green and hilly and has a great smoking mountain that erupts with fire sometimes."

"I have read about that," said Cleopatra. "The Romans call it Aetna. Did you know that Rome exempted your provinces from ten years of tax when their towns were affected by the mountain's anger?"

Apollodorus was surprised. "You are learned, Your Majesty. I heard something like that from my grandfather."

"Being kind to your people during times of need is a hallmark of a just ruler. That is why I exempted many from tax last year during poor harvests. It is a pity that my idiot brother does not understand these things," she said, gesticulating. But the other two had nothing to add, except to nod in acceptance.

"You became a soldier at twelve?" asked Charmian, changing the topic. The girl had indicated that Apollodorus spoke little of his past. Perhaps Cleopatra's questioning would force him to open up. After all, he could not lie to and evade his queen.

"No," he said, appearing slightly irritated. He turned to Cleopatra. "I started as a cook, Your Majesty. I also took care of the horses. I tended to wounded men and kept watch during the night."

"When did you join the fighting units?" she asked, leaning forward and fixing her eyes to his, causing him to squirm some more.

"About seventeen, Your Majesty. I caught the eye of a Pilus Prior, who recommended me to a Centurion, who inducted me to one of the cohorts."

"What is a Pilus–" started Charmian.

Cleopatra turned to her. "Charmian, I must speak of some sensitive military matters with him. Can you check on the progress of the baggage trains?"

Charmian gave her a knowing smile and jumped out of the carriage, leaving Cleopatra with Apollodorus.

"Do I make you uncomfortable, Apollodorus?" she asked mischievously, leaning forward to tap his knee with her finger and drawing a short line before she withdrew.

Apollodorus sat stiff and unsure of what to do. "I, well, you, I... you are my queen, Your Majesty. I am–"

"Now, Apollodorus. I will not have your head for not knowing what to say," she said.

"As you say, Your Majesty," he said, relaxing somewhat.

"Why do you not have a wife?"

"I have had no time, Your Majesty. Besides, what can I offer a woman if I can never be by her side?"

She appraised him. Over the years, Apollodorus had only grown more attractive. With his peppery beard and mustache, firm body, disheveled hair, broad face, and wide nose, he certainly drew the attention of many of her maids and women of the court. If only he were a king, or even a prince, a noble perhaps–someone from a family that mattered.

She shook her head to dislodge those recurring thoughts. "Well, perhaps your companionship, if not in marriage."

Apollodorus was quiet as he looked at her. "It is you I am devoted to, Your Majesty. I care for no other."

Something hidden deep in the recesses of her belly began to bubble up. She tried to control it, for as queen and the incarnation of Isis herself, she could not display such emotion, let alone to a common-born man who had risen in her army. But Cleopatra's chin began to quiver first, and hot tears welled in her eyes.

And then she began to shudder. The tears changed to sobs, and then shaking shoulders. She thought his strong palms were on her shoulders, or perhaps even his neck by her mouth. But she cried until the knots in her stomach and the tightness in her throat dissolved and vanished. She sheepishly wiped her face. When Cleopatra returned to a semblance of normalcy, her cheeks reddened at her moment of weakness.

She looked outside. The canyons were lovely, imposing, mysterious, and yet somehow cozy and kind.

Cleopatra finally mustered the courage to look to Apollodorus, whose eyes radiated a gentle kindness. "Keep your devotion to matters of the mind, Apollodorus. Not the heart. Or it will bring you great pain," she whispered.

Apollodorus nodded gently. "Her Majesty must seek the company of great men who do great deeds and come from great homes. It is ordained. But I still bathe in the glow of your proximity," he said sincerely.

At that, she cried again. And this time not with much shame, but with the knowledge of being in the presence of someone who cared and made no judgment.

They sat that way quietly for an hour, as dawn made way to dusk, as the blue bands of the glorious sky receded to the yellows and reds of impending darkness. The road had become gentler, even, and they shook less. She had refused to let him leave the carriage, and he did not begrudge her for doing so.

She cleared her throat. "I barely knew my mother," she said, her voice cracked and husky from crying. "I remember her walking me to the zoo or leaving me by the playhouse in the company of my maids. She spent little time with me."

"The royals have other duties, Your Majesty. I am sure her affection for you never wavered."

She exhaled. "I don't know. She did not have much to do. Do you know why I look different than Arsinoe?"

Apollodorus did not venture into speculation.

"My mother, like many others around me, was not entirely Greek. Her grandmother came from an Egyptian-Greek union. I do not think she spent much time with my father, and they say she died when I was only five."

Apollodorus bowed but said nothing.

"I grew up in the hands of respectful maids, stern tutors, and a father who loved me like... how many fathers do. At a distance. When I watch children being held by their parents or receiving affection, I feel lonely," she said, smiling.

She looked down at her feet and clasped her hands. "And now, a man who I saw as my father and advisor seeks to kill me. My sister thinks I plan to murder her. My brother wishes to see me dead. The Romans care little for me, *a girl,*" she said, shaking her head theatrically at the use of the word *girl*. "It seems all I have are Charmian, and you, Apollodorus," she said, wallowing in self-pity, even some false humility, and she let some more tears flow.

It was cathartic.

Apollodorus shook his head, and this time he summoned a boldness she had never seen in him by her side. He took her hands in his. "Your Majesty, you are ordained by the gods and Isis herself to be our queen. You are loved by millions in our land, by your soldiers, by Charmian, and by me," he said as she caught her breath.

"You governed an ancient land when you were just sixteen, Your Majesty. You have not just the blood of the royals of Macedonia, but you are also blessed by the blood of Egypt. You gave justice to thousands when, at your age, I cleaned utensils," he said, laughing. He was good to look at, with his twinkling eyes and even three crooked, yellowed teeth. She smiled.

Apollodorus continued earnestly. "The great Caesar did little at your age. Even the great Alexander simply headed away with an army at your age, but left governance to someone else."

She nodded, feeling confidence creeping up her spine. She wiped her nose and sniffled.

Apollodorus continued. "While it was foolish, you stood your ground during the riots. You survived an ambush and never lost the will to continue. You negotiated terms with Roman rascals. And here you are, having built an army in a foreign land, leading them back to claim your throne. And you are only nineteen, Your Majesty. What woman in the world is that extraordinary?"

Cleopatra blinked her eyes to suppress any more tears. He had given her pride and affirmations she had forgotten about herself.

He looked deep into her eyes and said in a low, definite voice, "You are Cleopatra. You are Egypt. You are goddess Isis. And you will be the rightful queen."

CHAPTER 31

ALEXANDRIA

POTHINUS

Pothinus sat under a canopy in the center of his beautiful garden. A little artificial stream snaked in between the greenery. He was surrounded by all manner of flowers–rose, lotus, jasmine, daisy, and chrysanthemum. The aroma, the explosion of colors, the soothing cool air as his slaves fanned him, all brought great joy. A woman painted his toenails while another gently massaged his aching shoulders.

He needed these diversions, because after months of tense quietness, news had begun to trickle in of Cleopatra's return to Egypt. Ptolemy's men–no, *his* men–had failed to intercept Cleopatra and Arsinoe as they made their escape to Syria. There were intermittent messages from spies in the last few months of the girl building some kind of army, and then news had arrived that she was returning. And this while they were dealing with disquiet in Egypt, and smattering news from the west about the Roman generals at each other's throat. He wanted it all to end so they could rule Egypt with him controlling the affairs. *A Pharaoh*, he mused. *He would be the first Eunuch Pharaoh. Maybe even depose the idiot little Majesty and take over the throne.*

Pothinus had done much work in gaining the confidence of the many priests, chiefs, leaders, administrators, and military men.

But his mind returned to Cleopatra. She was returning. With an army, at that! He smiled at her resourcefulness. And yet was frustrated by her temerity.

He shook his head and took a deep sip of his beer. What was Cleopatra trying to do, coming back? Was she going to declare war on her own people? On her brother? His Majesty was still deeply upset that his sisters had escaped, though in rare circumstances he hopefully wondered if they would return and 'become nice.'

He had hardened his stance in recent days that he wanted their heads.

Pothinus and Achillas had managed to keep Cleopatra's return a secret so far from His Majesty, but sooner or later the king would hear of it. He would be apoplectic. Achillas had already begun preparations to move his army farther east–though he did not know where Cleopatra would move her army. Would she come along the seaside? Would she go south and head to Memphis before turning north? Would she go to Herakleion? No one knew. The vast, deserted, hostile land made it difficult to track all her movements.

He heard shuffling feet. "Your Excellency," a polite voice addressed him.

One of his messengers from Achillas' side.

"What is it?" he asked, mildly annoyed at the interruption.

"General Achillas requests your presence immediately. He is unable to travel, but desires to share some urgent news."

What now?

"Can it wait?"

"It is about Cleopatra, Your Excellency."

Achillas had been loyal and faithful, so Pothinus was not overly irritated by this request. If the stodgy general wanted him, it must be with a justified reason. Pothinus hurried to dress. And then, a rider conveyed him to a location near the south-eastern edge of Alexandria, near the marshes. When Pothinus arrived, he saw frenetic activity in Achillas' camp.

Men moved about with purpose, and there was great energy among the troops.

What was happening? Was she already here?

He was guided to Achillas' tent in the middle of hundreds of others.

"Welcome, Pothinus. I am grateful you are here so soon," the general said. Achillas was dressed in dark-grey painted bronze armor with a ram's insignia, yellow-plumed helmet, and a blue cloak.

"Well, how could I ignore an urgent request from the commander of His Majesty's forces?" Pothinus said with some humility. He cracked his knuckles as he looked around. "You worry me. You do not look like a man about to take a stroll in Alexandria's gardens with one of his many admiring women."

Achillas laughed. "It seems the gods play with us. I have news of great importance."

Pothinus was intrigued. Achillas led him to a cushioned seat, and the men sat opposite each other.

"News of Cleopatra?" Pothinus asked. "Is she really re-entering Egypt?"

"Yes. Not just that, Pothinus. She has mustered an army of fifteen thousand–"

Pothinus was stunned. "Fifteen thousand? Could your spies be lying?"

Achillas shook his head. "Multiple sources. And sighting that we previously did not understand but realized too late."

"What do you mean?"

"She is clever and has been advised well, Pothinus. It seems she not only mustered this army somehow, but she then split it into four sections that entered Egypt surreptitiously, through the paths least taken."

Anxiety grabbed Pothinus' chest and squeezed it. "What do you mean she has entered Egypt?"

Achillas leaned back with his hands behind and supporting him. He looked at Pothinus quizzically. "It is what I said, Pothinus. She has entered Egypt."

Pothinus stood and began to pace. He tugged on his ear lobes. "How could we miss this, Achillas? How could we?" he said, his voice rising. He looked at Achillas accusatorially.

"It is a vast, barren land–"

"Not so barren that we could not see an entire army headed this way! The routes near Pelusium are dense and busy. Your men are incompetent! Do you realize how our Little Majesty will react if he finds out that his sister is within his borders without a challenge?"

Achillas stood as well. "Don't lay the blame on me, Your Excellency," he said, switching to formality. "You control most of the spies, so why is it I that must bear the burden of failure?"

The men glared at each other, but Pothinus knew that Achillas was right. His men had failed, just as the general's, or perhaps Cleopatra was too clever for them all. But to move an army of fifteen thousand *undetected*? There was no question she had the support of the remote towns, which had remained quiet as men moved in columns. He could not have his eyes and ears everywhere, as much as he wanted to. The northern ridges of the borders were observed, but obviously, she had evaded that route.

Pothinus calmed himself. These were not his first encounters with danger.

"What do we know?" he finally said.

Achillas gestured for Pothinus to sit, and they sat again.

"They appear to have split somewhere in Judaea, turned south far from Pelusium to evade our scouts, and then regrouped just two days south of Pelusium. They are camped there and fortified."

Pothinus was flabbergasted. "Just two days? Two days from Pelusium?"

"Yes, two days," Achillas said.

Pothinus put a hand on his bald, sweaty skull and wiped it. "This is disastrous, Achillas! We are unprepared for battle. We know nothing of their plans, and they are already here. If she captures Pelusium, we will have a major problem with our trade!"

Achillas nodded. "That is true," the general said, but looking quite relaxed. Pothinus found this nonchalance irritating.

"You look comfortable, as if all this means little, you moron! Do you realize what will happen to us if we lose the town?" he shouted at Achillas.

Achillas, for whatever reason, kept smiling. The wrinkles by his eyes grew deeper even as Pothinus yelled.

"What are you laughing at, Achillas?" Pothinus stopped.

"I enjoy conflict, dear Pothinus. It will be fun talking to His Majesty, don't you think? I really think you should lead the conversation," he said, grinning ear-to-ear.

Did this scoundrel know something? Why was he behaving like this?

"Are you defecting, you bastard?" Pothinus asked, unsure and confused.

Achillas laughed out loud. "Oh, Pothinus, it is amusing to see you worked up. No, I am not defecting, but I must present to you someone who has."

Pothinus froze. "What?"

"Come with me," Achillas said as he walked Pothinus to another camp. Pothinus' heart thudded. This short meeting had already stressed him enough. He gingerly avoided the ditches and tent stakes and wood heaps along the way, nodding at officers who bowed to him. The ground was mucky and dark, and his sandalled feet sank several times. Achillas said little on the way, except to smirk and say *just you wait*. Had one of Cleopatra's senior officers defected?

They arrived at a heavily guarded tent. Grim soldiers saluted as he and the general lifted the flaps and entered. The tent had multiple inner folds, making it dark inside with just a sliver of light.

Pothinus noticed the silhouettes of two figures, a taller, slender one with a shorter beside it.

And when he recognized who they were, Pothinus almost stumbled in shock.

CHAPTER 32

PERSAEPHARSALOS, GREECE

CAESAR

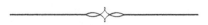

A mile separated his legions and Pompey's. Gaius Julius Caesar eyed the much larger opposing force. After days of Caesar attempting to draw him to battle, Pompey had finally decided to bring his forces down from a fortified higher elevation. Caesar, in final discussions with his commanders, inspected his formation. The two armies stood perpendicular to the river, which meant one side was inaccessible for a flanking attack.

With Caesar were the following: Markus Antonius, the exuberant, extroverted, often difficult-to-control officer, and leader of the Legions VIII and IX. Domitius, the commander of the central infantry unit. Sulla, the commander of the feared and trusted Legion X. Caesar took a position on the right, near Sulla.

"Final numbers, Markus?" Caesar asked Markus Antonius, *Mark Antony.*

"Twenty-two thousand legionnaires, one thousand cavalry on our side, sir. Thirty-five to forty-five thousand infantry and three thousand to five thousand cavalry on Pompey's side. Many of the troops are freshly levied, I heard, and not well trained."

"Domitius, formation?"

"All their infantry is on one side and four lines deep, and all his cavalry facing our right end, sir."

"Who is commanding their cavalry?"

"Labienus, sir. With slingers and archers behind his cavalry."

"Do we know if Pompey is behind the lines?"

"Scouts say that the general may not be in the active battlefield," Mark Antony said.

"He has grown old and nervous," Caesar said, smiling. "What do you think they plan to do, men?" he asked, testing their acumen.

"They rely on their numerical superiority, sir. They will bring their cavalry forward and hope to smash our flank," said Mark Antony.

"Very good. And what should we do?" he asked, smiling again.

Sulla, an experienced commander himself, was puzzled. "Our cavalry will protect our right, sir. We have a gifted force—"

"But we are outnumbered one-to-five or one-to-seven. Do you think each of our riders can kill five of the enemy?"

The commanders looked around sheepishly.

"You are exceptional men. Your men are exceptional. But the gods have not given men the strength of elephants, nor the eyes of hawks," he said, eyeing the vast array of men and horses far away.

Mark Antony grinned. "As usual, you tease us, sir. You have something on your mind."

Caesar smiled. "Indeed. Here is what we will do. Sulla!"

Sulla, who had wandered off to issue some command, came running. "Yes, Caesar."

"Send word for one experienced cohort from each line to pull out and form a fourth line behind our cavalry. They must remain hidden. Have them equipped with lances."

The commanders were puzzled. And then it dawned on them. They saluted Caesar, and each man went to head their units.

The battle of Pharsalus—one that would either make him the master of the Roman world, or see him dead or taken away in chains—was about to begin. What a strange turn of events, he thought, for he was now fighting who was once his co-consul, a man who was also his father-in-law, now his mortal enemy. Vastly outnumbered, Caesar was about to push his divine luck once more. He prayed silently, trotted to the right-wing of his force near Sulla, and gave orders for the infantry to advance and cover ground between his forces and Pompey's.

A great chorus of whistles rented the air, the glinting eagles rose high above the shoulders, trumpets signified advance, and the first line began to move.

As the supremely disciplined legions began advancing, each tightly packed, holding their javelins and with their shields up, Caesar looked to the heavens, seeking victory.

At first, two lines of the infantry advanced on Pompey's forces. While they were engaged, holding Pompey's men, Pompey's vast cavalry advanced on Caesar's. But Caesar's cavalry, instead of fighting them, drew in the enemy and split when near their hidden infantry. The infantry, with specific instructions to push their lances up on the riders' faces, caused such terror that Pompey's cavalry was soon in utter disarray and fled to the mountains. With the cavalry gone, Pompey's forces were exposed to Caesar's flanking attack. Soon, a defeat turned into a massacre, and Pompey fled behind his fortifications and eventually escaped arrest by Caesar's forces.

Days later, Caesar learned that Pompey Magnus was on the way to Egypt.

CHAPTER 33

NEAR ALEXANDRIA

POTHINUS

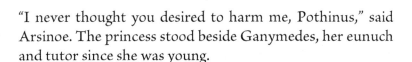

"I never thought you desired to harm me, Pothinus," said Arsinoe. The princess stood beside Ganymedes, her eunuch and tutor since she was young.

At first struck with surprise, Pothinus did not know how to react. He quickly recovered and stepped forward, embracing Ganymedes first, and then kneeling to Arsinoe. "There was never any desire to harm either of you, Your Highness. And yet your sister now seeks war. But let us put talk of conflict aside. How are you, and how did you escape?"

Arsinoe tapped on his shoulder. "You may rise. My sister is convinced that you were plotting to kill us both, but I know she was wrong. We left under the cover of darkness with a few faithful guards, and Ganymedes knew the way."

"My scouts intercepted them on the way to Alexandria and brought them here instead of going to the palace. I told Her Highness that His Majesty is still recovering from his sister's betrayal, and that she must remain in our protection until we present the case to him," Achillas said.

Arsinoe scoffed. "My brother would do nothing to me, but fine. I agree to stay here."

The strain of travel showed on Arsinoe's face. Just the last several months had aged her beautiful features. She had grown. There was a mature intensity in her eyes, and having lost weight, her face was gaunt and sharp. She had cut her lustrous and bouncy hair short, just to above her shoulders. Her demeanor told the story of a royal coming to terms with her opportunity.

Pothinus engaged in some small talk, inquiring about her health and whether she had sustained harm and so on, dripping concern and care. He had never really had a problem with Arsinoe and was still fond of her, in spite of her mercurial temper, though her presence had certainly complicated matters.

"I must confer with Achillas, Your Highness. The gods have blessed us with your return. You must rest before we prepare for our next steps."

He took leave of them and walked out with Achillas. "Why did you bring her here? Why not let His Majesty deal with this development?" he hissed at the general.

Achillas looked at Pothinus and shook his head. "Has this afternoon dulled your intelligence, Pothinus? She has Cleopatra's battle plans! We can use her presence to our advantage, maybe even force the defection of more…"

Pothinus slapped his own cheeks and laughed. "The stress! You are right. We now have three of the four Ptolemies on our side, and that is the message we will spread. But do not forget that Arsinoe is aggressive and might pose problems to our plans. Her eunuch Ganymedes is no fool himself."

"I know. If His Majesty starts listening to her, Ganymedes will take control, and we will be fighting for crumbs," Achillas said. By now the general, along with Theodotus, were fully immersed in Pothinus' scheming, and it warmed Pothinus' heart.

"I agree, Achillas. But right now, we must inform His Majesty of this development and ask what he wishes to do, or rather influence what he should do," Pothinus said, and the two nodded solemnly.

"How do you know she is not a traitor or one of those double-agents?" Ptolemy asked. He had calmed down after erupting and yelling around about his sisters and how Achillas and Pothinus had kept him in the dark.

"A double-agent can work effectively only if they are allowed to return to the other side, Your Majesty, or have messengers who can do so. She has none. We should confine her to the palace under watch, perhaps let her govern–"

"No! She will govern nothing! I am the king. She can be in the palace, but that will be it."

Pothinus and Theodotus failed to convince the king that keeping Arsinoe busy would be good for them all, and reluctantly agreed that she would be confined. Pothinus could only imagine Arsinoe's fury and the abuse he would have to endure.

But next came the much more delicate matter–His Majesty was still unaware of how close Cleopatra was. They would have to position this topic delicately before His Majesty flew into another of his rages and had someone killed on a whim.

"There is another matter that requires His Majesty's divine leadership, and your chance to shine on the theater of the world," Theodotus said, letting his voice soar dramatically. Theodotus, even if he was cowardly in many other aspects, was a master with his voice. He could drop his notes to a growl, like an unhappy lion, or let it reach an impressive pitch, but still rich and impactful, without taking on the sharpness of a woman's scream.

"What is it?" Ptolemy asked, adjusting the silk diadem affixed to his hair with silver pins.

Theodotus paused and rubbed his head. Perhaps hoping it would not be chopped off, Pothinus thought wryly.

"Your servant Achillas and His Excellency Pothinus have stalled your sister near Pelusium. We need His Majesty to soar like an eagle to the front and lead the army against her. His Majesty's army is clamoring and crying for his presence to take on this great threat!"

How theatrical!

Young Ptolemy's frail chest puffed, and his eyes lit up at the mention of leading an army. He had long clamored to 'lead his army against a great enemy,' except that no suitable enemy had materialized. And now, suddenly, a great chance had arrived. But His Majesty's mind had matured somewhat, and he thought more than ever before.

"How did she get into Egypt? Why was she not stopped?" he asked suspiciously. Theodotus meekly turned to Pothinus.

Pothinus stepped forward and fiddled with his golden bracelets. "It was intentional, Your Majesty," he said with a very grave tone. "For us to take our army far out to the east, exposing this city and straining our supplies, would be dangerous. What Achillas, that brilliant general, has accomplished—with Theodotus' and my planning, of course—is to draw them into a conflict where our strength shines. We might even be able to win with little bloodshed."

Ptolemy paced around the room. "Maybe that was clever. How can we win without fighting? Will we siege and starve them?"

"We will cut off their supplies, but that may not be sufficient. If her advisors and generals have planned well, and it seems that they have, they can withstand a blockade for months, which would be a waste of His Majesty's time. What we plan to do is sow discord–that on our side are the three divinities of the House of Ptolemy, and that their men should abandon arms and come to us. Not only will we win, but we might also gain her army at no cost."

Ptolemy smiled. Rare for the boy. "And what if that does not work?"

"Then His Majesty will strike them down with his own sword," Pothinus remarked, and Ptolemy nodded earnestly.

"What does His Majesty wish to do? We must move quickly," Pothinus asked.

Ptolemy made a show of thinking deeply. He expanded his chest and put on a stern face. "We will march towards them."

Young Ptolemy led his army of twenty-five thousand, including many of the Gabiniani, just in time to stall Cleopatra's advance to Pelusium. Apollodorus and Cleopatra were no fools, and they had foreseen that Arsinoe's escape meant their plans may be revealed, so they had changed their route and instead of coming in a straight line from the south, they had angled away to the east before turning to Pelusium. This gave time for Ptolemy's forces to first arrive at Pelusium and establish a defense.

But the hot and muggy months, with foul critters and mosquitoes swarming them, made everyone miserable. Cleopatra had put together a formidable army and established a strong defensive position. Achillas quickly realized that Ptolemy's army was unprepared for an all-out attack, and counseled the king strongly to wait as long as they needed to while they built the army, shored up their defenses, closed supply lines to the enemy, and looked for weaknesses in Cleopatra's defense based on what Arsinoe had revealed.

Ultimately, instead of a glorious battle with the clanging of swords, flying javelins, and shouts of victory, it was a tense stand-off with camps of both armies just miles from each other, neither willing to make the first move. But that did not stop Cleopatra's side from shenanigans. Once in a while, what appeared to be an entire Roman (or Roman looking) legion, attired in their kilts and plumed helmets and capes and Signifiers, and led by a giant man, made a show by marching in order and making great noise before receding. Another time, Cleopatra herself had arrived, fully bedecked in a combination spectacular Egyptian headdress of vulture feathers, asp, and sun-disk, with shining Greek body armor, trying to cause Achillas' men to lay down their arms.

Pothinus' attempt to try the reverse–bringing King Ptolemy, Princess Arsinoe, and even the younger Prince Ptolemy to the front in their regalia, had led to failure. Cleopatra cleverly had her army turn away and raised long horizontal banners in the front of their ditches to prevent her men from looking out. Finally, after sitting on their horses in the sweltering heat for hours, the royals had scolded Pothinus and Achillas, and returned. No one attempted the ruse again.

Achillas would not be drawn into a conflict or walk into a trap, and somehow, they had managed to hold off the frustrated and belligerent king from forcing an advance. *One false move against a fortified defense, Your Majesty, and our army will be decimated. You will lose everything. Remember the patience of your forefathers! Even the great Seleucus lost to the Indian boy-king Sandrocottus by advancing on a defense too soon.* To add to their woes, rascally merchants from Pelusium used boats to ferry salted fish and garum to supply Cleopatra's men. When captured, they begged for forgiveness, for after all they were just merchants. Some were put to death, but that inflamed local tempers, which jeopardized supplies to Achillas' men, so Pothinus had to give up on attempting any restrictions on the trade population of the town.

On this morning, when they all idled time and eyed the opposition, a messenger came running to Pothinus' tent. "Ships on the horizon, Your Excellency. We do not know whose!"

Alarmed, Pothinus gathered Achillas and a few senior officers and raced to the beach that was just a few miles north of their encampment. Far in the distance, on the open sea, were several ships with their masts flying high. Two small boats were making their way to the shore.

"Greek? Roman?" Pothinus squinted. Achillas was unsure. But whoever they were, the numbers were not too great to be alarming, and two boats posed no threat. The ships were a mix–in the front was a Levantine Trireme, distinct in its features, but surrounded by a mix of merchant boats and warships.

They waited an hour before the boats finally arrived at the beach. Several men, with their hands held high in the air, indicating no threat, waded onto the beach, exhausted. Achillas' officers escorted the men to Pothinus and the general.

"Who are you?" Achillas asked.

The man, a gaunt, tall Roman who spoke passable Greek, thanked them for not attacking. He was very pleased after learning the identities of Pothinus and Achillas, knowing that they held influence on behalf of His Majesty Ptolemy.

He then described his mission. "I am honored to be pleading our case before you, Excellencies. I have arrived here to bring a message from Egypt's friend, Rome's greatest general, a man–"

"Who are you here on behalf of, and why?" Pothinus asked sharply. They had enough to worry about already without sitting and listening to some Roman's grand descriptions of their leaders. He was concerned with whatever was happening between Caesar and Pompey, and he had not yet received word of those conflicts, and now it seemed some other chest-thumping Roman was sending messages.

The man, flustered by the interruption, bowed and sighed deeply. "General Pompeius Magnus, consul of Rome, an eternal friend of His Majesty and an admirer of his father, requests temporary asylum in Egypt."

CHAPTER 34

PELUSIUM

CLEOPATRA

"What holds us back?" Cleopatra demanded of Apollodorus and Kadmos. It was hot, and the slow southern wind was raising fine sand that was irritating her. The strain of waiting was beginning to affect her too–maybe it was better to put an end to this misery. She wiped some grains off her hands and squinted at the banners of her brother's army's forward positions.

"It is not the time to move, Your Majesty. They have dug forward trenches and have multiple layers of defense. Heavy casualties for us would be disastrous," Apollodorus said. He had been reticent to make any move other than shoring up their own defense and organizing their catapults for when the time was right.

Kadmos kept shaking his head, with his plumes dancing in the wind and his arms crossed over his barrel chest.

"You wish to say something, Kadmos?" Cleopatra asked him.

"We must move, Your Majesty. The longer we wait, the more our supplies will dwindle. We have few open roads, and sooner or later they will shut down the seaside transport. We won't die in battle, but we will starve to death!" he said, not looking at Apollodorus.

"We have enough supplies to last for months. This is not a skirmish, Your Majesty. One false move and everything you built will crumble in two hours."

"Let us take the battle to them in surprise! It appears we are equally matched, and my men are spectacular. I was a

Centurion–" Kadmos began, playing his *centurion* credentials for the ten-thousandth time. Cleopatra was tired of hearing it. Apollodorus had been patient so far, since Kadmos was effective and his men had great respect for him. But Apollodorus was the supreme commander of Cleopatra's forces, not Kadmos.

"I know what a Centurion is, Kadmos!" Apollodorus scolded him. "You led eighty men under generals. We have nearly twenty thousand here. Risking eighty men on a tactical move is entirely different from risking an army. I am your general. Now keep your mouth shut!"

Kadmos looked offended and was about to argue when Cleopatra raised a hand and put an end to it. "You will listen to Apollodorus," she said. "You are like a restless monkey, Kadmos, and everything looks like a banana to you."

Kadmos burst out laughing. It was to the man's credit that he took no offense and forgot what he was admonished for within ten minutes.

Cleopatra turned to Apollodorus. "The longer we wait, doing nothing, the weaker we will seem to our army and *my* people," she said emphatically. "As their divine ruler, I cannot be seen as idle and powerless!"

But their argument was interrupted by a breathless messenger who reported of ships on the horizon–definitely not military, but possibly Roman or Phoenician. And that a boat or two had moved onshore and were quite possibly received by Ptolemy's forces.

Cleopatra thought it might be trading factions or possibly messengers from Greece, since Caesar and Pompey were engaged in war there. Kadmos was convinced that it was the dastardly Parthians taking advantage of the unrest in Egypt and Rome. Apollodorus thought they could be merchant ships seeking permission from Pelusium customs. None were convincing, and all did little except cause further consternation.

She paced around and looked at the fluttering banners of her royal house. "I cannot be seen idle," she muttered again.

She had to do something, anything!

CHAPTER 35

PELUSIUM

POTHINUS

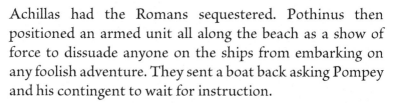

Achillas had the Romans sequestered. Pothinus then positioned an armed unit all along the beach as a show of force to dissuade anyone on the ships from embarking on any foolish adventure. They sent a boat back asking Pompey and his contingent to wait for instruction.

Pothinus, Theodotus, and Achillas hastily called a conference in His Majesty's presence. As regent, it was on Pothinus to make decisions that benefited the king, but Ptolemy was insistent on having his squeaky voice heard.

"If we give Pompey asylum, would that not benefit us and make us favorable in the Senate's eyes?" he asked, now a little more knowledgeable about the affairs of the world.

"That it might, Your Majesty, except that it might mean nothing," Pothinus said as Achillas nodded.

"What do you mean?" Ptolemy asked, sitting on his comfortable high chair, fanned by servants.

"The Senate is powerless. We heard that Pompey left Rome when Caesar began his advance, and it is quite likely there is no one there who will stand up to Caesar," Achillas added.

"And Pompey is here because he lost to Caesar, Your Majesty," Pothinus said.

Ptolemy thought hard. "What is the problem if we turn him away?"

It was Theodotus who spoke this time. "If Pompey is not granted asylum, you can expect him to be greatly angered at us turning our back on him when he needed us the most, after all he helped Your Majesty's father. It may also send a message of hostility to Rome."

"He has lost and is running. What can he do except stew in anger?" Achillas asked. The general rubbed the coarse brown leather on his scabbard and flicked sand from his corset.

Pothinus was deep in thought. He began to crack his knuckles, one by one, until Ptolemy yelled at him. "Stop it, Pothinus! You will break your fingers!"

Like father, like son.

"I apologize, Your Majesty," he said sheepishly. "But Achillas, you do realize that a general who has lost today does not mean he is vanquished. You saw Cleopatra run away in a little carriage. Is she now not teasing us with an army, just miles from here? Do you want one of Rome's formidable generals to leave with deep hatred of us? Pompey Magnus is held in great esteem by many loyalists. This is the man who once ruled Rome along with Caesar. He is a consul who has won multiple wars. Do you think he will walk away to admire sunsets?"

Achillas nodded and rubbed his stubble. "What if we arrest him, instead of granting a comfortable asylum, and let Caesar come and take him?"

Theodotus, the pudgy-nosed big-mouth, walked to the center of the room as if he were about to give a glorious speech. He arched his back slightly and lifted his right hand while folding his left on the chest. "Your Majesty. To hold Pompey will do nothing but invite Caesar's legions. Do we–"

"It's just us, Theodotus, don't hurt His Majesty's ears with your shouting," Pothinus interrupted. Suddenly, the group erupted into laughter, a small respite from the stifling tension and heat. Theodotus was miffed and tried to argue, but the king put an end to it. But when they returned to the topic, Pothinus understood Theodotus' reasoning.

"I see the point that the erudite Theodotus is making, Your Majesty. If we hold Pompey, Caesar is sure to arrive at our doorstep like a hound in search of a juicy bone," Pothinus said.

Achillas rubbed his sweaty and graying hair. "Pompey is like a hot and expensive honey candy–you cannot swallow it; you do not want to spit it out!"

Theodotus, undeterred by the previous slight, ventured in again. "There is a much bigger danger if we hold him, even beyond Caesar's anticipated intervention."

They were all puzzled. Theodotus looked around, his eyes glinting and conveying a message that he had an angle others had missed. As was his nature, he took his theatrical pose again. His fine voice rose in the soft afternoon heat. "The Gabiniani were sent by Pompey. Many of our Roman-trained troops still surely have fondness for Pompey. He can lead insurrection from within and take control of Egypt. All this might be Pompey's ruse to become king of *this* land!"

The council went silent. *The dramatic bastard may be right*, thought Pothinus. They all looked at each other, wondering who should speak next.

"We cannot keep him," His Majesty said, his young voice harder this time, demonstrating greater conviction. He was beginning to understand the complexity of the situation.

A man peeked into the tent. "I have an urgent note to make, Your Majesty," he said, kneeling in the entrance.

Ptolemy gestured for him to come in.

What now? Pothinus thought.

"Her Majesty Cleopatra–"

"She is not Her Majesty anymore!" Theodotus shouted at him—a wise move, before His Majesty threw another temper tantrum or had the poor messenger beheaded. Now was not the time for stupid distractions.

The man flustered and apologized profusely. "Cleopatra is moving her catapults forward, and one unit has advanced halfway between the camps, Your Majesty."

That caused much shouting, until Achillas calmed all fears that it was simply a harassment move. "They too have seen the ships and are trying to stir us up to do something unwise," the general said. "Such maneuvers mean nothing, and we are well beyond the range of their catapults."

He ordered two of his units to advance enough to be seen but do nothing else. But Cleopatra's move meant they had little time to sit and dither around–they could not have dangers on two fronts. She was forcing them to decide quickly, and the worry showed on Ptolemy's face as he bit his cheeks and gripped his chair's arms.

"We have to do something!" Ptolemy yelled. The Little Majesty stepped down from his high chair and gulped water like a fish. His thick black-brown hair bounced as he paced around in his crisp white tunic and golden-laced sandals. "Now! We have to decide now!"

While the men looked at each other with increasing worry about this seemingly intractable problem, Theodotus raised his hand and suggested that he had an idea worthy of consideration.

What does the big-lipped loud-mouth have this time?

And when Theodotus explained it to them, the reactions were divided. Achillas was unhappy, Pothinus was concerned, and Ptolemy looked worried but relieved for now. But they all agreed that this was the best course of action.

Pothinus summoned a messenger. "Bring Lucius Septimius here," he said. Lucius Septimius was a military tribune who had once worked for Pompey, but had now settled in Egypt as part of the Gabiniani.

The council sent a boat to the ships to convey a message to Pompey Magnus.

It was time to act.

CHAPTER 36

PELUSIUM

ACHILLAS

Achillas balanced on the gently swaying boat. With him were Lucius Septimius and another Roman Centurion (formerly) named Salvius, along with two rowers and two servants. Achillas had conveyed the king's orders upfront—that Pompey would be requested to join them in the boat, and that the men on the ships would not be allowed to disembark. This was for everyone's safety, and once Pompey was safely conveyed to the shore under His Majesty's protection, the men and the ships would be allowed free passage.

And now, they waited in the late evening sun. The warm and salty air still brought misery. The muddy water, not very deep in this section, gave no comfort to the eyes either. Achillas was surprised at the size of the fleet—there were many ships, and he surmised that the accompanying force, whatever manner of composition, was likely to be several thousand men.

"What is taking them so long?" Lucius asked. The clean-shaven, short and stocky man had long ago fought for Pompey.

"Probably still debating the arrangement," Achillas said, even as he held to the boat sides and wiped the sloshing water off his arms.

They could hear some sounds and possible yelling, but none of it was discernible. Achillas and Lucius shooed away some curious seagulls. They were running out of patience when they finally saw movement above.

A man peeked and shouted, "His wife and children will accompany him!"

Achillas shouted back. "No! Only Pompey and an attendant. Those are His Majesty's orders. His family may follow on a different boat."

Another head appeared beside the man. "Why would the king deny me the chance to come with my family, General?"

Achillas was surprised by Pompey's voice. But Lucius saluted his once-commanding officer and shouted, straining to be heard over the sounds of the sea and the creaking wooden boards of the boat. "I beg you to follow us, General, sir! I fought with you against the pirates."

Pompey stared for a while. "I remember you now. Lato?"

"Lucius Septimius, sir!"

"Ah, yes. Lucius. Let me speak with my wife," he said, and his large head vanished.

Achillas patted Lucius' back, and they waited.

Eventually, a ladder dropped from the bow.

A man, not Pompey, began to descend.

"Who are you?" yelled Achillas.

"Philip, General. Pompey's slave and now freedman."

Achillas muttered under his breath but let Philip come down. He waited for Philip to be seated.

Philip gripped both sides of the seating board. He tried to make small talk, but they ignored him, waiting for Pompey.

A colony of seagulls came sweeping from somewhere, making a great ruckus, and a few wings slapped them. Finally, a man in a cream toga began to descend the ladder. He came down slowly, gingerly, for he was large, and the ladder swung as he descended.

Achillas reached out to Pompey and helped him onto the boat, with Philip rising to help his master. Pompey Magnus' hands shook as he tried to find footing on the boat. Achillas had never seen the famed Roman consul and general before. Pompey was of similar height to himself, but he was wide, with broad shoulders, thick neck and arms, a prominent, bulbous nose, and heavy cheeks and jowl. He had an ample belly. His hair was curled, disheveled, and had thinned on the sides. He was sporting an unkempt grey mustache and beard. The man had deep, dark pits beneath his eyes, no doubt strained by recent events.

Lucius Septimius gave a half-hearted salute to his former commander and pointed him to a seating board. Pompey refused to sit, but instead asked that they wait for his wife and children to disembark. Achillas agreed, and eventually Pompey's wife Cornelia and their children came down and embarked on a different boat.

The rowers began to return to shore, swiftly putting distance between the ships and their vessel. The boat rocked, and Pompey tried to talk to Achillas and Lucius. The flags of His Majesty Ptolemy's tent were now visible, as were the rows of men waiting.

Pompey briefly reached to his side and touched Lucius Septimius on his shoulder in an affectionate gesture. "Lucius, I remember you now. You were a brave soldier!" Pompey said, trying to involve them in conversation. But Lucius would not look at the consul. Salvius maintained his silence and looked out to the sea.

Achillas and Lucius exchanged glances.

Pompey then addressed Achillas. "Why did the king not find it suitable to greet me in a manner worthy of my relationship with his father?" he asked, half-jokingly. After all, sending a little boat with a couple of men was hardly a rousing welcome, especially for the man who was a consul of Rome and also a patron to the late king.

Achillas grunted but said nothing.

Pompey, sensing some discomfort, addressed his former officer. "What is it, Lucius? What is going on?" he said, smiling broadly. But there was fear in that face.

Achillas lunged at Pompey.

Lucius, who was standing beside Pompey, swiftly moved behind him and held the consul's arms. At the same time, the servants went after Philip, who was weak and ineffective, and held him down by the neck.

Pompey yelled, "What are you doing? Stop!"

The consul pushed forward, heaving left to right, trying to dislodge the man holding him. He was surprisingly strong even for his age and demeanor, and it took Lucius all his strength to pull him back, even as Salvius pushed him down.

Achillas pulled a long knife from his waistband and plunged it into Pompey's ribs just above his abdomen.

Pompey grunted and gasped. He thrashed and tried to free himself.

Achillas pulled the knife and raised it again, higher, and stabbed Pompey, this time the blade going right through and puncturing the heart. Salvius joined, delivering blows to the chest. The acrid metallic smell of blood enveloped them, overpowering even the smells of seaweed and saltwater.

Pompey collapsed, spraying blood all over them. He had pulled up his toga to cover his face, even as he died. Philip was shouting, but they quickly restrained him. Achillas placed the body on its side and exposed Pompey's neck.

Lucius Septimius pulled a glistening sword hidden under two wooden boards. He then hacked the dead consul's head, sawing like a brute butcher until it was free.

Pompey's blood sloshed on the narrow boat's bottom, wetting their feet.

Achillas held Pompey's head in his hand and placed it in a bag. Meanwhile, the passengers in the second boat—Pompey's family and some others—had realized what was happening. They were close enough to have witnessed the attack. Achillas tried to ignore Pompey's wife's screams. When he glanced at them, Cornelia was hugging her children while closing their eyes.

Achillas raised his velvet-coated, glistening sword. "Stay away and return!" he shouted. Lucius joined and pointed his knife. Their boat turned and fled to the safety of the ships.

Achillas and Lucius lifted Pompey's body and threw it off the boat. They forced Philip to jump, for the water was only neck-deep here. Achillas then ordered the rowers to speed to the shore.

When they returned to the camp, there was much rejoicing, with the king praising Theodotus for his idea.

The rhetorician was very pleased. He nodded in appreciation for the kind words of the council. "Dead men do not bite," he said, grinning.

And such was the end of Pompeius Magnus, a great consul of Rome, famed general of eastern conquests, vanquisher of pirates, and father-in-law of Gaius Julius Caesar, near the muddy shores of Pelusium.

CHAPTER 37

PELUSIUM

CLEOPATRA

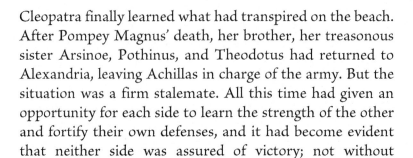

Cleopatra finally learned what had transpired on the beach. After Pompey Magnus' death, her brother, her treasonous sister Arsinoe, Pothinus, and Theodotus had returned to Alexandria, leaving Achillas in charge of the army. But the situation was a firm stalemate. All this time had given an opportunity for each side to learn the strength of the other and fortify their own defenses, and it had become evident that neither side was assured of victory; not without significant external assistance.

She called her council to decide the next move.

Apollodorus, Metjen, and Kadmos arrived at her tent. Charmian stood by Cleopatra's side as her handmaidens fanned the queen.

"You know what happened on the beach," she said flatly. They had heard, each man acknowledged.

Cleopatra rubbed the bridge of her nose and looked at the men seated before her. "This will bring Rome on us," she said quietly.

Apollodorus spoke. "What we heard is that it was Theodotus' idea to keep Caesar away."

Kadmos agreed with Apollodorus. "Perhaps your brother has saved Caesar from pursuit. Besides, I see the logic in murdering him–Pompey would surely engineer an insurrection in Egypt and take over the throne," the big man said.

For all their experience, these men can sometimes be idiots, she thought. The problem with these military commanders, none who were generals of vast armies or governors of people, was that they thought about what was in front of their noses, and not what transpired in minds and lands far away.

She shook her head. "I should keep you in the trenches and not listen to your strategic advice," she said, half smiling.

Apollodorus, unlike the argumentative Kadmos, had long accepted that Cleopatra's mind thought well ahead of theirs. She saw things he did not, and they had quietly agreed that he would be the military tactician but leave larger matters of policy and strategy to her and Metjen.

"You do not understand the minds of these men, and yet some of you are of similar stock," she said. "My brother's cabal miscalculated. Whatever enmity existed between those two men, Romans prefer to settle such things amongst themselves and not let others dictate those affairs for them. Especially not by killing off one of their own. Did those idiots not know that Pompey was Caesar's father-in-law and a co-consul? I am surprised that Pothinus sanctioned this stupidity!"

Kadmos tried to speak, but she placed a finger on her lips. He shut his mouth.

She continued. "Caesar will be in hot pursuit of his rival; of that, I am certain. He would not know that Pompey is dead. His legions will arrive in Alexandria. Knowing Pothinus and my brother, they will describe Pompey's death with glee and hope he will shower benefits on them."

"They seek to curry favor with Caesar and cement the alliance, thereby putting Ptolemy on the throne." Metjen said. The short and slim Egyptian with a sharp understanding of both Egyptian and Roman affairs had been her primary advisor. The soft-spoken man, once a priest of the temple of Isis in Memphis, was instrumental in shoring up her forces and keeping the people of the country by her side.

"But it will not work," Cleopatra said. "Caesar is going to be angry. He will interfere in our affairs. These fools have no idea how they think. What they *should* have done is hold Pompey, transport him to another Roman client-state like Judaea, and hand him off."

She gestured Charmian to bring her some beer and continued as she sipped at the cup. "If he arrives in Alexandria, he will sooner or later assume the mantle of the protector and arbitrator of Egypt. These Romans are sticklers to their laws when it comes to foreign parties, no matter how much they fight amongst themselves, breaking their own laws. Now it's too late."

Metjen was looking at her and nodding, perhaps knowing what was in her mind.

Apollodorus too probably realized her thoughts, whereas bull-headed Kadmos stood there, his eyebrows furrowed, still clueless and probably waiting for a message to charge.

"What we will do is wait. We will move our armies farther away from confrontation, and we will wait until Caesar arrives. And then I will convince him to put me on the throne. And as for my brother and my treasonous sister—"

She stopped and spilled the rest of the beer to the ground.

CHAPTER 38

ALEXANDRIA

POTHINUS

Pothinus was deeply upset. The last few weeks could not have gone worse. It was as if the gods conspired against Egypt, perhaps punishing them for their transgressions and failure to bring about a peaceful transition.

And now the devil was in the city.

Gaius Julius Caesar had arrived in Alexandria just a few weeks after Pompey's arrival on the shore of Pelusium. The Roman was unhappy at the news of Pompey's death, and even made a show of sorrow (*what a pathetic actor!*). And then, instead of returning, he had marched his legion into the city, much to the anger of the locals. Many Roman soldiers had died in the riots and ambushes on the streets, and now Caesar had cordoned himself off in a section of the vast palace complex. The cowardly Publius Cornelius, fearing Caesar's wrath at the state of affairs in Egypt, had snuck away one night and left to return to Rome.

But that was not all; he had summoned Pothinus on this day, wishing to speak of 'important matters.'

Pothinus hurried to Caesar's quarters. His Majesty Ptolemy had remained secure in the palace; after all, the king of Egypt would not travel to meet a harried general of Rome. It had to be the other way around.

Caesar had dressed himself up in a purple toga, posturing like a statesman instead of a rogue general occupying parts of the palace without invitation.

The general greeted Pothinus in Greek.

"I am pleased you are here, Regent Pothinus," Caesar said. "Your presence is appreciated in these disturbing times."

Pothinus regarded the general. "Cooperation with Rome is always high on our minds, Your Excellency. Alexandria can sometimes be wild, and the crowds take no direction from anyone."

Caesar acknowledged those words and smiled.

The two eyed each other quietly. It was as if both knew that Pothinus was likely lying, and knew that both knew that they knew. Pothinus had to suppress a smile. Of course, he had a hand in the disturbance and the attacks on Caesar's soldiers.

Caesar swept his lanky arm and asked Pothinus to sit. The two, not too dissimilar in height and composition, engaged in some small talk before Caesar, dry and direct in his methods, arrived at the heart of his summons.

"Roman law and His Late Majesty's will require that I act as guarantor and protector of the Egyptian throne," he said, fixing his piercing black eyes on Pothinus. "And circumstances here have greatly disturbed my ability to conduct that duty."

Duty indeed, by a whore's stinking bush, thought Pothinus. The gall of the man to pretend to suddenly care for Egypt's throne. He was finding an excuse to squat in Egypt.

"His Majesty Ptolemy is capable of settling matters of succession, Your Excellency," Pothinus said testily. "I am sure Rome eagerly awaits your return as the victorious general and consul."

Caesar smiled. It was a laconic grin, one without humor. "When I choose to return is for me to decide. I do not need a messenger to suggest my course of action."

Pothinus bristled at the insult but controlled his impulses. These were dangerous grounds. "I meant no disrespect, Your Excellency," he said, bowing. "What would you like to discuss, and for me to convey to His Majesty?"

Caesar leaned back. "First, you have not yet settled the question of debts. You owe Rome seventeen-and-a-half million denarii."

The nerve of this toga-wearing bastard. Owe Rome, by a donkey's arse. He means to him.

Pothinus shook his head vigorously. "A portion of which was settled by our assistance to Pompey Magnus."

"Who you killed. Who was against me. How does your assistance to someone's war help Rome?"

"Debts are between nations, Your Excellency, and your fairness surely recognizes that. Pompey was consul of Rome, and we rendered assistance. Should you have come to us, Caesar, we might have assisted you too. Egypt owed much to Pompeius Magnus," he said without a hint of irony.

But surprisingly Caesar did not litigate Pompey's murder. Instead, he accepted a revised payment of eleven million drachmas.

"You are gracious, Your Excellency," Pothinus said. *Bastard.* "I will convey this most acceptable settlement to His Majesty. We will work to secure the payment."

Caesar spread his legs and clasped his fingers, and then he stretched his back. "You do that, regent. I will remain here until then."

Son of a noble whore.

Pothinus was not very surprised by Caesar's proclamation. After all, this idiot had arrived in Alexandria and was now stuck, his troops attacked, his remaining legions still somewhere in Greece and Asia, and no doubt running out of money to pay his men. They might chop and throw his pieces to the seas if he sailed now without any money. Pothinus would stall the payment as long as he could until Caesar ran back to his dirty Rome, whimpering like a street dog.

He nodded and rose to leave. "We hope you will remain comfortable until–"

"I have not dismissed you," Caesar said without smiling.

Anger filled Pothinus' veins. *How dare he speak to me like I am a servant!*

"Is there more to discuss?" Pothinus asked, boldly this time.

Caesar stood. "I said in the beginning that as an arbiter executing the will of the late king, it is my duty to ensure stability in Egypt, for which Rome has assumed the mantle of protectorship."

Pothinus stared at the Roman.

Caesar continued, "By Roman law, and with me as consul, it is the will of the Roman people that quarrels in Egypt be settled before me, through proper debate and instruments of justice, than by the tip of the sword."

He stood straight, almost unmoving, his raspy, soft voice carrying in that tent. "It is my pleasure that you convey to the *boy* Ptolemy and the *girl* Cleopatra that they shall disband their armies immediately, and appear before me for arbitration."

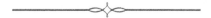

Kadmos and Fabricius tried to calm the furious lieutenants and legionaries that had surrounded them. They were away from Her Majesty's camp and would not draw royal attention.

"This is ridiculous, Centurion!" one man complained. "Look at these huge welts on my body! How long do we wait until the mosquitoes eat us alive?"

Another joined in. "All I do is scratch my balls, swat bugs, compete with others over how far I can piss, and rub my cock thinking of *Her Majesty*. Where is the loot? Where is the action?"

Some others complained of disease. "We have lost so many to dysentery and coughs. Not felled in battle but in puddles of their own piss. And some have died simply from boredom!"

Kadmos raised his hands in surrender and put on an apologetic face. "I am not the general, men. And she does not listen to me. General Apollodorus believes an aggressive move now would be a bad strategic choice."

"Why is it bad?" one of them argued.

"Well, would you prefer yanking your shaft to happy thoughts, or would you rather be impaled by Caesar's javelins?"

After some more shouting and shoving, Kadmos tried to bring sense to the men. "Listen. I have no great desire to sit and wait, miss the chance to earn more, and feel like I am wasting away. But our choices are limited. I will impress upon Her Majesty to break this impasse. But you must cooperate."

"We can wait, Kadmos. But at least give the men a chance to go out and be farmhands, or do something other than sit and fight with each other all day in this miserable weather!"

Kadmos knew that many camps had expressed similar sentiments. This was not a good development, and it could turn into mutiny. He would let Her Majesty know that not all was well with her army.

CHAPTER 39

NEAR PELUSIUM

CLEOPATRA

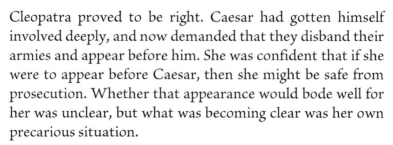

Cleopatra proved to be right. Caesar had gotten himself involved deeply, and now demanded that they disband their armies and appear before him. She was confident that if she were to appear before Caesar, then she might be safe from prosecution. Whether that appearance would bode well for her was unclear, but what was becoming clear was her own precarious situation.

Her army was becoming frustrated. After all, her coffers were dwindling, and with no battle, there would be no loot. Many of them had no interest in lingering near mosquito-infested swamps with nothing to see or do. The restless chatter had grown louder in recent days, and Kadmos hid no discontent, but instead kept her appraised of the growing pressure. Fabricius, the 'accountant,' kept complaining that he could not be sitting here, unable to conduct his business elsewhere.

If she were to advance on Alexandria, she would not only have to prevail over Ptolemy's more formidable forces, backed by the power of the state, but she would also be seen as a combatant of Caesar, and by extension, of Rome. Even if she won over Ptolemy, she would be weakened and unlikely to win over the legions of Rome.

And she knew what the Romans did to enemy rulers.

They paraded them like cattle in their victory marches, and then strangled them in front of everyone.

The Queen of Egypt was not going to squeal in front of hungry eyes and die while urinating on herself.

After much debate, she came to a decision that was acceptable to the various parties.

The army would not disband but move farther south and await orders. They would be allowed to seek additional farming employment and receive pay in the meanwhile. Those who remained would be eligible for bonuses and land once Cleopatra assumed the throne.

She, along with a few senior officers including Apollodorus and Kadmos, her principal bodyguards, with a thousand Roman-trained soldiers as protection, would travel to Alexandria wide of Achillas' forces and seek an audience with Caesar. The expectation was that Achillas would offer her free passage in accordance with Caesar's wishes.

The worst that could happen, she convinced the men, was that she would have to co-rule again with Ptolemy. "I will turn him into a sheep," she said, to laughing responses.

After bidding good-bye, Cleopatra's contingent swung south from Pelusium, traveled along a tributary, and crossed the river midway between Alexandria and Memphis, before turning north. The plan was that they would stay away from encountering Achillas' forces and make way to the city before sending a message to Caesar's men that she had arrived.

Cleopatra was tense during the journey–there were many unknowns. Where were Achillas' forces spread? Who controlled Alexandria? What if the missive from Caesar was a ruse? What if she was unable to contact Caesar upon arrival at Alexandria? But all factors considered, she was of the opinion that this was her best course, and that the rumblings in the countryside combined with Caesar's orders meant that perhaps Ptolemy, Pothinus, and Achillas would curb their enthusiasm for her head.

Such were her thoughts as they began to move up and angled towards Alexandria.

CHAPTER 40

NEAR PELUSIUM

ACHILLAS

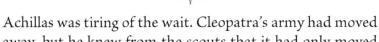

Achillas was tiring of the wait. Cleopatra's army had moved away, but he knew from the scouts that it had only moved south and re-fortified. He had received an initial missive from Pothinus that he must stay where he was and await further instruction. On this day came a letter from Pothinus, sealed in wax and only for his eyes.

The general retired to his tent. The days were becoming cooler now, the mosquitoes less aggressive but annoying, nevertheless. It wasn't war that killed the men, it was afflictions of various kinds–the shivering fevers, vomiting, dysentery, and other such misery inflicted on them during the wait that caused attrition.

Achillas sat on a chair and groaned. His back hurt from the training exercises in the morning with the cavalry. He had heard some rumors about Caesar's request, but without a formal communication, it was murky. Hopefully, Pothinus' letter explained it all and clarified what he should do next.

He broke the wax seal and opened the parchment. The neat, meticulous letters were by Pothinus' own hand. Clearly the regent meant for this to be most secretive, and he had not used a scribe for the letter.

Achillas' eyes opened wide as he read.

Dear Achillas,

Caesar demands that Cleopatra and His Majesty disband their armies and present themselves before him, so that he may, as executor of His Late Majesty's will, decide the future of Egypt's throne. Thus, this message bears urgency.

Caesar has arrived with one legion, and his troops are forced within a small area near the palace, and they lament their inability to occupy the larger part of the town, which is now lit with fires in places by angry mobs exercising their free will and indignation.

On the question of Cleopatra, it is our determination, and His Majesty's will, that she be disallowed any audience with Caesar, so that she may not charm her way with wile and lies, and put to risk His Majesty's claim to the throne. You are not to afford her passage and shall take every measure to prevent her person from appearing in Alexandria. May you be delicate in this matter as to not inflame people's passions.

His Majesty, with my counsel, orders you such. Prepare your army to walk on Caesar and lay siege to his men, drive them to despair, and rid Egypt of Rome. We shall provide sufficient enticement that should Rome remain at a distance across the sea, then they shall enjoy the fruits of Egyptian cooperation.

Let this be done.

The insinuation was clear–kill Cleopatra, but do it quietly so that she disappears.

March on Alexandria and destroy the Roman legions, and then Pothinus would send a message to Rome of Caesar's misadventures or some other made-up story, to calm an angry Senate. Knowing that Caesar had defied the Senate, it seemed that Pothinus' gamble was that they would not begrudge Caesar's end in Egypt.

Achillas took a deep breath. He smiled at the unique power he held at this moment–it was Achillas who would determine the life and death of Cleopatra, Caesar, and even His Majesty Ptolemy. He walked to the stove, lit up a fire, and burned the letter.

But if he lost? Then Egypt would be lost.

He then called a lieutenant to issue new orders. "Send orders to the legions to prepare to march in five days. Also prepare a half-legion, with two hundred cavalry and one-thousand five hundred troops to move farther south, to prevent any entry across the river and guard our rear."

"Yes, sir."

"And prepare a scouting trip with our best lookouts," he said. If there was one lesson from these past months, it was not to underestimate that wretched girl.

CHAPTER 41

NILE DELTA

CLEOPATRA

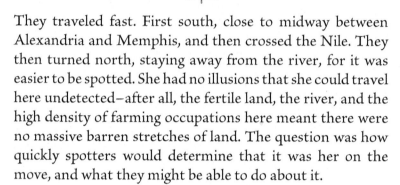

They traveled fast. First south, close to midway between Alexandria and Memphis, and then crossed the Nile. They then turned north, staying away from the river, for it was easier to be spotted. She had no illusions that she could travel here undetected–after all, the fertile land, the river, and the high density of farming occupations here meant there were no massive barren stretches of land. The question was how quickly spotters would determine that it was her on the move, and what they might be able to do about it.

She had argued with Apollodorus that Achillas and Pothinus would conspire to keep her away from Caesar or conjure stories that she was marching on the Romans. With no idea of what was happening in Alexandria, she only had her hunch while the horse-driven carriage shook as it trundled on a rough path that cut through grain fields.

The night was quiet as she rested in her tent, surrounded by her men. Charmian had traveled with her, while Iras had remained with Metjen. Apollodorus gave her a night report that no suspicious movements had been noticed. At this rate, she would be near the southern edges of Lake Mareotis, very close to Alexandria, in four days.

Kadmos reported that the men were in high spirits. "They will earn their pay, Your Majesty," he said, and flexed his biceps and danced his eyebrows.

She had to admit that he was entertaining, even if he sometimes flagrantly violated the protocol an officer must follow with his royal. She had overlooked his rude jokes about Metjen, insinuations of his conquests with the women in Syria and elsewhere, and even utterly laughable attempts of flirting with her, but someday she would have to tell him to behave. Now was not the time.

But she was amused that Kadmos had recently taken an interest in Charmian (*if not the queen, then her lady-in-waiting!*)–much to her chagrin, though Cleopatra knew that her lady-in-waiting had developed somewhat of an infatuation with the man. But in no uncertain terms had Cleopatra told Charmian to be careful. "Flirt with the man, Charmian, but under no circumstances shall you get pregnant," she told the blushing girl. "I have studied much about ending the growing seed in a womb, but those remedies are painful and dangerous. Do not make me decide that for you," she warned.

And of course, she had to embarrass the girl further. "There are many things you can do with a man without being penetrated."

A squealing Charmian had vehemently denied that she was planning to do anything with that rogue, but her eyes and giggles told otherwise.

Cleopatra had traveled with two lyre and harp performers who played a melodious tune in the night before she slept. The lyre's strumming provided a soothing background to Charmian's gentle singing.

Sleep, my little sun

Tomorrow you shine again,

Smile upon the grain and the flower

Smile upon the fruit and the bird

You shall not die today, you only hide,

You shall wake, and forever be by my side

Her body succumbed to exhaustion and her senses slowly dissolved in a haze of darkness as the song, the music, and the incessant *crick, crick, crick* of the night critters drew her into the arms of sleep.

Cleopatra dreamed of Apollodorus holding her hand and walking with her in a garden.

CHAPTER 42

NILE DELTA

CLEOPATRA

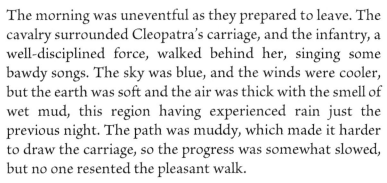

The morning was uneventful as they prepared to leave. The cavalry surrounded Cleopatra's carriage, and the infantry, a well-disciplined force, walked behind her, singing some bawdy songs. The sky was blue, and the winds were cooler, but the earth was soft and the air was thick with the smell of wet mud, this region having experienced rain just the previous night. The path was muddy, which made it harder to draw the carriage, so the progress was somewhat slowed, but no one resented the pleasant walk.

Two hours into the walk, they arrived at a plain with gentle hills to their north. They would have to climb up a small incline, and then she knew from the topography of this region that the ground would begin to descend. She had kept the curtains open and absorbed the air and the smells of earth, when she saw a scout rushing back towards them. He came straight to her, and Apollodorus rushed to the side of the carriage.

"We have been spotted, Your Majesty. There is an entire armed unit on the other side!" the messenger said, panicking.

Apollodorus sounded his whistle, and their contingent came to a halt. He turned to the man. "How big? Could you assess them? Is it the entire army?"

"It is definitely Achillas' men, General. Not the entire army. It seemed like they are of a similar size to our units, or perhaps a little bigger."

Just as he spoke, several riders of the enemy cavalry arrived at the top of the incline, not even a half-mile away, and sounded their trumpets. Her army's only chance was to retreat and run, or take on the enemy headlong. And there was not much time to decide.

Kadmos came running. "What are the orders?" he yelled, looking at both Apollodorus and Cleopatra.

She was tired of running or waiting.

Not anymore.

And in that quick instant, she made a determination that if Achillas had sent these men as rearguard, then it was unlikely that his best troops were here. And knowing the kind of schemers Pothinus and Theodotus were, it was more likely that they were planning to march on Caesar than acquiesce to the orders. If that were true, then the bulk of the army was either preparing for a march, or was already on one.

If she was right, she had a chance. If she was wrong, she would die. At least she would die trying in a battlefield—a rare, almost unheard-of glory for a woman—instead of in a prison or a forum.

Her lips curled up in a smile. "Kadmos, let us see if your men earn their pay today. General Apollodorus, bring us glory!"

Kadmos laughed. "Finally! Finally!" he yelled, and the impetuous ass took a quick moment to grab Charmian's hand and kiss it, surprising her, before he rushed away.

Apollodorus nodded in agreement. "Yes, Your Majesty, and may Isis bless us!"

With that, he screamed, "Formation!" and the well-trained unit organized itself with impressive speed. Two men hurried to put a corset and armor on her, gave her a blade that she knew somewhat how to wield. It would come to use if she were to want to kill herself, rather than be taken. They put a bronze helmet with beautiful purple plumes on her. Since she was adamant that she would not be carried away to safety or hidden from danger, she was asked to get down from the carriage and go to the center of the infantry unit, ringed by soldiers. But Charmian was whisked away, protesting, to the back of the unit.

The cavalry, like the wings of an eagle, split in two and arranged itself on either side of the infantry, while the center mass arranged itself in Roman Testudos, like turtles, closely huddled square masses with shields up and swords drawn. A small row of Scythian archers ran up to the front for the opening volleys. If Achillas' men formed their center like a Macedonian phalanx with their twelve- to thirteen-foot *sarissas*, then the cavalry attack on their flanks was critical to break them. If the cavalry lost, then the battle would most likely be lost.

Her heart thudded with fear and excitement. She had never been in the middle of a battle, and now, her fate hung in the balance of this force. The armor was heavy, and the helmet a burden.

Just as she gathered her thoughts, the enemy cavalry appeared on the horizon, kicking up mud and rushing down at them.

"Charge!" she heard someone scream, and her cavalry rode up to meet the enemy. The sounds of hoofs on the wet mud was like thunder in her ears. The infantry shifted to a trot, and with her heart thundering, she began to jog with them.

Did I make the right decision? To attack? And to stay here instead of being whisked away to safety?

She shook those thoughts and focused on the scene ahead. Between the bodies of her soldiers, she got the first glimpse of the enemy, *her people*–in a classical Macedonian phalanx, first put to use with terrifying effect by Philip, Alexander the Great's father, and then honed to perfection by Alexander.

The House of Ptolemy had maintained this structure for three hundred years.

She could not see the clash of the cavalry, except for sounds in the distance–metal against metal, neighs of horses, screams and shouts. *Where was Apollodorus? Kadmos?*

The infantry was called to halt by a captain, and then as she strained to look beyond her protective cover, she was mesmerized by the Scythian bolts that flew from the archers' bows and dotted the sky like a swarm of long, deadly insects. At the same time, shields went up all around her, and a large guard by her side roughly held her elbow and forced her to push her shield up.

Incoming arrows!

Thwack, thwack, thwack, thwack.

The arrows made a soft and squishy sound as they hit the wet earth or impacted the leather and wood shields, like a mother's wet kisses on a chubby baby's cheeks. And sometimes those sounds were interrupted by screaming. She kept her shield up until her arms tired, and then two guards by her side, noticing her struggle, pushed themselves against her and protected her with their shields.

Would the rain of arrows end, she wondered, but it did. And then, just like that, with a huge blood-curdling shout, the infantry charged ahead. She ran with them, shouting herself, the sole female voice, unheard in the din of battle but energizing to the men around her.

Bring me glory, Isis, Ra, Dionysos! she implored, even as the pain in her shoulders and feet vanished with the rush of battle-fury. At first, there was nothing but a mass of bodies around her, all with their shields up and their javelins out. They launched the javelins and drew their swords. All around her was absolute madness–the cavalries were still at it in the distance, but the inexorable force of the infantry was moving forward. But then, slowly the lines around her began to part, and the frightening reality of the battle began to emerge. Even as she was protected, she was only a few lines deep from the front, and what was happening became clear.

The mass of spikes was impaling her men, even as some made it through and were hacking at Achillas' men. Her cavalry had made some headway but were nowhere near breaking the enemy cavalry. The battle quickly descended into a mass wrestling match in the slippery muck. She ran with the men, stumbled, flailed about, sometimes afraid, and sometimes exhilarated. Twice, an enemy sarissa's blood-stained tip, with pieces of an unfortunate soldier's innards still sticking to it, came close to shearing her. At one point, exploiting a gap in the fighting formation, an enemy soldier almost made it to her, perhaps imagining that she was a small and weak boy. She clumsily fought him off–hitting him with the shield and swinging her sword, connecting to his, causing pain to shoot up her shoulders. But one of her royal guards jumped into the melee and killed him, severing his arm first and then stabbing him. She recoiled in horror as blood sprayed all over.

She was tiring. The gray and black mud hardening in places made it difficult to walk. The sounds were beginning to ring in her ears, and limbs and bodies piled up around her, soaking the mud and the grass shoots with blood. She refused entreaties for her to be taken away–if she had to die, it would be here. She shouted at one of her guards for a report. "Where is Apollodorus? Get him here!" she ordered.

Luckily, her general was not too far away, and he came jogging to her with guards protecting him. The situation was dire, but not entirely hopeless. Neither side was gaining–the skill of her forces was counter-balanced by the numerical superiority of the opponents, and neither side was willing to concede. But the situation was slowly growing worse for her, Apollodorus said, as his men fell in greater numbers.

"We cannot hold on for too long, Your Majesty," he said, gasping for breath, his face almost unrecognizable in layers of blood, skin, mud and sweat.

She looked around, clearing the sweaty hair that obscured her vision. "Do you know if Achillas or any of his senior men are here?"

"None that I recognize, Your Majesty," he said.

She could sense the line in the front falling back, struggling, their muddy shoes sliding, unable to hold against the weight of the enemy forces.

She remembered a story from a war three hundred years ago. She was going to try the same.

A gamble that could lead to death, but what did she have to lose anymore?

"Apollodorus, I order you to–" and she continued, as Apollodorus' eyes widened in horror.

CHAPTER 43

ALEXANDRIA

POTHINUS

"Well?" Caesar asked, his voice tinged with irritation and impatience.

"The riots and unrest are hampering our efforts to secure coin for repayment, Your Excellency. We have managed a thousand talents, but the remaining two will take more time," Pothinus said, putting on a concerned voice.

Caesar looked at him with those intense eyes. "You are stalling, Pothinus. I know that."

Pothinus smiled politely. "You know the situation outside the palace grounds, Caesar. The shouts in the nights, the fires, the mobs. Would you want me to risk bringing treasure wagons through our streets without the right protection?"

Caesar appraised him coolly but said nothing. He walked around in the grand hall that he had set up as his headquarters. His senior officers milled about, looking at maps on the tables or lounging on luxurious velvet seats.

"What of the orders to the siblings?" he said.

Orders? You cannot order the king of Egypt to anything.

"They have been dispatched, Your Excellency. Cleopatra's hostility towards her brother, His Majesty, makes it difficult to ascertain what her move will be. But should you want to know, she despises the Romans as much as she hates her brother."

Caesar raised an eyebrow. "Does she? She spent time in Rome and was treated well."

"She resents Rome in Egypt, as many do," Pothinus said pointedly. He was right. What self-respecting Egyptian, whether of local stock or Macedonian heritage, would accept the meddling of these blowhards?

"Is she coming?" Caesar asked, harder this time.

Pothinus shook his head. "The order has been conveyed, Your Excellency. But we hope that you understand that His Majesty's messengers cannot guarantee her presence. It is up to her."

"And has His Majesty disbanded his army?"

Pothinus nodded vigorously. "The order has been conveyed. It will take some time, as you can imagine," he said unctuously, clasping his hands. "The soldiers need to be paid, their release orders prepared, and we must guard the rear for any misadventures by Cleopatra's forces. But it is in progress."

Caesar stepped closer to Pothinus. He was wearing a general's attire on this occasion, perhaps trying to drive home a point, or having just returned from one of his trips to put down some unrest nearby. His hair was thinning, so he had a habit of smoothing it time to time, conscious of its state.

"You know who Caesar is, do you not, Pothinus?" he said, with the slightest smile on his thin and menacing lips. He slipped to the third person when the conversation turned very serious.

"Yes, Your Excellency," Pothinus said.

"And that Caesar has been a consul and vanquished many enemies who thought they would get the better of him."

"Yes, Your Excellency, I do–"

"Quiet!" Caesar admonished him.

Pothinus controlled his anger but bit his tongue.

"And that Caesar will be the ruler of Rome, and controls the power of Rome?"

"Yes, Your Excellency," Pothinus said, his voice hollow and a strange dread in his belly.

"And that when Caesar issues orders, he expects them to be carried out, without deception?"

"Yes, Your Excellency."

"Well, then. This is what we will do until the situation is clear. You will inform His Majesty that he will be an honorable guest, in my custody, until the debt is repaid and royal disputes are settled in my presence. And I shall be magnanimous–the island of Cyprus will be returned to Egypt for Arsinoe and the youngest Ptolemy to rule."

Pothinus was surprised at the generous offer of returning Cyprus, but he also had an inkling where this conversation was headed.

Caesar continued, "You are to bring His Majesty here," Caesar wagged his bony finger and then pointed to the floor, "and arrange for his comfortable stay in these quarters."

Pothinus was stunned. He knew what this was: *hostage situation*, plain and simple.

He hoped Achillas would be here soon.

But for now, Caesar would keep the king of Egypt as hostage.

Achillas' men moved with purpose. Of his total of seven legions, each about four thousand, he had left a half-legion as rear-guard against Cleopatra. Four-and-half he left waiting midway, south-west of Pelusium and Alexandria, and two moved with him towards Alexandria. The plan was to foment as much trouble in Alexandria as possible, recruit the rabble-rousers and convicts as a force to add to his men, and wear out Caesar. And then, if needed, he would summon the rest of his reserves and finish off the Roman.

He and Pothinus had their reasons for not moving the entire army to Alexandria, for the mind of the mob was fickle, and one would never know what a full-scale invasion of the city might cause.

Achillas was in full agreement with Pothinus–there was no question of disbanding the army, and they would teach the Roman rascal a lesson he would never forget.

In just a few days, they would be in Alexandria and put an end to Caesar's foolishness.

CHAPTER 44

NILE DELTA

SABU

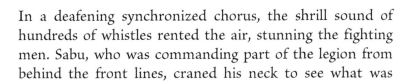

In a deafening synchronized chorus, the shrill sound of hundreds of whistles rented the air, stunning the fighting men. Sabu, who was commanding part of the legion from behind the front lines, craned his neck to see what was happening.

Are they signaling retreat?

But following the whistles came loud trumpets and several hoisted flags bearing royal insignia. The spectacle caused a sudden slowing of the fighting as men on either side paused the slashing and stayed in a pushing position, and those in loose clusters quickly put distance from their opponent and stood, exhausted, panting, but seeing what was happening.

Then rose the murmurs and shouts, and he could hear the rippling waves of the opponents' shouts–"Surrender to your Queen!" said in Egyptian and in Greek.

What was happening?

A great roar rose from the opposite end, and before Sabu could determine if this was a renewed push by the enemy, all eyes gravitated towards something near the front-center.

There, rising up by standing on the soldiers' shields, was a woman–

Queen Cleopatra?!

Sabu was hit by a mix of reverence, loyalty and fear. His directions were vague but insinuated–if they were to come upon her in a vulnerable position, then to kill her. He had been horrified at that order but never thought it would come to reality. Even when they had chanced upon this armed unit, his hope was that this was some kind of expeditionary force, but not with the queen in it.

And certainly not with her in the middle of a battle!

His cheeks burned with shame at what they were doing. She was Isis, she was the embodiment of their holy gods, and he knew that she had governed well before these disputes arose.

He, like many others around him, watched astounded.

There she stood, petite, with a shining diadem around her loose hair, her face tinged with mud and blood, but unmistakable in conveying her bearing. She had removed her armor, and instead in her hand she held a crook and a flail. She wore a long, elegant gown, now caked with dirt. But she stood with dignity, even if wobbling on the shield.

A sudden hush descended on the field, and as if by instinct, Sabu blew a specific tone on his whistle: 'stand down!'

And like a runner coming to sudden halt, both sides disengaged with speed. The cavalries were still at it, but they had noticed too, and he could sense consternation based on the haphazard movements.

The men suddenly stood quiet, their eyes glued and lips sealed even as captains shouted at everyone to be silent. Sabu pushed his way to the front, and there he was, only a few tens of feet from her. The Queen!

She stood with dignity. He had never realized, but she had reddish hair. Her nose was certainly not as beaked as it was on the coins, and she was not as tall as he imagined. In fact, she was not tall compared to even the women he knew.

But she was *regal*. And how immeasurably bold of her to be among men, in battle, and to stand up on the shield without fear of archers!

His chest expanded with pride.

Then, her voice pierced the calm air.

"My dear subjects, I speak to you in the god's tongue of this land, in the tongue of my forefathers, and in the tongue of the brave men from lands far West and East," she said to the captivated audience.

And she said that *in his language!* And then in Greek, and then in Latin, and then in Aramaic. Who other than a goddess could speak the language of every man here? His hair rose at her speech. Many of his men simply dropped their weapons and sank to their knees, even as her men kept a watchful eye for any misadventures. They had created a cordon around her, with three huge men standing on shield-platforms by her side, looking for errant arrows.

What a sight!

His Queen had a soft but commanding voice. It had no harshness. Instead, the words were carried by sweetness, soft, perhaps only heard by the few in the front. But enterprising soldiers nearby shouted the words verbatim for others to hear, and she knew when to pause and let them convey her speech. It was masterful!

She continued, "Lay down your arms. Why are sons of this land forced to lay their hands upon their queen, ordained by the gods, protector of their homes, forced to this situation by conspirators with no honor?"

There were murmurs of assent.

"Who among you wishes me harm? For what harm have I caused to your person?"

The silence was pierced by a smattering of answers. "None, Your Majesty!"

"Lay down your arms and grant me free passage, my men. Let your queen bring honor to this land. Let your queen make her case with Caesar, and may the wheels of fate turn where it does. But may it happen with your queen's voice, rather than in its absence!"

With that, she raised her hands to the sky and at an oblique angle towards them in blessing. The few who shouted objections were quickly shut down, and Sabu was thrown into confusion.

Her Majesty's men raised flags for truce and discussion, and Sabu, while taken by this event, was no fool. He ordered a defensive posture and called the cavalry to stay alert. The two sides put distance between them, and each side allowed the others to collect their dead and wounded.

Queen she may be, but his line of duty extended to general Achillas, and through him, His Majesty.

It was time to parley.

CHAPTER 45

NILE DELTA

CLEOPATRA

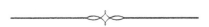

Cleopatra sat dejected. Her performance at the battlefield had earned her enormous respect, if some hysterical responses from those dear to her, for putting herself in such danger. But while it put an end to the fight, they were now stuck in a standoff where Sabu, a captain who seemed very remorseful for his role, was unwilling to give her unhindered passage.

"I am humbled by your presence and your grace, Your Highness," he had said sincerely, "but I am bound by duty to my general and His Highness."

None of the threats or cajoling had worked, and with the losses on her side, it made little sense to fight again. Besides, there was a high chance that Sabu's messengers were already on the way to Achillas' larger forces with news. Moving forward with an armed unit was now out of question.

Sabu, risking his life and limb, had offered only one way out. That they would not attack Cleopatra's forces provided she moved her men south again and stayed out. "I seek not to have your blood on my hands, Your Majesty," he had said, "but I beg you to move south, for that gives me an opportunity to state that you withstood losses and left the battlefield."

After bidding him farewell, she had decided to bless the last rites to the dead, and then to rest before engaging in any conversation.

And now, as the night approached, she had to decide what to do. She called her war council, with Apollodorus,

Kadmos, Charmian, and a few other senior officers from the army.

"Do we have a path to Alexandria?" she asked. The men all looked at each other but had no response. Kadmos had been injured with a bright red gash on his forearm, and she could not help but notice the glances between him and Charmian. He certainly played it up, making fake noises of distress. *What a rogue!*

"Apollodorus?" she pressed on him.

Apollodorus bowed. "There is no military path, Your Highness. Not unless we return to our army and have them march again. But it will be too late and take too much time. Many may have already left and headed countryside, waiting for summons."

She entwined her fingers and paced around in the tent. *All these men, and none with a bright idea!*

"What if we convince Sabu's men to join us instead?" she asked.

Kadmos stepped up. "What good will that do, Your Majesty? The combined forces would still be nowhere near Achillas' army's size, which Sabu says is nearly seven legions. And we risk defection in the ranks–for some, their reverence to you might not hold once they hear their general invoke their king's name."

He was right, as frustrating as it was. A king's name held more weight. Even if the king was an ineffective little twat. He was a man, and for many in the army, that was all that mattered.

She glared at him, but he did not back away, for he knew the truth in his words.

Suddenly, Charmian spoke. She had a soft, lilting voice. Sometimes it sounded like a little girl's. "Why did you risk your life so, Your Majesty? Why did you think it would work?"

Cleopatra paused. Perhaps they deserved an answer. Their devotion to her came not just from a higher purpose, but because she explained her rationale and thinking to them. They were in this journey not out of fear, but admiration. She had to remind herself of that.

"Has anyone here heard of Craterus?" she asked. They all shook their head.

Not surprising, considering they had nowhere near the education she had.

"He was a general of the great Alexander. After Alexandria's death, his men broke into different alliances as they fought for the empire," she said, smiling as she let her eyes fix on each man's and woman's in the audience, moving from one to the other.

"So, it came to pass that he would have to fight Alexander's royal secretary, called Eumenes. Eumenes was a clever man, a Greek scribe who rose in the ranks and became a capable general. But Eumenes' men, many hard Macedonians, resented the fact that he was Greek. And Craterus knew this."

They were captivated by her story, of course, wondering what this had to do with what she did today, foolishly getting on a shield and exposing herself to the opposition, even though that brilliantly mad move had worked.

Cleopatra continued, recollecting the intriguing story her tutors (including Pothinus) had told her, and that she had read in the scrolls in the library. One of those, termed *The Atlantis Papyrus,* had an interesting story from a man called Deon, from her founding forefather's time, and this man had personally fought on Eumenes' side.

"So, when the two armies faced each other, Craterus decided that he would expose himself to Eumenes' soldiers, causing them to see the famed and well-respected general. What would they do? Fight for a Greek secretary they had little respect for, or a brave, decorated general who led armies for their divine king?"

Kadmos laughed. "What a brilliant man! To end a battle before it begins. The scribe learned his lesson, just as you taught Achillas' men."

Cleopatra smiled.

Charmian, a smart girl herself, caught what Kadmos missed. "That was not how the story ended, was it, Your Majesty?" she said.

Cleopatra shook her head. She adjusted her diadem and crossed her hands as she looked at them. "You are bright, Charmian. And you, not so much, Kadmos," she said, much to everyone's guffaws. He seemed not a bit embarrassed.

She was enjoying this moment. Telling them stories... like how her tutors did for her.

She continued, "But Eumenes was a smart man. He guessed what Craterus might attempt to do, so he positioned a non-Macedonian Cappadocian cavalry against Craterus, and spread word in his camp that it was not Craterus in the enemy position, but some warlord named Pigres. Craterus was caught by surprise when the Cappadocian cavalry bore down on him, had no idea who he was and paid no respect to his stature, and he was eventually surrounded. He fell from his horse and was trampled to death. Eumenes won the battle."

"What?" Apollodorus was flummoxed. "Why did you—" He stopped, and Cleopatra noticed a strange look in Apollodorus' eyes. She avoided looking at him and addressed the group.

"It was the idea, for the gods know that great ideas may work sometimes and not the other. I am Queen of Egypt, and I would not let us all die in vain, in foolhardy attempts, without the use of—" she said, and tapped her head.

Charmian began to sob. "You might have died, Your Majesty," she said as she sat by Cleopatra's legs.

Cleopatra was filled with affection for her, and for the others, who had unquestioningly followed her orders and stayed by her side. But the saga was not over.

"We have not accomplished what we set out to do. Without an agreement with Caesar, assuming he is still alive, none of you will ever be free. They will hunt me down, and you, and all we did will come to nothing," she said.

There was a solemn agreement with what she said. Such was the nature of battle and enmity. The losers paid with their life and freedom. Unless, of course, some were willing to turn for coin or loyalty.

But Cleopatra wanted to live up to another fame of hers, for what good was her intelligence if she had no other method at her disposal?

She looked at Apollodorus and nodded.

It was time for the backup plan that they had hoped they would never need to employ.

CHAPTER 46

ALEXANDRIA

POTHINUS

The man's wailing finally stopped. One pulled fingernail and a dislocated shoulder were enough to get him singing. He dropped all pretense of loyalty and bravery. No one withstood torture for too long, and it was only in plays that brave men held on until death.

"Did she send you here to kill me? Someone else?"

The man lay on his good shoulder as he shook. He looked up at Pothinus with fearful eyes. "No, Your Excellency," he gasped. "Only to report details."

"What details?" Theodotus asked.

This man was one of the two who were found engaging in suspicious conversation and behavior in the palace grounds, and even with the Romans near the docks. The other had escaped when they were accosted by Pothinus' spies.

A quick discussion with the people (not the Roman bastards) who they conversed with revealed that the men were curious about the configuration of the palace, the location and position of the Roman garrison, whether the Romans or His Majesty's navy was ready at the harbor, and so on. Questions of the nature of military intelligence, along with mundane, seemingly normal discussions about trade and merchandise (were the Romans interested in carpets?).

What were these two up to? Some normal questioning yielded nothing useful, but the man's demeanor had suggested something more.

"What details?" Pothinus repeated, and he kicked the man in his injured shoulder.

He wailed and rolled around in pain. They waited. They had plenty of time.

The man finally spluttered the words while clutching his shoulder. "Queen Cleopatra, she sent us."

Knew it. That bitch.

"What did she want?"

The man put his head against the floor. "About where the Romans were. About where His Majesty's navy was. That is all, Your Excellency," he spluttered, his saliva wetting the floor.

What use was that information? he wondered as he exchanged glances with Theodotus.

"What else? What else?" they pressed on him. But he had little more to say except to keep repeating and crying that all they were to report back was what was happening here, and where the Romans were. He also made some other grand claims that Pothinus recognized as coming from a man in pain and doing whatever he can for relief.

They finally gave up. Pothinus gestured for a guard to take the man and throw him off the harbor deck.

"What is she trying?" Theodotus asked.

"Well, for some reason she wants to know where the Romans are, and where the navy is," Pothinus said.

Theodotus tapped on the arm of the chair, and then pulled his hand away in disgust when he noticed the bloody nail sticking to the side. He yelled at a servant to take it away.

"Is she planning a naval attack?" Theodotus wondered.

Pothinus was about to reprimand Theodotus for such a *stupid* thought, but then he checked himself. *What if?*

He had learned not to underestimate Cleopatra. All the intelligence he had received was that she still held on to her army, and that they had moved south. There was nothing about a navy. What if she had secretly constructed a navy, used her army as a diversion, but was planning to arrive by sea?

Was she planning to attack Caesar, or join him? Was she his reinforcement?

The possibilities were confusing and confounding.

They debated what this meant–and they finally settled on the most plausible, logical theory.

That Cleopatra was going to force her way into the harbor with maybe a small naval force, thereby avoiding His Majesty's army, and connecting with Caesar to make her case.

But the whole thing could be a diversion. A ruse. A tactic to keep Achillas' men needlessly occupied at the beaches.

Pothinus was not going to take chances. Not when the kingdom was at stake.

CHAPTER 47

NEAR THE RIVER

CLEOPATRA

———————⟡———————

The day after the battle, Cleopatra moved her army farther south, away from Sabu's forces.

Then, she summoned her senior council and announced that the remaining army would retreat south and join the main group, awaiting orders. Kadmos would lead them back to Metjen, who would assume leadership.

"With Apollodorus, Charmian, and Kadmos' help, I shall go into exile until I find a way out for all of us," she said.

The officers protested loudly. The protests made way to lamentations, and lamentations made way to reluctant acceptance, and reluctant acceptance made way to sadness. But Cleopatra was adamant. With her amongst them, there would always be conflict, and nothing meaningful would come of it. Besides, she knew that as much as many protested, some would soon turn, and betrayal would not be far behind. At that point, she would have lost most of her army, her money, and then it would be her life. Pursuing armed conflict would lead her nowhere.

In the afternoon, after the orders were propagated, there was a solemn ceremony conducted by Egyptian and Greek priests, blessing her. And then, wearing the mantle of the goddess and assuming the role of the chief priestess herself, she blessed the men and the women for their onward journeys. "I will see you again as queen," she said to many teary eyes, "and you will suffer my command again," she concluded, to many laughs and sniffles.

Apollodorus arranged a scouting trip to ensure there was no danger around them.

Cleopatra trusted Kadmos. She could not help but smile as he managed one final, flirtatious farewell to a blushing Charmian. *My sword stays high and hard waiting for you* he said, that rascal. Cleopatra knew that Charmian yearned to be in Kadmos' loud and boisterous company.

When the sun began to set, Cleopatra departed the camp with Apollodorus, Charmian, and four mounted royal guards closest to Apollodorus and fiercely loyal. They walked a short distance from the camp and watched as her army began to move south and slowly vanished from view.

They first set on foot, walking north-east, towards the direction of the Nile. The Great River flowed gently at this time of the year. Apollodorus had planned this trip, and she knew that a boat waited for them. She had dressed like a simple Greek woman wearing a drab olive-grey gown, and on her waist was a faded leather bag with some jewelry, coin (*those bearing her name!*), and the one item that she, and she alone, was allowed to wear in the entire kingdom–her diadem, signifying her royal status.

The guards on the horses stayed out of sight, keeping an eye out for any threats. Cleopatra, Apollodorus, and Charmian walked together.

Cleopatra enjoyed looking like a peasant. She once horrified Charmian (*Your Highness Charmian, would you like me to serve you some beer?*), causing her to make all kinds of gesticulations. "Such words shall never come from your mouth, Your Majesty," she almost scolded her queen.

It took three hours, until nightfall, when they finally arrived at a desolate section of the river, near a very particular landmark with a cluster of trees and a small hill. There, a man waited with a lamp. When they approached, Apollodorus shouted a secret phrase, to which the man responded correctly.

They halted for the night, and Charmian helped Cleopatra settle comfortably. They washed in the cool water and dried their clothes. Charmian cooked some salted fish and prepared some bread with gravy for the group.

They ate quietly, and Cleopatra knew that each one contemplated their future. She slept fitfully, tired and leaving tomorrow to the gods.

When morning came, they completed their rituals and ensured that all supplies were loaded onto the boats, and that there was not coin just on their person but also hidden in specific crevices and pockets of the boat. Charmian helped with preparation, cleaning, and the final inventory of goods to go on the boat. Bread, beer, mattress sheets, physician's items, even strong liquids to repel mosquitoes.

And then, it was time to leave. They all walked towards the small boat. The morning birds still chirped. The water was cool, quiet, and relatively clear. It would grow turbid farther north.

The burly guards stood and waited.

Apollodorus nodded to Cleopatra, who turned to Charmian.

"Charmian?"

"Yes, Your Majesty?" the girl said enthusiastically, holding a small bag in her hands, her belongings. Even after all these months of difficult living, Charmian had lost none of her radiance. Her glass-grey eyes still shone bright, she still took meticulous care of her long, shiny black hair, and she had blossomed into a beautiful girl. And Cleopatra knew that she was unquestioningly loyal and could not bear the thought of being away from her queen.

"You will not be coming with us," Cleopatra said softly.

Charmian was aghast. Her face changed in an instant—surprise, shock, bewilderment.

"Your Majesty! How can you—"

Cleopatra moved closer and held her shoulders. "This requires only me and Apollodorus. I need your assistance, but you must render that from afar."

Charmian began to sob. She cried and begged to stay with Cleopatra, stating that it was her duty to be by Cleopatra's side, no matter what. And that she would stay by the queen's side until death.

Cleopatra chastised her that she had no plans of dying, but to return as queen, she needed Charmian to do as she was told. She then explained Charmian's mission—one that would require the lady-in-waiting to ride with a guard as fast as she could, and meet someone Apollodorus knew near the eastern borders of Alexandria.

Charmian was pleased at being of use. Very few knew who she was, and she was at low risk of detection. After making sure that Charmian had her instructions memorized and accurate, and that she would not speak of this to anyone, they bid good-bye to her.

It was one of those rare times when Cleopatra was moved to tears.

As Apollodorus helped her onto that little boat, Cleopatra wondered if this journey would end with her as queen, or as a forgotten rotting corpse in the northern marshes.

CHAPTER 48

NILE

CLEOPATRA

For five days they traveled north, carried by the gentle flow of the Nile, and with Apollodorus' skill at rowing–something he had learned a long time ago.

It was not the officious customs patrols that harassed them, or the inquisitive traders, or the odd military naval boat that shouted challenges, but the mosquitoes. As they neared the northern marshes, the insects' ferocity increased. Mosquitoes swarmed them at dusk, like a thick blanket, and hounded them relentlessly.

Without her retinue of servants, fanners, physicians, and well-designed protective layers and covering, Cleopatra experienced the misery of the marshes and its most hated denizens. Her skin broke out in hives; on her neck, arms, shoulders, cheeks, nose, forehead, feet, and waist. No part escaped the miserable itch, and the salves she had were insufficient. When tears welled up, she looked away, so as not to put doubt in Apollodorus' heart. She had learned, like common people, to swat and crush the mosquitoes as they sat on her, creating a disgusting red streak of blood. After doing it a hundred times, revulsion changed to sport, and she proudly began to point out to Apollodorus how many she had killed.

The journey was part terror of being discovered, and part pity at the misery, but Apollodorus told her multiple times that he admired her strength, for not once did Cleopatra desire to abandon this mission and retreat. As they entered deeper into the marshland, the river grew turbid, the vegetation was wilder, and they were soon surrounded by an endless expanse of swamp, with not a life in sight. She worried whether Apollodorus knew where he was going—but the river was an excellent guide, for here it flowed in a single band, and it was clear to anyone on it that there was only one way; the way that led it to the sea.

But there was one wonderful aspect of this boat journey.

Their unfettered conversations.

She asked him many questions while sharing her own stories of growing up. She exhaled. It was as if a heavy sack had been removed from an aching shoulder—for who knew if she would be queen again? They laughed about common enemies (*how is Pothinus slim, if he is so full of gas?*) and reminisced about the good days at the palace when she was regent (*the trip to the zoo and seeing the magnificent lions*). His life was so fundamentally different from hers, and she was amazed to learn new things about how he lived and grew up. He told her more of his military stories (*he surely exaggerated some feats, which made him endearing to her*) and had to be cajoled into speaking of the women in his life (*not many, really, Your Majesty, and certainly no one like you!*).

Only on the seventh day, now close to the sea, did the weather and the landscape change. They came to a quiet, uninhabited bend of the river. The water was much clearer, and there were a few tall trees near the bank.

They decided to halt for the night.

Cleopatra took the time to wash in the river as Apollodorus established a simple camp. The wind was calm and cool, and after days of stress, the ability to sit in a pretty location, spared from the mosquitoes and the heat, with no one to bother her about one crisis or another, was liberating.

They ate the basic staples of salted fish and coarse bread. She wondered if she would ever return to the magnificent feasts of the palace. The roasted boars, fowl, the wine, cheese and beer; the palms, dates, figs, olives, oranges; the spiced lamb, puffy soft bread, pig; the sweet and sour *sherbets*, rice, aromatic lentils… her stomach churned.

After dinner, they sat together watching the flow of water, even as the sky began to darken, the orange-yellows slowly turning to dark blue, and then only the slightest hint of light. At some point—she never realized when, for it only seemed natural—her fingers were entwined with Apollodorus'. The man whose unwavering loyalty, bravery, and fortitude had gotten her this far.

He had his head held low, refusing to look at her, and she knew why. *She was his queen!*

Cleopatra turned and put a hand under his coarse, bearded chin, and with some effort turned his face to her.

"Apollodorus?"

"Yes, Your Majesty," he said, his voice cracking but his eyes transfixed on her face.

"You cannot say no to your queen," she said, smiling.

Apollodorus reached back to her neck and pulled her into a gentle, yet passionate kiss. The smell of sweat and the salty taste of skin meant nothing.

CHAPTER 49

NEAR ALEXANDRIA

APOLLODORUS

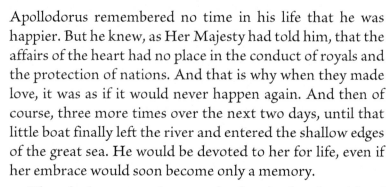

Apollodorus remembered no time in his life that he was happier. But he knew, as Her Majesty had told him, that the affairs of the heart had no place in the conduct of royals and the protection of nations. And that is why when they made love, it was as if it would never happen again. And then of course, three more times over the next two days, until that little boat finally left the river and entered the shallow edges of the great sea. He would be devoted to her for life, even if her embrace would soon become only a memory.

They had to stay close to the beach, for the risk of currents dragging them to the sea and to their lonely deaths was high if they ventured too far. They stopped again for the day, waiting for dusk to travel. The sea was calm, with the usual fish trawlers, a smattering of customs vessel, some merchant ships on the way to the harbor, and at a significant distance, a fine Egyptian bireme with the recognizable mast of the royal navy.

They would be inconspicuous.

When the sun began to set, but with some time before darkness, they set out on the sea again. The distant light of the magnificent lighthouse of Alexandria was visible even here, more like a pinprick, but would be awe-inspiring once they got closer. It would be another day.

That evening, they finally made rendezvous with Apollodorus' contact. The man, Basilius, hailing from a little village, was a faithful follower of Apollodorus and an ex-soldier. He could not believe his eyes when he saw Her

Majesty Cleopatra. He prostrated before her in disbelief, and she had to scold him to get up and not draw attention.

They stayed in his isolated little mud house, with him panicking over how to treat his queen, and Apollodorus had to calm him down. Basilius' wife almost fainted but recovered enough to treat them to a sumptuous meal. She cried twice, overwhelmed, but eventually settled into a comfortable conversation with Her Majesty. Watching them speak, Apollodorus was struck by a remarkable trait of the queen, on how easily she picked up local dialects and imitated the accents, making the speaker taken by her familiarity with their ways.

From Basilius they received intelligence about Roman arrangements and the situation with Ptolemy's forces.

"The news is that General Achillas has left many of his legions midway between Pelusium and Alexandria and is still advancing with the rest."

"So, His Majesty Ptolemy has not disbanded his army?" Apollodorus asked.

"No, General. Alexandria is in a state of unrest. It seems His Majesty and his senior advisors are all in one section of the palace, heavily guarded and cordoned off from the Roman section, which is by the harbor."

"Any other rumors?"

"That Caesar is angry at the regent stalling debt repayments and the royals not appearing before him. And that His Majesty does not want," he said, looking at Cleopatra fearfully, "for Her Majesty to return."

She nodded but said nothing. It was not surprising that they wanted her dead.

"How reliable is your man?" Apollodorus asked.

"By my life, my wife's life, and all the gods dear to me. He thanks the divine forces for giving him this opportunity."

Apollodorus knew that every link in a long chain would have to hold; otherwise, this mission would be futile.

They retired after receiving further information on the state of affairs. He longed to hold her but knew that the tide of fate was turning. The future of Her Majesty Cleopatra, the manifestation of goddess Isis, the woman he was hopelessly in love with, would be decided the next day.

But late into the night, Apollodorus was awakened by Cleopatra, who had come out of the room Basilius and his wife had vacated for her.

"I can't sleep," she whispered. "Come inside with me. Just stay beside me."

He went back with her quietly. She did not lie down—instead, she put her back to the wall and sat. And he sat beside her.

"These houses are so small."

"As they are for most people, Your Majesty."

"What are they made of?"

"Usually sun-burnt brick and clay. Some are made of packed mud and stones with hay for roofs. It depends on what they can afford."

She contemplated the situation. "I can understand now why some have trouble paying taxes."

Apollodorus preferred not to comment. "The poor struggle every day to eat and have a roof over their heads."

"That is why I allow for tax reliefs," she said, returning to her favorite subject. "Maybe I should do more if I become Queen."

"The people will always adore a queen who cares for them and not just collects taxes," Apollodorus said. He felt consciously as if he was accusing her.

"Well, that is what some of my ancestors did. Just collected taxes and gave nothing in return. But others, like the second Ptolemy, did much to improve agriculture, roads, and buildings. I want to be that Queen."

"Yes, Your Majesty."

"Was your house like this, growing up?"

"It was."

"Did you eat thrice a day? Is the food really that simple every day?"

Apollodorus marveled at the questions and how far removed she was from the life of a commoner. "Sometimes thrice, but often twice. Yes, it is simple, Your Majesty. Most people cannot afford boar or fowl on a regular basis."

"My father never once took me to see the life of the commoners. My tutors never said I should. I never thought about it. Maybe I should."

"That would make you a rare Queen. You also learned the language of Egypt, which no one else did."

"And they always smell so much. Do they not shower or clean their mouths?"

"Baths are a luxury. Most go to the river for a cleaning once a week. They clean their teeth once every three or four days."

"Maybe I should approve more bathhouses. Where people can come and wash themselves," she said, examining her grown and dirty nails under the lamp.

"That would be a good idea, Your Majesty."

She laid her head on his shoulder.

"Do I stink?"

"Well, it is natural, since you do not have your perfumes or your daily wash."

"We both stink, everyone here stinks, so one needs to feel embarrassed."

"Indeed, Your Majesty. But you stink far less."

"You say that to please me. You are a fool, Apollodorus. And you never ask me questions."

"Your Majesty, it is not my place to ask you questions."

She yawned. He noticed that her eyes were losing focus. She switched topics. "But I don't like the Jews."

Apollodorus laughed. "But they are important residents of Alexandria. Their trade relations with Parthia and Judaea are important to us."

"I don't like people from Northern Macedonia either. They are rude."

"They are all your subjects, Your Majesty. And there are rude people from everywhere."

She sighed. "I suppose so. What if we get captured tomorrow? Do you think they will kill us right away?"

"I hope not, Your Majesty. It depends on who captures us. If Pothinus' men, then maybe. If the Romans, maybe they will hand us over to Caesar?"

"I have heard he is a good man. Intelligent. Maybe he will listen to reason."

He held her hand. "I hope that as well, Your Majesty."

"Why do you Greeks and Romans wear the same drab gowns every day? It is boring. The Parthians are so colorful."

"Dignity in simplicity, Your Majesty. The Parthians are pretentious peacocks."

"You should wear a long, flowing silk gown, a green scarf, and a tall pointed red hat with peacock feathers. Then put several chains around your neck and a few rings on your fingers."

"You should pay me more then, Your Majesty."

"I am sure you were not paying me taxes from your farm."

"I was."

"Do you think I should investigate your crimes?" she said, running her palm on his beard, yawning loudly.

"I think you should go to sleep."

CHAPTER 50

ALEXANDRIA

APOLLODORUS

They waited until evening approached before getting on the boat again. Basilius and his wife conducted prayers and bid them farewell. Apollodorus could see the worry and fear in Cleopatra's eyes, but she was resolute when asked if she wanted to proceed. *Don't ask me again!* she chastised him, her eyes blazing at the question. A day at rest had significantly improved her countenance–the various inflammations from insect bites had reduced, and her face was back to its radiant, purposeful self. She still had angry red welts on her shoulders and an thin, unsightly gash on her cheek, but she said she was ready for the task at hand.

The boat hugged the quiet coastline as Apollodorus rowed carefully. The fire from the top of the great lighthouse reflected off the waters as dusk arrived.

The vast palace complex, Her Majesty's home, would soon appear on the left. From here, on the calm gray-green sea, one would never know the tumult in the palaces and homes of the city. A few larger naval ships were stationary off Pharos Island, far ahead.

He hoped that their little boat would go unnoticed.

A hope that was dashed soon when a small, curious patrol boat made its way towards them. There were two men on it, naval guards presumably, definitely not Romans.

"Halt, halt, stop rowing!" the man yelled in Greek, holding up a lantern. It had become dark enough not to be able to see faces from this distance. Then the other man yelled in Egyptian.

Apollodorus cursed under his breath.

"Be quiet, Your Majesty," he said in a low voice. He patted his waist to ensure that his knife was intact, and he reached down near his feet to check that the short, sharp-edged metal pole was where he had placed it.

Cleopatra bent her head and pretended to be sick, with her face on her knees.

Apollodorus greeted them loudly, but he did not slow.

"I said stop rowing, you bastard!" the man shouted again.

Apollodorus had to act quickly. If he continued, there was a chance that the boat would sound an alarm with whistles or trumpets and attract others. Not knowing who they were or their intentions, this would be an incredible risk.

His chest tightened. He placed the oar inside and raised his hand in a friendly gesture. "I did not hear, my friend. I have stopped!"

The boat swayed gently as the patrol boat neared. They were patrolmen, and one held a sword in his hand while the other held up a lantern to look closer. The patrol boat aligned itself in parallel. Apollodorus looked around–there were no other vessels nearby.

"What is your business? Why are you here?"

"My wife is ill. I was taking her towards the great temple of Isis. With all the unrest in the city I thought a boat would be safest," he shouted.

The second man lifted the lantern to better illuminate the boat. Cleopatra kept her head down.

The first man, the hefty, pot-bellied Greek, put a leg on the boat's rim and brandished his sword. "You shouldn't be here. You are too close to the palace."

"We will go wide, sir. I just want to get treatment and blessings for her. I have gone this way before, so why not now?"

Potbelly thought for a while. "Some rumors about Queen Cleopatra invading with a fleet."

Apollodorus managed a fake, hollow laugh, like a spoon rattling in an empty brass vessel. "I better get going before her fleet gets here!"

But Potbelly would not go. He continued to stare at the boat. "Why is she hiding? Tell her to show herself."

Apollodorus was alarmed. "She is sick, sir. She carries a disease that attaches to those nearby."

"Why are you not sick, then?"

Apollodorus stammered. "I– I do not know, sir. Maybe because I am her husband."

Potbelly was not satisfied. He gestured for the second man to maneuver the boat closer. "Tell her to show herself," he said, harder this time.

He had to change tactics. It was dark now, and even whistling or trumpeting would not get far. It would take significant time for anyone to triangulate their position. He saw no other lights nearby–boats or ships. The flames and lanterns by the palace lit the side, and ripples of light danced in the water, and then there was the ever-present blaze of the lighthouse. But all these sources were far away.

"I won't. She is sick, sir. I must hurry. We seek no harm and would like to proceed," he said, and reached below.

Potbelly bellowed over the wind, "How dare you defy an order, goatfucker! We are His Majesty's officials, and you will identify yourself, now!"

They angled the boat to hit them broadside, even as Potbelly balanced the sword in one hand.

That was it. No more taking chances.

Apollodorus dropped the oar, but surreptitiously picked up the metal spike and held it behind his back. Potbelly's boat touched theirs, and he barked an order again. "You, remove your cloak, show yourself! Now!"

Apollodorus wished she hadn't, but without waiting for an instruction from Apollodorus, Her Majesty removed the hooded cloak and defiantly looked at the man. Her auburn hair shined beneath the light of the lantern. "I am your queen," she said, in as much of an imperial voice she could muster. "Now stand down!"

Stupid! Stupid!

Potbelly's jaw almost hit the sea. He staggered with shock. "What? You–"

And then he turned to the man beside him and bellowed, "It's her! It's her!"

He reached into his waistband, and that was when Apollodorus knew there could be no more conversation.

Apollodorus swung his metal spike up in a violent upward motion and rammed it beneath Potbelly's jaw. It rammed through his mouth and brain and exploded up the skull. He never even knew what happened, and Apollodorus pushed him off the boat. He then jumped across to the other boat, attacking the second man.

The Egyptian was not weak either. He had his sword out, and it glinted in the flickering flames of the lantern that was rolling about on the boat floor. Apollodorus managed to grab one of his opponent's hands and, before he could swing his weapon, stabbed him in the side. The man screamed and dropped his sword. Apollodorus grabbed him in a chokehold and sliced his neck. He pushed the man forward to avoid being drenched in blood.

With the unpleasant deed complete, he hopped back to the boat. His heart was still thundering in his chest, and his mind still disturbed from how close they were to being uncovered. He knelt by her.

"You should not have done that!" he hissed.

He could not see her expression in the shadows. "You can't tell me what to do!"

"I can, if you trust me with your life and your future. You almost got us both killed," he said, not backing down.

"Well, you killed them. How did it matter? I thought maybe hearing my voice would force them to stop, and maybe even aid us."

He shook his head. "It does not always work that way, Your Majesty. They may have had a special whistle or code. You don't know if there is a great reward on your head. Your enemies are not stupid. I am certain they are on the watch."

She was breathing hard. He knew that as his queen she would never apologize, nor did he expect her to. But he hoped she understood the risks.

Finally, her fingers grazed his cheek. "Are you alright?" she asked.

Apollodorus laughed. "Yes, I am, Your Majesty."

"Come here," she said, holding his hand.

Apollodorus sat by her side as they calmed down. The boat's gentle swaying soothed the nerves, and the glinting lights promised a new future. She lit up their lantern and held it to his face to examine the blood streaks.

"Clean yourself," she said. He used some of the seawater to wash himself.

"What do I have to lose anymore?" Apollodorus said to her puzzled expression.

And then he boldly kissed her one more time. She did not resist, but when they ended it several minutes later, she whispered to him, "Can you live with me being with other men, Apollodorus?"

He always knew that he would never take the place of a king or a prince. "It will be difficult, but I will do my duty."

I know my place.

She turned to him. "Do you think we will get rid of the Romans? Speak your mind. Can we be truly independent?"

She had rarely expressed doubts in this regard. It always appeared to Apollodorus that Cleopatra's goal was to rid Egypt of Rome's influence. But then, she always thought at a level he rarely understood.

He decided to be truthful. If there was something he knew far better than her, it was the understanding of military power.

"I do not think so, Your Majesty," he said nervously.

"Go on."

"We have been weakened for years. Our navy is depleted, and our army cannot match Rome's legions. Building such a formidable force is a combination of training, incentives, practice through conquests, a pipeline of experienced generals, the ability to raise armies on demand, the ability to pay and handle idle armies. We have had little of that since—" he said, and stopped.

"My grandfather's time. I know. Continue."

"Rome has many alliances and vassal states. They claim us as a client-state under their protection. The only way we can extricate from them is if we announce an all-out war and sustain the bloody battles for years."

She played with her hair and itched her neck. "And they do not forget defiance."

"No. Look what they did to Carthage. They can attack us from the sea, and then they can march their legions through Syria and Judaea."

"What do you know about Carthage, Apollodorus? I thought you were just a cook and cleaner," she said teasingly.

He laughed. "I may not be able to read well, Your Majesty, but I can hear and understand!"

She patted his hand and fell silent. No doubt that she was thinking about how she would engage Caesar, if they ever managed to get in front of the Roman.

He hated that they had to appear before him to decide on their fate, but such was the affair of their nations. But things changed.

She caressed his hand and sighed. "Let us go."

And Apollodorus began to row again, curving the boat towards a section of the royal quarters under Roman control.

CHAPTER 51

ALEXANDRIA

CLEOPATRA

———◇———

They neared the empty docks near the eastern edge of the palace. It was quiet here, with just a few flickering flames and shadows of a few sentries patrolling the edge. Apollodorus held up the lantern and began to swing it slowly, in a specific rhythmic pattern. Thrice to his left, thrice to the right, and then stationary for some time. And then repeat again.

He did this for several minutes, but she saw no indication from the dock that anyone noticed.

This went on for a while, with her becoming increasingly anxious. "Should we just get to the dock and tell them to take us to Caesar?" she asked.

"Not just yet, Your Majesty. It is possible that the guards are a combination of His Majesty's men and Caesar's, just to maintain a truce, and we don't know who might object."

She let him decide. So Apollodorus continued his lamp swinging. They were beginning to get disheartened when suddenly a new point of light appeared at the edge.

A man stood there, swinging the light from a quiet corner, following the same pattern. And then he moved the light up and down several times–another code agreed upon.

"It's him!" Apollodorus said excitedly.

He rowed the boat towards the rocky section and maneuvered it until he found a spot between the rocks. The edge rose sharply and ended in a fenced section. He asked her to stay where she was until he returned.

Apollodorus hopped off the boat, clambered up the slope, and vanished. She could not hear what was being said, but she waited anxiously. Her heart beat like it would explode, and blood rushed into her ears, dimming all her senses.

What if he had walked into a trap?

It took some more time, but eventually Apollodorus came back. She could see his form due to the light from the Pharos lighthouse that was closer now.

He kept his voice low. "It is time to go, Your Majesty," he said, his voice betraying his nervousness. "He can take us inside the Roman perimeter."

He held her hand as she disembarked. As she stood on the cool rock, he went back to the boat to bring the large hemp sack. He then helped her climb up the slope, with her slipping multiple times. The gravel was loose and slippery, and it took her considerable effort to manage her way up the incline until she had a good foothold.

As she reached the top, she came to an opening in the fence, and the man reached out his hand to pull her up. It was dark here. He had turned off his lantern. He kept his voice low, but he bowed to her. "Your Majesty. It is my honor."

Her heart fluttered, and familiar memories of sounds and smells flooded her. It was *her* home and yet here she was, as if a fugitive, sneaking back into what was *rightfully hers*! It brought back memories of happier days with her holding the bronze railings, standing beside a massive granite statue of Pharaoh Ptolemy II Philadelphos, builder of the Pharos lighthouse, and gazing into the deep blue sea. Pothinus would stand by her, telling her thrilling stories of the ancient past. Arsinoe would complain about the seagulls and the smell of seaweed. How things had changed.

She nodded. "What is your name?"

"Euaristos, Your Majesty," he said.

She admired his restraint. "I shall remember your service, Euaristos."

Apollodorus, who had arrived by then, clasped Euaristos' shoulder. "Shall we?"

"You must get in the sack, Your Majesty," Apollodorus said. She never thought it would *really* happen.

"Do I have to? Can we not be escorted inside?"

Euaristos shook his head. "Very risky, Your Majesty. Too many factions. I can get Apollodorus to the final perimeter, but you must not be seen."

She looked unsure. Apollodorus was careful not to show too much familiarity. He knelt before her, in the shadows. "We do not have time, Your Majesty. The shift will change soon, and those who may help Euaristos will move. We have to go. Now!"

She made up her mind. She reached into her leather purse, pulled out an elegant gold bracelet and put it on. Then she put on a thin silver-gold necklace adorned with quartz and amethyst.

She smoothed her hair to wear the one piece of ornamentation that signified her stature–the beautiful white silk diadem studded with pearl-pins. Charmian was not there to help her, so the clumsy hands of Apollodorus and Euaristos aided in tying her hair in a parted bun, wrapping the diadem, and securing it with the pins.

They both bowed to her and wished her success. "I long to see you as the queen, Your Majesty," Euaristos said. She smiled and readied herself.

They held the mouth of the bag open. She stepped into it gingerly. The hemp smelled strange, unpleasant, like uncooked fish in an open basket. Apollodorus had padded the bag with some cloth–that way her shape would not be too evident. She arranged herself like a fetus and whispered, "I am ready."

Apollodorus tied the bag's mouth. Her chest constricted and she could barely breathe in this claustrophobic arrangement, but they had practiced this maneuver before. She breathed in and out several times–controlling her panic and getting accustomed to the sensation.

Her bottom left the ground, and her back thumped against his. Then, Apollodorus set off.

CHAPTER 52

ALEXANDRIA

CLEOPATRA

---◇---

Her back bounced off Apollodorus' back as he walked, causing dull vibrations in her stomach. She heard them greet someone, other sentries perhaps, the conversation muddled. She knew that the eastern quarters where Caesar had situated himself was not a short walk. From their location, they would have to walk the length of a long seaside corridor lined with basalt sphinxes and granite falcons, past pink columns and two gold-lined gates. She heard a gate open, and he walked again.

At some point, Apollodorus stopped. Strong hands, possibly Euaristos', supported her bottom. He said cryptically, "Almost near the third perimeter. It's only Roman guards from here. Please stay still, Your Majesty."

She held her breath. It was another hundred steps or so before Apollodorus stopped again.

Euaristos began to speak. He had switched to Latin, a language he appeared to be familiar with and comfortable in. Cleopatra wondered if Apollodorus and Euaristos had served together at some point long ago, and what he owed Apollodorus.

"Message for Caesar," Euaristos said. "Bring Centurion Atticus."

"Caesar is preparing to rest. What is your business?"

"Don't act all official. You know who I am. This is an important message. Bring Atticus, or Caesar will have your balls nailed to a cross tomorrow."

There was some argument, including the guard demanding to see what was in the sack. But Euaristos threw some big names around and Apollodorus said he carried gifts that would lose their exclusivity if anyone gazed upon it. "Do you think a hairy monkey will jump out of the sack and assassinate Caesar, you idiot?" Euaristos chastised the guard. Cleopatra was briefly offended but let it be. *Hairy monkey?*

After a few tense moments, it seemed the guard went away to bring Atticus. Apollodorus and Euaristos engaged the other guard in some light, bawdy talk. "Forced to stand here instead of banging a hot woman somewhere private?"

"Banging is for the rich. We are fools. I fight for Caesar while he looks for rich people's wives to seduce."

"Very true," said Apollodorus. "We will never know what it means to be with a beautiful queen."

The cheeky bastard! Kadmos' influence had rubbed off on the serious Apollodorus.

Eventually, there were more voices. Atticus appeared to know Euaristos. Apollodorus walked again, and it sounded like they had moved to a secluded corner away from the guards. Atticus was whispering, but since he was nearby, she could hear him better.

"Yes, he may come and unveil the gift to Caesar. But if your queen's handmaid tries anything funny, we will gut her on the floor."

It had worked! Charmian had managed to make contact with some palace officials to get the message that one of Cleopatra's maids would be bringing a message to Caesar. She had almost forgotten this aspect of the plan. This way, it was easier to convince Atticus to let them through.

"She is half-unconscious in a sack. She won't be able to assassinate a toddler," Apollodorus said helpfully.

She did not hear Atticus laugh.

And then, after a few moments of silence, they began to move again. She could hear more speaking noises now, surely getting nearer to wherever Caesar was. Was he in one of her favorite halls? The one with soaring ceilings and magnificent paintings of bulls, gods, flowers, and children's palm prints on the walls? Her heart was beating wildly now. She was also feeling cramped, and her back and thighs hurt. She could hear Apollodorus' loud breathing–he was tiring as well. He was a strong man, but to carry another adult all this way, after rowing for hours, would take a toll on anyone.

Almost there, and with hers and Egypt's fate in her hands.

She heard salutes–the Romans had a way of thumping their chests and yelling something. It meant she was getting closer to where the supreme commander was. Suddenly, it was cold. She must be in the great hall, where there was a duct running along the walls that cooled the air.

Give me strength, Isis!

Finally, there was silence. She breathed deeply. What was happening?

"Message for you, sir," Atticus said.

The response was a dry, gravelly voice. Not loud, but clear. Commanding. "I am waiting."

Apollodorus set her down. The polished ground was welcome beneath her feet. She adjusted her diadem even as she was being placed on the floor.

She made sure to orient herself in a seated position. They had practiced this routine many times to ensure that she was not set down splayed, with her legs apart, for all the world to see. Or in some other un-royal position.

The sack fell around her, and the entire world opened again. It took her a moment to get adjusted to the lights around her and focus her vision. She had one hand on the floor, supporting her.

Cleopatra looked up at the man who called himself Gaius Julius Caesar.

CHAPTER 53

ALEXANDRIA

POTHINUS

Pothinus was mediating another argument between Arsinoe and Ptolemy. The two siblings, now forced to be together, both under Caesar's 'custody,' would not and could not agree on the separation of powers and the role of a king and queen. Pothinus had decided to bring the king under Caesar's protection, to avoid any confrontation with the Roman consul and general. While Caesar had made no announcements (*I am waiting for the other sister*), he and Ptolemy had struck an unusual but cordial relationship. Caesar spoke to the young king about his conquests and advised him on politics, and Ptolemy extolled the virtues of Egyptian grain, food, and glass. At times, Ptolemy advised Caesar too, which the Roman took with dry humor (*Yes, perhaps I should have led my troops that way, very interesting!*). The same could not be said of Arsinoe, who refused to engage with Caesar. The two times they had crossed paths, she was pointedly rude and insulting, which Caesar ignored.

And now the brother and sister were at it again.

"You will be my wife and listen to me. It doesn't matter that you are older!" Ptolemy yelled, red in the face. He was now nearing fourteen and had developed an independent streak, unwilling to be cowed by his fiery sister's harangues.

Arsinoe, having regained her strength, color, and spirited streak after returning to the luxury of the palace, would have none of it. "It matters. I have more knowledge than you, and the king and queen should rule as equals. Tell him, Pothinus!" she said, pointing to him. She had dressed herself every bit a queen, with only the diadem missing, for she was not authorized to wear it. That was a line she had not crossed yet.

"I am sure that when we come together in council, with Caesar's assistance, we can come to an agreement that brings peace and joy to all," Pothinus said.

Not a chance.

"Why does that half-bald, thin old man get to decide?" Arsinoe challenged. "Cleopatra is not coming back, so what are we waiting for?"

Pothinus had to do everything to keep his patience, having had this argument more than once. "His Late Majesty has chosen Rome as the executor of the will, Your Highness. And that means we must wait until Caesar decides."

Arsinoe's temper was rising. "No wonder you cannot decide one way or the other, Pothinus. Maybe because you have no cock!"

Pothinus inhaled sharply. But this was not the first time he had cruelty heaped upon him, even from his own wards. And unlike Cleopatra, who was wise with her words and rarely stooped to cruelty by personal attacks, Arsinoe had no compulsions or remorse for employing such tactics.

Theodotus, who stood nearby, wisely chose not to intervene.

"My decisions as regent to His Majesty are bound by the words of His Late Majesty and our obligations," Pothinus said, politely but firmly. "And until we know Her Highness Cleopatra's fate, and we are certain she is attempting to find audience with Caesar," he said, dropping the *Her Majesty* for Cleopatra, quietly signaling that she would not be queen.

"What do we know about her plans? You said her army has not entirely disbanded but moved farther south,"

Arsinoe said. She fiddled with her bracelets and yelled at a servant. "It's too cold here. Bring some fire!"

"Only that she may be planning arrival by sea. We have a few patrol boats out to watch the waters."

"What can we do if she comes by sea?" she said.

"With enough notice, we can block them with our navy, some of which is out of Caesar's reach and under Achillas' control."

"Is it possible she was building a navy without anyone knowing?" Arsinoe laughed. "Brother, you should execute your spies. They must be the dumbest spies in this world!"

Ptolemy and Arsinoe began arguing again as Pothinus waited patiently.

Finally, Arsinoe turned to Pothinus. "Why are you so sure she will come with a navy?"

Pothinus and Theodotus looked at each other. "She has no army, Your Majesty. The roads to Alexandria have been blocked. We have our eyes and ears everywhere. Achillas' army is on the move. There is no way for her to arrive by land. Every traveler is inspected."

Is she going to fly? She may be an incarnation of Isis, but the goddess does not fly.

Arsinoe shook her head vigorously. "No, Pothinus. Do you not know her? Why would she do the obvious and come with a navy that everyone can see? What makes you think she will not disguise herself and come on a boat, like a trader or fisherman?"

The hair on Pothinus' neck rose, and his blood turned to ice. *How could they not have considered that!*

Theodotus' face fell as well. Pothinus regained his composure. "You may very well be right, Your Highness, though a boat escaping our eyes, and then making her way through rings of security, and then somehow appearing before Caesar is extremely unlikely," he said, his confidence growing as he worked through the possibility. But perhaps he should have had more patrol boats with precise instructions.

He would take care of that the next day.

"How long must we wait?" Ptolemy asked. He had become a little more comfortable with Caesar. Pothinus had to remind His Little Majesty that he was a hostage in his own palace and country, and never to forget that.

Before Pothinus answered, a messenger came running into the room and locked eyes with him.

The messenger was breathless, but it was his face–pale, white, and absolutely terrified.

CHAPTER 54

ALEXANDRIA

JULIUS CAESAR

———◇———

Caesar, rarely surprised by anything, was dumbfounded by the scene before him. A young woman sat on the floor as the bag fell away. Nothing about her said handmaid, or any type of maid. The first thing he noticed was the diadem, a symbol he was acutely aware of, and the auburn hair. She sat there, her eyes shining from the flickering lights, resting on one hand, smiling.

For the briefest moment he turned to his Centurion. "Atticus–" he said, and then it dawned on him.

For a man not given to outwardly exuberant behavior, the utter gumption and audacity of what had unfolded before him, combined with his own passion for bold and unexpected moves, made Caesar laugh out loud.

The woman before him raised her hand, still smiling. "Will you not welcome the Queen of Egypt, Caesar?"

Caesar, still laughing, walked to her and offered his hand for her to hold and rise.

"An unusual appearance, Your Majesty," he said, bowing very slightly and speaking in comfortable Greek.

"For unusual times," she said without breaking eye contact.

Caesar turned to Atticus. "You both have done well. Go and rest while I speak to her. Atticus, ensure that this man is well cared for," he said, gesturing towards the man who had brought Cleopatra in a sack.

Cleopatra turned to the man. "I shall meet you tomorrow, Apollodorus. Your service will be amply rewarded."

The man, Apollodorus, bowed and left, though very hesitatingly.

Caesar turned to her. "A better welcome could have been arranged, had I known the truth," he said, smiling. Caesar consciously touched his head and adjusted his garment–he was wearing a disheveled toga and had not had the time to carefully arrange his hair or wash his face after the last bout of drinking. He was supposed to be meeting a servant!

"You know that I could not, Caesar," she said as she walked comfortably to the couch and reclined on it.

This is her home. She knows every corner.

Caesar appraised her. He had last seen her perhaps a decade ago, when her father was in Rome. Pompey was their patron, but Caesar had met the father and the daughter once or twice. He remembered a shy but well-spoken girl. She was not very tall. Her auburn hair was tied in a bun, but it was curled and wavy. She had an angular face, a straight nose slightly curved at the tip, thin lips, but beautiful gray-brown eyes that sparkled. An attractive dimple formed on her right cheek when she smiled. Caesar had known many beautiful women, and Cleopatra would not rank anywhere among the most bewitching. But none were so bold and adventurous as the one now reclined before him, exuding the haughtiness and confidence of a queen even while dressed like a peasant and smelling like a fish bag.

She snapped a finger at a Roman officer, who looked utterly confused as to how to behave. Caesar nodded at him. The man came before Cleopatra and bowed.

"Bring me some water. And arrange for my quarters," she said, switching to Latin.

Caesar was surprised. He had received reports of her personality and skills, but now he was witnessing it himself. And it still filled him with a strange amusement that here she was, having arrived in a bag, seeking his audience, needing his approval, and ordering *his men* like she was their queen. He chuckled to himself. He had seen many driven to desperate acts when their power was at risk, but he had not seen this version before.

"Well, there is much to discuss. But I suggest you rest," he said, looking at her state.

"This is my home, Caesar. I grew up here. I lived here until I was driven away. I will do what I want. Do you see those colored palm prints on the wall to your left?"

He peered at two deep orange palm and finger imprints nearby.

"Those are my hands," she said.

"Of course," he said, smiling. "I will–"

"I shall summon you when I am ready to discuss this," she said, "for surely the executor of my father's will is grappling with how to deal with two sisters, a brother, and a cunning regent?"

Caesar let out a dry laugh again. She was amusing. Playful. "Of course," he said, humoring her. When had a supplicant of a client-state spoken to him that way? *Never!*

Even the formidable leader of the Gauls, Vercingetorix, had quietly laid his shield before Caesar's feet. Now the Gaul was waiting for his demise in the Mamertine prison in Rome.

But he was no fool to be manipulated in any way. He turned to Cleopatra. "Your Majesty, you know that it is my duty to bring about a reconciliation. I admire your entrance today, but you will remain in my custody until I summon you. Go now and rest," he said firmly.

The girl needs to know who decides her fate.

She did not react. Instead, she stood and looked at the officer readying to take her. "Do what you must, Caesar, but know that I know Egypt better than anyone else."

Caesar nodded but said nothing. He turned to another officer. "Send word to Pothinus that Her Majesty Cleopatra has arrived before Caesar."

CHAPTER 55

ALEXANDRIA

POTHINUS

Arsinoe sat in one corner, aghast and speechless.

Ptolemy looked like he was about to cry. "How could this have happened? How did my sister get in front of Caesar?"

Pothinus, himself still recovering from the shock, knew that if he did not control the situation quickly, it might end with his head on the ground. "We are surrounded by treasonous malcontents, Your Majesty. Surely your brilliant mind has seen that there are many ways she may have established this contact, perhaps with Roman collusion."

The young king looked despondent. He was afraid of his older sister, and also hated her with all his being. "Bitch. She will probably–"

"She will seduce him. I know her. She will trick that old man!" Arsinoe shouted. "Then she is going to come after us. We will die if we don't do anything!"

Theodotus finally stepped into the conversation. "She cannot do anything, Your Highness. Remember that Caesar is more than twice her age, very experienced, and will see through any silliness," he said, his voice loud and firm. The siblings turned to him but did not interrupt.

"She does not have the legitimacy of His Majesty or the support of the people of Alexandria, so she is of little political relevance. She does not have the beauty of Her Highness," he said, squarely looking at Arsinoe, who was pleased at this description, "and is unlikely to seduce a man well known for his various affairs with many beautiful women."

Pothinus took the cue to continue. "What he will do is use and discard her. You have nothing to fear, Your Majesties. We will dissuade him from bringing her back to power and convince him of her duplicity, and the risk she poses to relations with Rome and peace in Egypt."

Arsinoe was not convinced. "How can you be so confident, Pothinus? Do you not know her? When in Syria, with no power and the will of Egypt behind her, she convinced two governors to give up their palaces for rest. She built an army while deep in Roman governed territory. She had an adjutant to a Syrian chief stripped and executed for an insult, with no repercussions. She is manipulative, and you do not see it."

Pothinus found his voice. "As that may be so, Your Highness, but so are we. Do you not remember that we outmaneuvered her twice already? And that her Syrian army sat scratching their balls, unable to do anything? And that while she may have presented herself in front of Caesar, she had to do it not on a triumphant procession or while seated on a golden carriage, but like a common thief?"

Arsinoe shook her head. "But still. She is going to find a way to kill us. You must speak to Caesar as soon as you can."

"I will. He listens to me!" said Ptolemy. The boy walked to a temporary fire pit nearby and placed his palms over the flames.

"Yes, yes, imperator know-it-all bald-head listens to you," Arsinoe said, rolling her eyes and slapping her thigh with her palm.

"He does! We speak politics and military. Have you spoken to him? He probably thinks you are a dimwit with boobs."

"He does not talk to me because he knows I am not swayed by his nonsense. He probably thinks you are a stupid little–"

"Enough!" Pothinus raised his voice.

The stunned siblings looked at him, an instinctual reaction to his *teacher* voice.

"We are facing a crisis, Your Majesties. This is not the time to argue and descend into crass behavior. As regent, it is my duty to ensure that you are safe and returned to power without bringing Rome down on us. But you must allow me to do my job!" he said, with an edge still in his voice.

Arsinoe scrunched her face. "Fine. Do what you must, Pothinus."

Ganymedes, Arsinoe's other tutor and advisor, so far silent, finally spoke up. "Pothinus, let us open our minds to the reality of the situation. Caesar will attempt reconciliation between His Majesty and Cleopatra. That union still leaves Her Highness Arsinoe at significant risk. Any option discussed with Caesar must make provision for Her Highness as well."

Pothinus glared at Ganymedes. If it were not for Ganymedes' constant meddling, he may have had a better chance at controlling, or even disposing of, Arsinoe. But he had to deal with them.

"Of course, I know that," he said, dropping his voice and deliberately patronizing the man. "I will send word to Caesar that we wish to discuss."

Arsinoe looked at Ganymedes and shook her head. "It will be useless. Mark my words," she said, and stormed out of the hall.

Pothinus whispered to Theodotus. "Keep an eye on those two. Meanwhile, let us convince Caesar that it is in his best interests to put Cleopatra to death."

CHAPTER 56

ALEXANDRIA

CLEOPATRA

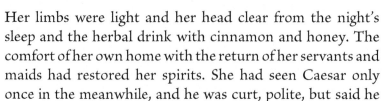

Her limbs were light and her head clear from the night's sleep and the herbal drink with cinnamon and honey. The comfort of her own home with the return of her servants and maids had restored her spirits. She had seen Caesar only once in the meanwhile, and he was curt, polite, but said he had matters to attend to. Still, she could see he was amused by her company.

But the situation was deteriorating rapidly outside, and she knew Caesar was getting desperate. He also had muttered that he could not trust anyone in the palace except his men. She was quietly pleased at the misery heaped on him, but also worried that a weakened Caesar would be a great danger to her.

But Caesar had sent word that he would be arriving for extensive discussions to bring an end to hostility and find a way for reconciliation. She waited anxiously.

She had learned much about the man. Stubborn (*like her*), dry and not quite a man of humor (*not like her*), womanizer (*not her*), a brilliant general (*she was brilliant too, if not a general*), polyglot (*he knew maybe three languages; she knew eight*), handsome (*some said she was pretty*), an experienced statesman (*she as well, even if younger*), astute, and exceptionally bold (*her as well!*). She knew he was over fifty years of age, more than twice hers, but she had been surprised when she first laid her eyes on him. He was slightly shorter than she thought (*Apollodorus was taller*), there were bags under his eyes (*strain*), but he had firm, lean limbs; a soft, commanding voice; inquisitive eyes; and an attractive, long and angular face. She did not like it that he was mostly bald, even if he tried hiding it under his helmet. She had enjoyed running her hands through Apollodorus' thick and luxurious hair.

Her mind turned to Apollodorus. She had lain with men before, in controlled methods, not with much feeling but to fulfill desires of the body. Her earliest infatuation, oddly, was with a Roman cavalry officer stationed in Alexandria when she was fourteen. It was a man called Marcus Antonius, though she never had the chance to talk to him. But Apollodorus? She had to fight to control the urge to summon him to her. She sent him a coded letter and told him he must be quiet and await orders. Her body and mind ached for him, but there were far larger considerations at play.

She awaited Charmian as well. News of her arrival would be spread soon, and Charmian would know. It was difficult to function without her most trusted lady-in-waiting.

Caesar arrived in the morning, looking rested and comfortable. He had also made sure to dress like a general for the occasion, sure that it would be more impressive to a young woman than the fatherly toga. He had even combed his remaining hair forward, trying to hide his baldness.

She smiled at his vanity. And his vanity was good for her.

"Your Majesty, you look lovely and rested," he said. She marveled at his almost flawless Greek. She hoped to practice her Latin with him at some point.

"And you look general-ly," she said, smiling. She held her hand out for him to hold and bow, which he did. "You are already a conqueror, Caesar, and need not come to me as such."

Caesar smiled sheepishly. "For one that is conquered, you are quite bold and vocal, young lady."

They both rested on separate luxurious cushion-lined seaters on which they could recline. They made some small talk, and she liked that while his style was quite to the point, he was very well educated in the matters of the Egyptian royal family and the complexity of the situation.

"We do not have time, Your Majesty," he said. "And I am running out of patience."

More like running out of men and options.

"And you seek my counsel?"

He grinned. "Venus has limited my options. An amusing twenty-one-year-old, or an impetuous and temperamental fourteen-year-old."

"A twenty-one-year-old who has governed a land of seven million since she was sixteen and built an army at twenty, Caesar. What were you doing at my age?" she said, cocking an eyebrow.

Caesar ran a hand over his head and smoothed the strands of his remaining hair. "You supported Pompey," he said, abruptly changing the subject and fixing his piercing eyes on her.

CHAPTER 57

ALEXANDRIA

CAESAR

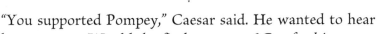

"You supported Pompey," Caesar said. He wanted to hear her response. Would she find an excuse? Beg for his mercy and consideration? Or would she scoff?

Cleopatra did not waver. "You know very well, Caesar, that Pompey was our patron and you were not. I did not know you or your intentions. I thought you would lose."

Caesar was surprised by the honesty. "I was given to understand you were well tutored. Caesar has never lost a battle."

She propped herself up and returned to a seating position. A thin gold chain hung from her neck, and she played with it. "Caesar had never gone up against an accomplished general like Pompey."

He nodded. She was no fool. "Pompey lost."

"And I am here before Caesar."

He smiled.

He stood and began to pace slowly, with his hands behind his back and his cloak following him. He did this when he wanted to discuss serious matters of politics and state. "Alexandria is burning, Cleopatra," he said, dropping the honorific title. This young woman had to understand that it was he who determined her fate, and for her not to foolishly attempt influencing him.

She did not respond but instead watched him quietly.

Caesar continued. "There is a saying that civil strife is not caused by inequality in property and coin–"

"But also by inequality of honors, which you are partially responsible for, by insulting my people," she said.

Caesar was taken aback. "You know your Aristotle."

"I know my Aristotle, Homer, Plato, and Eratosthenes."

What a contrast she was to the Roman women he knew! There was none of that piety or supplication. "Indeed. I would have no reason to be here, were it not for what your regent did to Pompey and the small matter of ten million denarii."

"But you have stayed past your welcome, Caesar. The fires are burning because your soldiers occupy my city, and you cannot control Pothinus or my brother."

He appraised her. She had the slightest dimpled smile, which he found attractive, though he was no great admirer of that nose. "What is your suggestion?"

"I am willing to compromise, but Pothinus will prevent such a development. You saw what they did to Pompey—their rationale was likely that you would take his head and go home. They have no interest in engaging you. I do."

She kept surprising him with her insight and turn of conversation.

"They tell me you hate the Romans. My men tell me you have not disbanded your army, contrary to my orders," he said as he picked up a small goblet of red wine.

She scoffed. "And let myself be captured and executed? My army is not against you, Caesar. But *their* army is. They have not disbanded either. They are marching on you as we speak."

"I am told Achillas' army has halted. Perhaps they seek peace. If Caesar disposes of you, all this might end," he said.

Her brilliant eyes burned with defiance. "If you dispose of me, that will be the end of you. They are treacherous.

Pompey had restored my father to the throne, and look what they did to him. I, on the other hand, can make Egypt prosperous and be an exceptional ally to you and to Rome. And I am not stupid like my brother."

Caesar laughed. *What a fine family.*

"Well, his advisor is clever, and his general has proven himself a worthy adversary."

"Pothinus' regency will lapse in two years. And then do you want to deal with my brother as the sole power?"

Caesar rubbed his clean-shaven chin. She had a point. The young Ptolemy was difficult to predict. Rome was far, across the sea, and he did not want to deal with a rebellious Egypt when he was away.

He changed subjects again. "Alexandria is magnificent."

They then left the serious subjects aside and spoke of the city, of Egypt, of how she was so learned, and of his family and upbringing. He laughed several times, including when she sarcastically said *Alexandrians get enough entertainment from their royal family that they have no desire to see dangling Roman penises under their kilts for additional amusement.*

She could also flatter easily, knowing fully well he recognized it for what it was, and that he knew she recognized it. *They say Alexander and Caesar are the two brightest stars in the world, who have accomplished equally. But you have lived far longer.* Whether that was a compliment or a subtle insult, he could not tell. Someday, he would ask her to take him to the great conqueror's tomb.

She also had a beautiful voice and knew how to play with the words. The pitch rose and fell as needed, and she recited little poems to make her point. She could quote Homer at will and was not above making lewd comments on her opponents (*Why does Theodotus give speeches to his women when in bed? Because they would fall asleep if he used his mouth in any other way*). He recognized some of Theodotus' style in hers, but she was far more pleasant to listen to. He could not remember what young woman of her age had such a beguiling character.

Finally, he returned to what he was set to advance on. "What is it that you think I should do?"

"Tell them that I will co-rule and mend relations with my brother. And that I am the rightful queen to the throne and look to build a prosperous kingdom. But I will need Rome to protect me until I have established myself. This is in your and my best interests."

"And do you believe that the regent eunuch Pothinus and General Achillas will cooperate?"

"Their cooperation can be bought," she said dismissively.

By then, Caesar was more than impressed. His desire to execute her father's will, collect some money he desperately needed, and keep the grain, ship, and troop supplies from Egypt, meant that a stable co-rule with this girl on the throne was a much better alternative to leaving it all in his little screechy-voice's hands.

"I will summon His Majesty and the eunuch Pothinus to convey my intention. The affairs of Rome require my presence. And if you so desire, I wish to seek more of your pleasurable company," he said, bowing slightly.

"The pleasure is all mine, supreme commander," she said, her eyes smiling brightly.

CHAPTER 58

ALEXANDRIA

POTHINUS

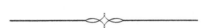

It took a further two weeks before Ptolemy and Pothinus arrived before Caesar. But in that time, Pothinus had engineered enough agitation so as to convince Caesar that there was no other way but to quickly put His Majesty to power. Pothinus knew that Caesar was fed up, constrained in his quarters, besieged by the crowds and some of Achillas' soldiers. Caesar, who was a man of controlled habits, had taken to drinking. His officers spoke of how the generally mellow leader was losing his temper often and despairing his terrible situation. Caesar's two legions were wearing down, and many had died when they ventured out to the city. But Caesar's engagement with Cleopatra was much less clear. That they had established a good rapport had been evident, just as His Majesty feared, for the devious girl had found a way to ingratiate herself to Caesar and was now safely under his control.

In a theatrical show of anger, the young Ptolemy had forced himself to the street, lamenting loudly to growing crowds that he was being insulted and that the wretched Cleopatra was planning to gift Egypt to Rome. He had ripped his diadem, thrown it to the ground as horrified subjects watched him, and stomped on it. A Roman battalion had to go in and fetch him back, facing a barrage of stone-throwing, slippers, and rotten fruit. Then, Pothinus managed to have a massive crowd outside the Roman quarters, screaming for Cleopatra's blood and Ptolemy's crowning.

Pothinus also conspired in other ways to make life difficult for Caesar and his legions. He had the worst grain supplied. Often the sacks had worms or rat droppings in them (*unrest in the city has made supplies unreliable*). He had their mail intercepted (*attacks on the couriers, we have little control!*). Delivered diluted wine and spoiled beer (*we will teach the rascals a lesson when order is restored*).

All this, of course, he claimed happened without his knowledge and through the spontaneity of Alexandrian spirit. *All they want is for their king to claim his throne, what can I do?* he said, with a very sad face, to the Roman officers who confronted him angrily.

Pothinus made sure to bring His Majesty before Caesar with all the pomp of a king. Ptolemy sat on a gold-handled, blue-silk cushioned litter carried by oiled, almost nude Nubian and Egyptian bearers. He carried the flail and the crook, and wore the hooded crown of a Pharaoh. His arrival was heralded by trumpets and drums.

Caesar likely anticipated this, for the Roman had eschewed his toga and waited like a conquering general. He wore a deep-green, metal-plated cuirass carved with images of a lion and an eagle. A purple cloak hung from his back and was pinned to the cuirass in the front with a large gold ring. His *pteruges*, the skirt-like garment below the cuirass, had deep-brown leather strips hanging from the top. He wore fine sandals with straps that ran up to his knees. In an unusual move, he wore a general's helmet with bright red plumes. An ornate orange scabbard hung from his waist.

Pompous peacocks trying to outdo each other.

The group first engaged in elaborate formalities, including a sumptuous dinner, courtesy of Pothinus. For over two hours, they engaged in polite talk, forced laughter, tired jokes, and reminisced in each other's glorious pasts that neither cared for.

After the formalities, with Caesar being gracious enough to recognize the king's rank and bow to him, they retired to a small adjacent room set for discussions. A Syrian cedarwood table with several plush chairs had been arranged with jugs of water, fruit, and a selection of cheese.

The king took his seat, followed by Caesar and Pothinus. Arsinoe and Ganymedes would not accompany them, for Pothinus had persuaded Ganymedes that Her Highness' temper could pose problems. Curiously, neither of them had objected. Pothinus surmised that they had accepted whatever outcome, so long as they were safe. Cleopatra would not be present; both parties recognized that having her there would lead to no progress. Pothinus hoped that he could keep her away permanently.

Pothinus opened the meeting. "Gaius Julius Caesar, Consul of Rome and commander of the Roman legions, we thank you for the mediation and your willingness to settle the questions of succession in Egypt as protector designated by His Late Majesty Ptolemy Dionysos. His Majesty Ptolemy Philopator has graced this occasion to move the process forward to conclusion."

Caesar made a curt acknowledgment of the welcome. As much as he was dressed like a proud peacock, the Roman looked tired. Perhaps Cleopatra had been harassing him since her arrival–how much could the man take?

"I speak to you, King Ptolemy, my young friend, that it is time to reconcile and bring this unrest to an end. You hold the power," Caesar said modestly, "to convince the people that as king and queen, you and Cleopatra–"

"No!" said Ptolemy. "She will kill me, and then she will destroy this kingdom with her greed."

Caesar was unfazed. "No. Have I not treated you with fairness? She promises me that the past is forgotten, and that a bright future awaits you as co-rulers. The world of statesmen is such that one could be foe in the morning and friend at dusk. She recognizes your skills in these months, and that you have grown to be king."

Ptolemy looked surprised. "Did she say that?"

"Your sister thinks of you as an ascendant sun," Caesar said, leaning forward and placing his palms on the table.

Pothinus leaned in and whispered into Ptolemy's ear, "A knife covered with the sweetest butter is still a knife."

Ptolemy puffed up his chest and wagged the crook. "My sister lies. She bids others to do her will. If you are my friend, you should declare me king. No harm will come to Cleopatra."

Caesar fixed his stare on Pothinus. "His Majesty knows in his heart that a reconciliation, as desired by his late father, is in the best interests of Egypt and Rome. Perhaps it is time His Majesty recognizes that his advisors may be preventing a just settlement."

Pothinus bristled at this (correct) insinuation.

Caesar continued. "The will of a king is best exercised in solitude after recognizing all merits proposed before him. May we speak in private, Your Majesty?"

Pothinus was alarmed. Before the king spoke, he interjected, "The regent must at all times stand by to counsel the king, Caesar."

Ptolemy looked undecided. Caesar's entreaties, including how Ptolemy adorned the hearts of the Alexandrian people and that Caesar must speak to him alone, all fell on deaf ears. Caesar also promised to declare Arsinoe queen of Cyprus, which elicited little interest. Ptolemy, while positively inclined towards Caesar and desiring good relations, would not go alone without Pothinus or entertain a conversation that involved Cleopatra.

Frustrated, Caesar finally declared. "Very well, then. I shall allow His Majesty to consult his advisors before we speak again. At this time, I shall make no proclamation, as the equation with Cleopatra has not been resolved. I lay that responsibility at your feet, Pothinus," Caesar said pointedly.

Pothinus did not take the bait. "We will all come to a conclusion in the best interests of Egypt and His Majesty, Caesar."

How long would this toga-wearing goat be able to bear his situation?

Or maybe he would need to bring an end to the toga-wearing goat and not wait any longer. But he was also frustrated that Cleopatra had poured enough poison in Caesar's ears that the man would not relent and bring these sorry affairs to an end.

And then, just when they were about to end the meeting, a messenger from the royal quarters made his presence known. The orders were for all interruptions to wait, and yet what had been so important that this man could intrude with such impunity?

"What is it?" Pothinus asked, angry and irritated.

"Her Highness Arsinoe, Your Majesty and Excellencies!"

What now? Was she on the way to create more trouble?

"What about Her Highness? Is she joining us?"

The man looked afraid to share what he came to announce, but with all eyes on him, he willed himself to declare, "Her Highness has escaped from the palace with her advisor, His Excellency Ganymedes…"

The group erupted in shouting and recriminations, with each side accusing the other of masterminding it. Pothinus accused Caesar of doing this to foment mistrust, and Caesar accused Pothinus of doing it to foment trouble. But once it became more obvious that they had all been caught by surprise, they calmed down to ask the messenger.

"Where has she gone?" Pothinus asked.

"They say she is headed to meet Achillas."

CHAPTER 59

ALEXANDRIA

CLEOPATRA

———◇———

The day had been eventful. Charmian had arrived in the morning, rushing into her chamber. Cleopatra was thrilled to see her lady-in-waiting, even going so far as embracing the girl. The two shed tears of happiness. With Apollodorus not being by her side, and Metjen far away, Charmian's presence gave a comfort she had been missing since she arrived.

She shared all her Caesar-related gossip with Charmian, but said little of her journey with Apollodorus. Whether Charmian suspected, she could not say.

But the stream of events outside brought anything but joy. Her sister Arsinoe had escaped and was on the way to meet Achillas. Cleopatra guessed why. Caesar had not been sleeping well, fearing assassination attempts. And she had managed to keep him on her side so far, but if these pressures continued, he might one day abandon his current position and feed her to the wolves.

He came to her in the evening, as he did every evening. But on this day, he was tired and stressed. "They are unwilling to reconcile," he said. "That wretched Achillas murdered two of my men bearing messages to lay down his arms. And now your sister is meeting him. What does she want?"

Cleopatra dropped her voice and spoke soothingly, hoping to convey her sympathy and understanding. "She has always fantasized about being the queen, Caesar. She sees this as an opportunity to assert herself, take control of Achillas' legions, and wage war on you. That is my assessment."

Caesar seemed unconvinced. "The brief times I met her, she did not seem the type that would inspire confidence in her armies. Your brother is under Pothinus' grip, and that is where I see the dangers."

"Pothinus is a learned man. He eyes a prize greater than that of a regency," she said, walking over and sitting by his side.

"How so?"

"It is no doubt, Caesar, that men of your import have little patience or time to meander about in Egypt, when the larger affairs of the world await your presence. Pothinus controls my brother and Achillas. And once left to his own devices, he will work to finish my siblings and me. He will spur Arsinoe and Achillas, and then have Achillas turn on her."

Caesar arched an eyebrow. "Will the people not rise and crucify him? They see you as gods."

"I am a manifestation of Isis," she said seriously. "But Pothinus speaks the language of the land, he is Egyptian, and most importantly, he was once a priest and holds cordial relations with the most influential men of god."

Caesar looked thoughtful. "So that he may usurp the throne for himself, with the confidence that so long as Egypt behaves as a compliant client-state, Rome will stay away," he said. "The eunuch is clever."

"Pothinus will bide his time. Do you believe that he is not behind the unrest in Alexandria? He has everything to do with it. Achillas travels unfettered between his army and the city, and foments trouble."

Caesar, no doubt accustomed to large-scale battles with thousands of soldiers on the plains of Greece, forests of Gaul, and hillocks of Hispania, had never really encountered urban warfare. Even though his men were of exceptional bravery and quality, they were outnumbered, and Achillas' men were no minnows either. And Caesar could not run away at night, because with no money to pay his men and the affairs of Egypt in disarray, things might turn terribly for him.

Most importantly, his pride would not allow him to retreat.

"What made you learn so many languages?" Caesar asked. "My men tell me that the kings of the House of Ptolemy learned no other language, let alone seven."

She smiled. "Eight. I always had an ear for languages. I picked up Egyptian easily from the visitors on my mother's side. But others? Well, when I was thirteen, my father had me read a sacred diary of our dynasty's forefather, Ptolemy Soter himself."

"And?"

"In his diaries, he wrote of a couple named Deon and Eurydice, whom first he suspected of foul behavior, but later enlisted their help for a most enticing mission. The woman, Eurydice, Deon's wife, he writes of her talent for many languages, and how she employed those languages to great benefit. I also read an interesting account written by Deon himself, speaking of her feats, and that was when I decided I would be the first Ptolemaic queen to learn many languages. I then surrounded myself with those who spoke the many languages, and had them speak to me in their tongue. And Caesar, nothing else has given me power over the people as the ability to speak their tongue."

"I must admit, the strength of that skill surpasses many others. There is much I do not know about your dynasty, and you," he said, smiling.

Cleopatra placed a palm on his shoulder. "It is true wisdom in knowing…"

"That you know nothing. Socrates," said Caesar. "I am yet to learn much about the desires and insidiousness of Alexandria."

"And you have me beside you, Caesar. With me as Queen of Egypt, and you as consul of Rome and custodian of the Roman empire, we can create a world no one else has. Who else dreams this big?" she said as she ran her fingers on his neck.

"Your dimple is enchanting," he said. "And for a girl of your age, you are exceptionally articulate."

She pouted. "Oh, Caesar. You think so little of the women of Egypt. I was taught by the greatest mathematicians, philosophers, rhetoricians, and physicians. Rome does not value education for its women, but we Ptolemies do. You forget that I governed the Nomes of Egypt for years."

Caesar reached up and held her hand. His palm was warm, and his grip strong. Even at his age and with the strain he was experiencing, she thought, he had a certain attractiveness, all the more enhanced by his stature. Her heart palpitated briefly, thinking of Apollodorus.

"I know a way you can ascertain Pothinus' true intentions," she said, and outlined a plan.

Caesar listened intently, even as he caressed her face. But from his look, then the intensity of his embrace, and the ferocity of his lips against hers, she knew that his mind was as far from politics and war for the night as Alexandria was from India.

CHAPTER 60

ALEXANDRIA

POTHINUS

———◇———

Pothinus sat in his quarters. A servant fanned him while another attended to his nails. A third massaged his throbbing oiled skull, and she was exceptionally talented, soothing the knots and causing waves of pleasure as she kneaded his painful temples.

He too was under house arrest following Arsinoe's escape, with not much freedom to go about his business outside the walls of the palace. He had to account for his travels and return before sunset. Not that these threats meant much, but they were an indication that Caesar was unwilling to settle the disputes and was willing to prolong the stupidity of the situation.

Messengers brought back news that Arsinoe had indeed joined Achillas, but that it was unclear what they were attempting to do. Half of Achillas' legions remained out of Alexandria, following Pothinus' instructions, while the rest engaged in incessant warfare with Caesar. But Pothinus was not too worried about Arsinoe–Achillas would be able to handle her. And once things returned to normal, they would deal with the temperamental girl.

But this ridiculous charade with Caesar had gone on for too long.

His intention was to tire Caesar and drive him out, and then find a way to maintain a distant, yet harmonious relation. But Cleopatra had muddied it, and Caesar was clinging on with no intention of leaving. How much could he coddle the Romans?

Would Rome miss its rabble-rousing dictator-in-waiting? Had he worried too much that injuring or killing Caesar could bring the might of Rome upon Egypt?

And now, this bastard had the *audacity* to order him to send a missive to Achillas to stand down immediately, disband the legions, and come to Alexandria with Arsinoe for final settlements. And that Caesar would decide one way or the other, if they did not follow his orders.

"There, there," he muttered to the massager, pointing to a specific spot behind his ears. He groaned as the actions eased his throbbing headache, allowing him to think clearly.

They bathed him after the massage, cleansing his lean body. A stylist lined his eyes with kohl, wrapped him with a new shendyt, applied balsam oil behind his ears, and helped him wear his amethyst-and-topaz studded chain. Pothinus' spirits rose like a falcon soaring in the sky, one ready to shake the status quo and resolve the situation.

He ordered for two messengers. He could not risk sending one.

CHAPTER 61

ALEXANDRIA

POTHINUS

The banquet was boring and listless. Another pathetic attempt by His Excellency the bald, toga-wearing goat to curry favor with Pothinus. What was so great about Caesar, he wondered, for the man had not only found himself in an insanely stupid situation, but was now unwilling to leave. It was a quiet affair. His Majesty sat sullenly at the head of the table. Men whispered into Caesar's ears during the dinner. Pothinus was feeling sleepy. Cleopatra was nowhere to be found. He had not seen her since her arrival at the palace, but he could sense her effect on Caesar.

"Have you received word from Achillas or Arsinoe about their plans?" Caesar asked.

"I have sent a clear and unambiguous message, Your Excellency."

"And what message did you send?" Caesar asked. He had stopped eating and stared at Pothinus intently.

What kind of a question was that?

"That they must disband and come to settle the question of succession, put an end to the unrest, and allow Caesar to execute his duties to the people of Egypt."

Caesar, dressed in a disarmingly friendly loose white toga, tapped on the table. "Was there anything else?"

Pothinus' heart galloped like an Arabian horse. What was he implying?

"I beg your indulgence, Caesar. I have followed your orders."

Caesar looked at him, unblinking. "You are intelligent, Pothinus. Few nations entrust a eunuch with their troubles."

Pothinus did not respond, not knowing the direction or intent of this conversation.

Caesar continued, "But you forget that Caesar has dealt with many who think they possess the acuity to make a fool of him."

Pothinus' skin turned cold and clammy. "Of course, Caesar. Only those without the right mental faculty would underestimate you."

Caesar seemed not to hear. He continued, "Caesar has faced many deceptions in his life. He has won battles of scales you cannot imagine, against insurmountable odds. And he understands the nature of those who wish to deceive him, and the tactics they employ. He knows people better than they know themselves."

King Ptolemy was looking at both of them intently, unsure what was happening. Two of Caesar's armed guards moved closer, and several soldiers surrounded the banquet.

"What is happening, Caesar?" His Majesty spoke, alarmed. Caesar ignored him.

"Caesar!" Ptolemy yelled.

Caesar turned to him menacingly. "Not now, boy, not now."

Ptolemy fell silent. Pothinus was tongue-tied, unsure of what to say.

"Seize him," Caesar ordered, and a Centurion swiftly came forward and grabbed Pothinus.

"Get your filthy hands off me, you bastards, I am the regent of Egypt!" Pothinus shouted, struggling with the man. But the highly experienced soldier pinned Pothinus' arms to his back and quickly immobilized him.

Did Caesar find my other message?

Even as others kept watch over Ptolemy, the guards dragged Pothinus out, and Caesar followed. They took him to a small open portico and sealed the entrance.

"You cannot hold me, Caesar! You need me for peace and settlement!" Pothinus shouted.

How dare this man! How dare he!

And then, from behind one of the columns, stepped Cleopatra. Pothinus' heart jumped into his throat. It was a mixture of emotions; hate, fear, admiration, and even love—for he had held her in his hands as a child, taught her, played with her, tutored her to regency.

She looked radiant, dressed in an elegant blue silk gown and with a diadem over her head. A thin silver-threaded chain hung over neck, pulled by a single ruby. Her eyes sparkled, but it looked like there were tears in them.

She stood beside Caesar, not uttering a word.

"This must be a misunderstanding, Your Majesty!" Pothinus said, addressing her. "I have always strived to bring peace."

She did not respond. Caesar extended his arm to a guard, who placed a papyrus scroll in his hand.

Pothinus' eyes widened.

Caesar made a theatrical show of opening it, and then he read slowly.

I order you not to desist in your endeavors to march upon Caesar. He is reviled in Rome as he is here, and he has overplayed his hand. While your brave men march, I shall employ other culinary attempts.

"That is not my message!" Pothinus shouted.

"We have the second messenger," Caesar said with little expression. "Her Majesty warned me of your duplicity and the methods you are fond of."

Pothinus knew then that to protest more would only make him look like a peasant who protests an accusation that he has stolen his master's donkey while riding it.

He turned his attention to Cleopatra. "This conflict is for us to resolve, Your Majesty. Why allow a foreigner to meddle in our affairs?"

"Your resolution was to have me killed, Pothinus. I saw you as my father, and yet you turned on me."

Pothinus would not allow her to lay blame at his feet. Not so easily. "You turned on me first, Your Majesty. Why did I lose your grace to be your principal advisor? What wrong had I committed? Had you forgotten that it was I who campaigned for your regency?"

She shook her head. "You never lost my grace. I wanted your mettle to manage the complex relations with Rome," she said, laying a palm on Caesar's shoulder.

"You had my appointment murdered, Pothinus. What crime had he committed?" she continued, referring to Philippas, the man she had chosen soon after assuming regency.

Pothinus shook his head. "Oh, how I have tried to protect you, Your Majesty," he lamented. "It was not I who had Philippas murdered, and yet I held my tongue in reverence to His Late Majesty's children."

"What do you mean?" she asked, her voice rising, surprise evident on her face.

She had put on a little weight, he thought, distracted.

"It was your sister! It was she who conspired to kill Philippas, for she worried that sidelining me would cut the connection she had to your thinking. I had no hand in it!"

The reveal shook Cleopatra. He saw her clench her fist, and yet a single tear fell from her already full eyes. Perhaps she had realized the depth of her sister's resentment and ambition.

Pothinus pressed on. "Her Highness Arsinoe is joining Achillas. Her ambition, combined with his abilities, will bring fire and destruction to Alexandria. You need my insight to fight them effectively."

Caesar, who had been quiet so far, stepped into the conversation. "How can you be of help when you have conspired to kill Caesar?"

Cleopatra responded even before Pothinus considered an answer. "Oh, Pothinus, how little you know those who you cradled in your hands. Arsinoe and Ganymedes will never reconcile with Achillas. The general is loyal to you and Ptolemy, and they have their own agenda. Whatever the nature of the attack, it will not be with all of them acting in concert. Caesar, there is nothing to consider here," she said, dismissing the conversation.

"To be rid of me is unwise, Your Majesty," he said, his voice shaking. "The shadow of bad decisions is long, and in it wither bountiful trees that would otherwise bear fruit."

"Or if that decision is good, in that shadow grow flowers that would otherwise wilt in the summer heat," she said.

"We can reconcile by the blessings of the gods, Your Majesty, and return to the glorious days where we walked the corridors engaged in stimulating thought. We can work towards a greater good," he said.

"No more, Pothinus. It will be I who will decide what is right for Egypt," she said, even as Caesar stood quietly, listening to them squabble.

How shameful that the Roman witnesses family disputes.

Pothinus scoffed. He had run out of patience. He fought the men who held him as he shook his shoulders. "What is right? What do you know about—"

Cleopatra nodded to a man behind him.

The hot, searing pain of a dagger thrust through his back exploded inside Pothinus. In the most fleeting moment, he felt betrayed by her. She had shunned him when such action was unwarranted. His last picture of his abrupt end was the bloodied tip of a blade emerging from his ribs.

CHAPTER 62

NEAR ALEXANDRIA

SABU

By virtue of his valiant efforts against Cleopatra and his abilities in organization and inspiring his men, Sabu had gained the confidence of Commander Achillas and marched with him to lay siege to the invader Caesar's men in Alexandria. But such was the hand of gods that Her Majesty, having subdued them by false proclamation of divinity, had smuggled herself to Caesar himself. When he heard the news, Sabu was greatly pained—how could he have knelt by her, who, having shorn herself of all shame and dignity, made peace with Caesar? When his actions were revealed to Achillas, the commander dealt to him ten lashes that caused fever and angry red welts on his back, shaming him in the presence of his men. But many entreaties of loyalty and recommendations by the men of his battalion caused Achillas to reconsider his position, maintain Sabu's rank, and allow him to continue on his march.

Still, Sabu was devastated by the betrayals; by the queen, and then by the commander who failed to see the reason for his actions, sanctioned by divine laws and obedience. And this he believed the gods acknowledged, for they presented to him an opportunity so splendid that he did fall to knees and pray.

Four days ago, Her Highness Arsinoe had arrived at the camp. By her side was her advisor Ganymedes, a eunuch of great importance and intelligence—like the regent Pothinus, who, at this time, was in the custody of Caesar, leaving to Commander Achillas the affairs of the army. Such was her boldness that she made a hasty escape from the

Roman's custody and made way across the marshes to the camp, much to the men's surprise. But her arrival posed a vexed problem—would the men have to follow the orders of Her Highness, or Commander Achillas, still under the orders of regent Pothinus on behalf of King Ptolemy?

And so she did make a speech to the officers, including Sabu. *I am the queen*, she declared, for Cleopatra had vacated her rights by surrendering to Caesar, and that since His Majesty was prisoner, he too had relinquished his authority to command an army. And thus, she said, she was by rights and law the royal that the army must pledge to. To this Achillas objected. *I have received no missive from Pothinus or know of his fate*, he protested, without which he was still obligated by duty to act on behalf of His Majesty Ptolemy and wait for orders to proceed to Alexandria.

The situation so deteriorated that with neither accepting the other's position, each endeavored to secure the support of the men, now divided into factions and cunningly offering their loyalty to whoever offered the greatest enticements. For each coin Achillas offered, Arsinoe offered a coin and a bag of grain. For each plot of land Achillas offered, Arsinoe offered a plot and exemptions from future tax. Such was her power and her acute understanding of the state's ability to confer bounties on its citizens, that Achillas lost the battle for loyalty, with the majority of the captains now pledging theirs to Her Highness.

With that settled, Achillas, if he were of the right mind, would submit to her authority and lend his exceptional capabilities in service. But he did not—instead he took to quarreling with Ganymedes on who would be Arsinoe's advisor, and refused to heed her command that he control the army but follow Ganymedes' orders.

Into that maelstrom Sabu was drawn, now as captain to Her Highness Arsinoe's guards, as Achillas and Ganymedes shouted at each other in Her Highness' presence.

"A eunuch must stick to matters of administration, rather than tell a general how he must move his armies. Surely you see this, Your Highness!" Achillas raged. The general's neck veins throbbed, and his eyes were red with anger.

Ganymedes, soft by his appearance but sharp with his tongue, responded thus: "Has your mind dulled, Achillas, you fucking idiot? Is it not a general's duty to obey the commands of his queen, and by virtue of her authority, her advisors? What man can call himself general that does not obey the fundamental tenets of rank?"

Whatever arguments were going on before Sabu stepped into the tent, Achillas, a man of singular and exceptional boldness, ignored where he was and who he was arguing with, and launched at Ganymedes. He gripped the advisor by his neck and squeezed it so hard, and so quickly, that Ganymedes let out a squawk and struggled with Achillas' powerful arms.

Sabu was stunned but unsure of how to act. And that was when Her Highness Arsinoe came in front of him, her eyes full of fury.

"Arrest him!" she shouted. Sabu knew then that the decision he made would be the most important in his life. He signaled his guards and rushed towards Ganymedes and Achillas. They tried to pry Achillas' fingers off Ganymedes' neck, and the eunuch was turning blue, with his eyeballs rolling up and exposing the whites.

Sabu pulled out his dagger and sliced Achillas' thigh, drawing a deep gash in the exposed flesh. Achillas screamed and let go of Ganymedes, who stumbled to his knees.

Achillas turned to Sabu, spittle flying from his mouth. "Disloyal son of a whore!" he screamed and tried to grapple with Sabu.

But Achillas was subdued, done by the pain of his injury and the strength of three guards. They dragged him out of the tent, with his blood leaving a wet trail on the muddy ground. Her Highness Arsinoe followed, screaming expletives at the general. Sabu's heart was heavy for having treated his once-commander thus, but he dismissed it, for such was fate and direction from the gods. Besides, who was Achillas to stand up to Her Highness? Sabu was taught to bow to the House of the Royals, the embodiments of the great gods themselves!

They threw Achillas on the ground, where he lay clutching his thigh. Achillas' helmet had fallen off, and his matted wet hair was coated in dust. Ganymedes, having recovered from Achillas' attack, followed Her Highness and stood over Achillas. He spat on the commander and shouted, "Bleed, bleed like a pig! How dare you attack me?"

Achillas would not relent. The commander tried grabbing Ganymedes' legs, and the frightened eunuch kicked Achillas' hands and jumped back. One of the zealous guards swung his sword and almost hacked Achillas' arm off, severing it to three-quarters at the forearm. Achillas bellowed and rolled on the ground. But Sabu knew that this was an end unbecoming of a general who had shown much courage and led his men with discipline, so he ordered the guards to step away. He knelt behind Achillas and held the commander's head–Achillas was still protesting, but his strength was waning with the blood loss. His half-severed arm dangled, and he gasped as Sabu cradled him.

Sabu looked up to Arsinoe and put on the most pitiful voice he could muster. "Spare him, Your Highness, for he has served us well," he implored.

Her Highness, her eyes still blazing and her face showing no pity or consideration for Achillas' long and illustrious career, looked at the two other guards. "Execute him," she ordered, her nostrils flaring and face still red with anger. She turned and stormed away. Ganymedes still waited on the side.

To give Achillas an end worthy of his stature, Sabu pushed up the general to a kneeling position, holding him at the waist. He then secured a robe from a waiting guard and tied it to the severed arm, covering the deep wound that had cut through to the bone. Sabu then made prayer to Achillas, wishing him glorious life in the afterlife.

Meanwhile, an impatient Ganymedes shouted, "Finish him! What are you waiting for?"

Sabu regretted the side he had taken—Achillas had led honorably, but how would Arsinoe do? He hoped he had done the wise thing. Sabu then pulled out his dagger and placed its tip at a specific point by the hollow of the collar bone, a place he knew that when a blade was plunged, it would puncture the heart and cause a quick death.

Achillas did not resist. Instead, the general hung his head and waited bravely.

"May the gods smile upon you when you cross the rivers of the afterlife, general," Sabu said as sorrow rose up his throat like a river through the gorge.

"And may you live well, captain. Now, do it," Achillas said with great effort, even as a rivulet of blood dripped from his bandaged arm, his skin already clammy and his face turning white.

And so Sabu did. And once Ganymedes walked away, Sabu wept for the great Achillas, whose long and loyal service to the kings and queens had come to an end not in battle against a worthy opponent like Caesar, but by the ill tempers of those who saw little beyond their ego.

CHAPTER 63

ALEXANDRIA

CLEOPATRA

Charmian washed Cleopatra and wiped the queen's body. She, along with two other maids, then applied a fine lavender perfume to Cleopatra's neck and back, and helped her with her lapis-lazuli earrings, a gold pendant, and a luxurious silk gown. Iras was still far away, and they missed the little girl whose enthusiastic (though not always) application of perfume was a joyous event every day.

Cleopatra then moved to her adjacent quarters, the one with gold-embroidered couches, color paintings of Pharaohs and animals, life-sized bronze lamps, a giant, multi-layered soft bed with lush green drapery, and a huge window that opened out to the dazzling blue sea. Here she spent much of her day, listening to reports from outside, trying to gauge the sentiment of the people and her kingdom, even as she wondered how to regain control from a terrible situation.

Much to her disappointment, the sentiment on the streets was not very favorable towards her, and many mobs blamed her for how their lives were upended. The king, as incompetent as he was, she thought, was still held in higher esteem. She had survived great odds, but how long Caesar's protection would last was a matter of how dire the situation became for him. The Roman was enchanted by her, no doubt, for she presented a front unlike any woman he had encountered or seduced. They spent hours debating politics, history, and philosophy. Caesar was an exceptionally gifted man–demonstrated through his arguments, his experiences, his knowledge of the arts and philosophy. In fact, at one point, Cleopatra had teasingly asked Caesar if he were willing to renounce Rome and take up the role of Egypt's supreme general, causing Caesar to be at once offended and tickled. She learned much from him: of the nature of men, of the nature of politics, of power and ambition, of the benefits of moving fast even under disadvantageous conditions (though he admitted that his misadventures in Alexandria were not his best examples), of alliances and the shifting sands of loyalties, and of forgiveness and punishment (he was a forgiving man, even to those that fought against him). She was as enthralled by him as he was by her. And the more she understood him and the capability of his empire, the more it became obvious to her that there was no conceivable way, in the near future, for her to get rid of Rome—Apollodorus was right.

Her reverie was disrupted by Charmian, as much her confidante as she was her most trusted lady-in-waiting.

"Are you sure about this, Your Majesty?" she asked as she combed the queen's hair, untangling the curled knots and sometimes receiving *be gentle, are you trying to rip my hair off?* admonition.

"I have no choice. Besides, I do not know, myself."

Charmian's breath was warm on her neck, and Cleopatra knew that she wanted to say something.

"Go on, what is in your mind? I know you want to ask."

Charmian, now the head of all Cleopatra's servants and slaves, dismissed the other women from the chamber. She then knelt by Cleopatra and placed a gentle palm on her knee. "Does Apollodorus know?"

Cleopatra was surprised. She had spoken about everything with Charmian *except* her brief affair with Apollodorus. She held Charmian's palms and sighed. "He knows. And he understands."

Charmian nodded and said nothing.

Cleopatra whispered to her, "Was it that obvious? Did others know?"

Charmian giggled. "Obvious to me, Your Majesty. I do not know about others. But there was some gossip about an affair that I quickly put an end to."

"Kadmos?"

"Him too, but I scolded him and told him to keep his mouth shut if he wanted to keep his head attached to his body."

"What about you two?"

She blushed. "Nothing until we left. Hopefully..."

Cleopatra slapped her hand and smiled. But there was sadness in Cleopatra's heart, for Apollodorus had been her rock, and now Caesar was in the picture—larger-than-life, and instrumental to her survival.

But there was something else that no one in her close quarters knew. That she was aware Caesar had only one child, the wife of Pompey, who had died during childbirth. For a man known for his many affairs and dalliances, no one else had claimed a child that they said was by him, to the extent she knew. Was it that sickness he had–the shaking and pains in his chest? She had seen him in that state twice. She had never questioned him, but instead cared for him during those episodes.

Why?

Caesar had shown experience in bed, but he lacked the vigor of Apollodorus, perhaps on account of his age. But what was more telling was how casual Caesar had been regarding the chances of her getting pregnant–almost as if he did not think it could happen, even if he spilled his seed in her. And all this knowing Roman law and its restrictions around marriage with foreigners, and the rights of foreigner-born children.

Why?

Charmian cut in again. "He will be here soon. You are certain, Your Majesty? And you are sure no harm will come to you?"

She took a deep breath. She had taken on monumental risk by smuggling herself to him. And now, she would take another. Such was her life.

Caesar arrived soon, not as a general, but in his usual purple toga. He acknowledged Charmian and waited until she left.

Cleopatra's heart beat like a drum. Her cheeks became warm like fresh bread out of an oven, and she struggled to breathe. But it had to be done.

She made Caesar sit on the bed. He already knew by her demeanor that there was a matter of concern. "What is it?" he asked, touching her cheek with the back of his hand. She held it and looked into his eyes.

Now.

"Your child grows in me now, Caesar," she said softly.

CHAPTER 64

ALEXANDRIA

CAESAR

Caesar was besieged. It had been rare for him to feel this way–almost helpless, questioning his own decisions, and worrying whether his men would desert him. But so far, his exemplary legion had held on. The battle-hardened veterans, knowledgeable in all matter of defense, had stubbornly held against the relentless pressure from outside. Ganymedes' men trained and helped the mob come up with improvised siege-towers, they launched greased stones into the complex, they tried climbing over compounds at all hours, they tried poisoning waters, they tried setting the palace on fire, and they made a great din at all times, depriving Caesar and his men of precious sleep. Caesar also had received conflicting news about Achillas' death. Whoever was in charge, whether it was the girl Arsinoe or the eunuch Ganymedes, they had not stood down. King Ptolemy's main legions still waited outside Alexandria and had not marched on yet, but those that were in the city continued to wreak havoc. Yet on Cleopatra's insistence, he had allowed her to send some of her trusted spies to scour the city for sentiments on Arsinoe, and it was clear that the people did not want her either.

The Alexandrians were getting fed up with the months of unrest. They wanted the king to appear and take charge. And the king, of course, was in Caesar's custody, making everything complicated.

"As much as you resent it, Caesar, my brother is key to breaking this siege," Cleopatra had said.

Cleopatra. Oh, that girl! She had complicated everything for him. How foolish was he to be enchanted by her! A girl of his daughter's age. And now, she claimed his child bloomed in her. Caesar doubted that–for he had not fathered a child since Julia, and he had bedded many. Was this a ruse? Was the Egyptian queen cunning enough that she would impregnate herself with another man, and use that as a way to gain legitimacy with Rome by announcing that her child was of Caesar? She was resourceful, clever, and cunning. Was she *that* devious?

So, he had spluttered, argued, and then stormed out of the room that day when she said his child grew in her, leaving her weeping. But Caesar found himself in the greatest quandary–could he release her from custody and let her family deal with her as they wished? This, of course, meant they would kill her at the earliest opportunity. But there were benefits of letting Cleopatra go–it could reduce pressure, even sow enough confusion among his opponents and give him an opportunity to bring them to negotiations, or engineer an armed settlement.

But.

But.

He had seen what she could do. They had been trying for years to get rid of her and failed. She had ruled boldly. Escaped and built an army. And then risked her life to come to him. She had accurately predicted what Pothinus would do. What was the guarantee that she would not somehow unite them all under her, and then march on him? Besides, if what she said was true, that she carried his child, she would use that in any manner possible to either shame him or cause his own men to rebel. And for a man who had lost his only daughter years ago, Caesar wondered if the gods were blessing Gaius Julius Caesar with a son who might carry the legacy of the father—or perhaps a daughter, Julia the Younger, who might even become Queen of Egypt.

Oh, that girl!

He could just have her executed.

Caesar sighed loudly.

Could he do it?

Could he?

Because deep inside, he knew, as a man so accomplished himself, that there was simply no one like Cleopatra.

CHAPTER 65

ALEXANDRIA

CAESAR

———◇———

Caesar knew that fate turned on two qualities–opportunity and grit. Sometimes, you had to move rapidly to seek advantage where none was evident, and other times, you had to wait until an opportunity presented itself.

It was the second that came to him on this day. After weeks more of relentless attacks, rioting in the streets, disruption to water supplies, naval attempts, and fantastical rumors, a negotiating party sought Caesar's consideration. And when that news arrived, he had been on Cleopatra's side, having reconciled to the situation and reluctantly accepting the position that the child may be his, and that he quite possibly loved her, though she offered little by way of a tactical benefit. In fact, she was a burden that he was now carrying.

"What do they want?" he asked the Centurion.

"They seek to parley, Caesar. They say they will only speak terms to you."

"I must be present," Cleopatra said, much to Caesar's surprise. "If there is anyone who understands their true intent, it would be me."

"But you will not speak," Caesar said sternly. "Because they seek to talk to me, and their anger towards you will blind them to rational conversation."

She reluctantly agreed, but Caesar knew it would be a gamble allowing her to stay in the same room as whoever was coming to meet him.

And thus, under careful arrangement, his men allowed the Alexandrians to come to him. He sat on a chair with Cleopatra beside him. He had compelled her to not wear her diadem, should that send a mistaken message that she had already assumed the position of a queen when that was not settled. The boy-king Ptolemy was still under house arrest and would not be present.

The first two were military officers—a man named Sabu, a Greek-speaking Egyptian; and another man. Along with them was a delegation of Alexandrian citizens—an influential merchant from the western quarters, a leader of the fishers, three local administrators, two orchard owners, and a representative of Jewish interests. A senior Egyptian Alexandrian administrator called Unasankh had also accompanied them.

Their eyes flashed in surprise when they saw Cleopatra. They bowed to her and politely enquired after Her Majesty's health. And she, likewise, said she was pleased to see them arrive for a discussion, but noted that it was Caesar who would speak and decide. And she said this in three languages—Greek, Egyptian, and Hebrew—once again impressing Caesar with her methods.

Caesar opened the conversation. He was a direct man, and these times afforded little by way of elaborate Alexandrian formalities. "Where is Achillas, and what is your position?" he asked bluntly.

Sabu was a well-built, articulate officer dressed in his military garb. "Achillas is no more, Your Excellency. Ganymedes and Her Highness Arsinoe accused him of insubordination and had him executed," he said plainly, though the unhappiness of the event floated in his tone.

Cleopatra whispered into Caesar's ears. "As I predicted," she said. "They must have quarreled."

"And what do you seek?" Caesar asked. Ganymedes had turned out to be a formidable foe–causing enough trouble that Caesar had been compelled to set fire to docked ships to prevent them from building a navy, and in the process burning several buildings, granaries, and even a small section of the famed library. It was one of those rare circumstances where Caesar had received an earful from an angry Cleopatra. If these men had a way to end Ganymedes' reign, that would be most welcome.

"The people clamor for the king, Your Excellency. His continued incarceration makes any negotiation difficult. Passions are inflamed, and our attempts to quell the riots are failing," Sabu said, clasping his hands together.

"Why do you not disband and allow me to make peaceful declarations?"

Sabu looked at Unasankh and ceded the stage to the senior man.

Unasankh looked around, and on receiving approving nods, he bowed. "If Caesar will allow me to be frank."

"Go on."

"The great people of Alexandria hold much influence, Caesar. The royals must keep the people in their confidence. Asking for the king's army to disband, without the king by their side, is a great affront to Egypt. Her Highness Arsinoe will never agree to lay down arms, for to do so puts her, and all the senior officers, at risk from angry mobs," he said, his eyes darting between Cleopatra and Caesar, as if to seek her opinion. "The army is ill-equipped to handle city-wide riots or a national civil unrest. And that will only anger the people further towards you, Caesar."

The old, sagely-looking Greek merchant, dressed in fine robes and sporting a generous beard, joined the conversation. "We are faced with a vexing issue, *Imperator*.

The people and the army are fed up with Ganymedes and Her Highness Arsinoe. They are tyrannical and unwilling to find ways to compromise. The army wishes to stand down, but cannot do so on account of loyalty and lack of royal decree. They need the king. The people long for peace. It has been months now."

Caesar leaned towards Cleopatra.

"He speaks the truth," she whispered. "No one will win. Not them. Not you."

"What do you propose?" Caesar asked, turning to the delegation.

The merchant, the one who called himself Archippos, spoke. "Free the king and let him join the army. Let him announce a truce, have the army stand down, and then arrive peacefully at a negotiated settlement, as Caesar pleases. At the moment, I beg your pardon for saying so, Caesar, but your actions have led us to a situation that we cannot resolve."

Unasankh, the senior administrator, nodded solemnly and warned of unrest in the south as well if the situation was not resolved quickly.

Caesar bristled at the accusation but knew that he had to find a way through the impasse. "What other options do you have, other than me letting him go?"

Many in the delegation looked at each other, and finally, Sabu, the officer, spoke. "There is no other way than the presence of their king to secure settlement, Caesar."

Caesar knew that his chances were dwindling. It was only a fortuitous circumstance that Arsinoe had not marched on to Alexandria. Messengers said that the army had stalled several days away on account of rain, and because of officers still coming to terms with Arsinoe at the head of the army. Issues with logistics, leadership, and some opposition from the people had caused the delay–but he knew that this would not hold much longer.

Where was Mithridates? Months ago, Caesar had sent for help to the nobleman from Bosporus, but there was no news yet on whether the relief army, which had to arrive through Syria and Judaea, was anywhere nearby. Timing was of paramount importance. If Mithridates was too slow, then it would be too late for Caesar, and Ganymedes' remaining legions near Pelusium could intercept Mithridates' army and destroy him.

After some more wrangling that led to no concessions on either side, Caesar dismissed the party, saying he would meet with the king and decide the course of action. They were asked to return the next day for an answer. Meanwhile, Caesar's demands to end hostilities were rejected, for the delegation said they had no power to do so with Ganymedes still in charge.

Once the delegation left, Caesar turned to Cleopatra. "It is time for you to accept the state of affairs and agree to a settlement with your brother. Every time I meet him, he complains about you and questions my decisions, but a reconciliation must be made."

She chewed on her bottom lip. "Do I have a choice?"

"No. Do you have sufficient support to remain unharmed if I leave you as queen?" he said firmly.

"I will have to bring some of my closest advisors and officers from my army to ensure my protection. Will you leave a Roman garrison behind?"

"Yes. But you must manage your affairs until I can bring additional support."

She agreed to the arrangement; but it remained to be seen whether the young king was willing to go to his other sister.

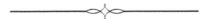

The boy-king burst into tears when Caesar met him to discuss his release to the army. *Please do not send me away, Caesar, for I learned much from thee, and it is thee who hath kept me safe from the treachery outside these walls,* he implored, his cheeks wet and his eyes brimming with sorrow.

"The people need their king, and it is you who they seek to bring peace, Your Majesty," Caesar said gently, holding the boy's shaking shoulders.

"You know them, Caesar. What if they choose to kill me when I leave? I so desire to end this all, stand my army down, and seek your guidance," he said, surprising Caesar with his mature words.

"The delegation strongly conveys the words of the army that they need their king by their side, and for him to convey to them to lay down arms and restore sanity. They are not happy with your sister and the eunuch Ganymedes, who now control the conduct of your army."

Ptolemy hung his head low and sobbed. "You are throwing me to the wolves, Caesar. Why?"

Caesar placed a hand on the boy's shoulder and squeezed it. What a family this was–he had seen many quarreling families, but the Ptolemies were truly a breed apart. A father killed his daughter, a wife had her husband strangled, siblings married amongst themselves, they fought and tried to kill each other… it was a bloodthirsty dynasty. As someone said in the Senate, Egypt always presented a vexing problem. To leave it alone would create a challenger. To destroy it would lead to depriving Rome of a strong supply source. To annex it would bring a great deal of administrative headache. Nothing seemed sensible. But this intractable situation presented no easier options.

Caesar, who for this occasion had dressed himself as a general, crooked his arm theatrically. "A king of the Ptolemies is a god, Your Majesty, and they clamor for you. This is what we must do, and this is what will bring calm to this troubled land. Will you reconcile with your sisters and order the army to stand down?"

Ptolemy nodded sadly. He looked up at Caesar with his wet eyes. *Still a boy, shouldering the responsibilities of grown men*, Caesar thought. "If you say so, Caesar, for you have the experience. I wish to end this all."

Caesar was pleased. And he hoped that Cleopatra, who was listening from a chamber behind the room, would comply with this arrangement. He spent some more time talking to the king, helping him draft the disbanding orders, proclamations, and decrees to bring peace. He then sent the weeping king back to his quarters, asking him to prepare for departure. He summoned Theodotus and told him that he would need to go with the king, to which the rhetorician reluctantly agreed.

Caesar grunted as he stretched his back. He would first talk to his officers, and then head to Cleopatra's room, where he knew she would be waiting to opine on what had just transpired.

CHAPTER 66

ALEXANDRIA

CLEOPATRA

———◇———

Cleopatra rubbed the growing bulge in her stomach as she stretched her legs on the couch. The days were becoming harder, and the experience of bearing her first child weighed upon her. Her back hurt, her mornings were nauseous, and the daily lower-back massages gave immense relief. As Charmian wryly observed, even queens farted no less than commoners, and promptly earned a slap on her wrist.

Caesar walked in, relaxed, his eyes sparkling with mirth.

"You are a family and city of such deception," he said. "One never knows whom to believe and whom to berate."

She laughed. "Of whom do you speak, Caesar? The delegation, or my sorrowful brother?"

"The boy seemed reluctant to leave," he said.

Cleopatra looked at Caesar. For a man of such vast experience, he was quick to give the benefit of the doubt, and mercy came easily to him. And for that, his officers often gently mocked him. *I see that you are here to stab me, you rude fellow. I shall make you my bodyguard!* they said, to much laughter. She wondered if this characteristic of Caesar's would one day betray him, for not all men who sought forgiveness deserved it, and not all those who benefited from generosity chose to repay it in kind.

"Do not let him go, Caesar," she said, this time without a smile. "Those tears are not real. If he leaves, he will continue the war with energy."

"That thought came to my mind," Caesar said. "He is not a very good actor. What of the delegation?"

"Their intent seems sincere, only they misread what their king might do. Do not let him go!" she said anxiously. "Is Mithridates on the way?"

"I do not know if he is on the way. I shall send scouts–"

"Let me support you. Let me send scouts from my waiting army near Memphis. We cannot take chances," she said. "But hold Ptolemy until then."

Caesar sat and looked at her quietly. She could see the strain on his face.

"What if I simply annex Egypt and put an end to this entire sordid affair?"

Cleopatra dreaded hearing *annexation*. Rome's current policy was to leave Egypt's rule and administration alone, treating it as a client-state and securing grain supplies, war materials, and men. Annexation was a different situation– they would depose the royals and replace the throne with a governor or administrator, and it would be the end of her dynasty.

Cleopatra had to think fast, for every hour was critical. She walked towards a richly detailed mural of a map on the wall. She pointed to where Rome was, and then Gaul, Hispania, and other provinces. "Look at this, Caesar. You are the master of those domains, are you not?"

He walked to her side and looked at the map as well. He nodded.

"Look how far Egypt is from all those provinces connected to Italy. You have spent time here; you have seen this land and its people. How similar to you do you think we are?"

Caesar did not answer.

"You seek to be the master of the Roman domain when you return. You are still dealing with unrest in the East. How stable and compliant do you think Egypt will be if you depose me and leave this in the hands of one of your governors, most of whom can barely muster two sentences in Greek? You know you need me, Caesar. No one knows Egypt better. No one can manage this kingdom while being firmly on your side."

He still stared at the map, not answering. *Employing the same tactic as she did with some of her supplicants. The power of silence.*

She continued, "The Ptolemies administer seven Nomes with millions of people through an elaborate system of taxation and property rights. Our senior administrators are either Greeks or bilingual Egyptians, but the most influential priests are Egyptian. I know how to deal with them and extract what I need. This is not Gaul with its tribes or Hispania with its barbarians, Caesar. This is an ancient land with very deep-rooted cultures and norms. Do you really want to annex us and deal with every pain that comes after? Do you want to impact the flow of revenue, men, and goods?"

"You underestimate my administrators. I can easily find a man who is loyal to Caesar and knows Greek. It could be one of your senior men."

"You have seen how my senior men have been in the last few months," she said, dropping her voice conspiratorially.

Caesar laughed.

"There is no substitute, Caesar, none, to having Cleopatra on the throne—by your side, with your child, ruling Egypt as she knows best, with the people bowing to her divinity while she continues the supply of grain, gold, and gruff men to Rome," she said as she smoothed his thinning hair. "And my oracles tell me that it will be a son. And do you think that without me in charge, they will let me, and *your son*, live?"

He held her hand for a while, and then Caesar paced around the room. She knew that the master general's mind worked through scenarios, and he saw things she did not. Caesar probably knew, as did she, that the people of Alexandria were no great fans of her. They probably hated her as much as they hated the others, for she had been by Caesar's side. But if they prevailed, with Caesar reigning supreme, she was confident she could convince the men of her autonomy and regain her confidence. She would then convey to the people that what she did was in their best interests and to preserve the kingdom, preventing it from becoming a Roman province.

Finally, Caesar spoke. "My men will chide and mock me for letting Ptolemy go. Perhaps he lies, or perhaps he does not. But go he must, Cleopatra, and this is why: if he wages war on me, we will prevail, and his act allows me by law and posterity to punish him and remove him from attaining the throne. But if he follows my order, then peace will come from it, and you shall still have the opportunity to remove him in due time. I do not trust the boy, but we must force his hand rather than prolong this agony."

Cleopatra was quietly glad that he saw her reasoning. But once again, this was a gamble. What if Ptolemy marched on Alexandria with all the legions and the people of Alexandria with him? How would they survive? When she posed him the question, Caesar only laughed.

"This is not the first time, my love," he said, speaking the rare endearment which she desired from him but received modestly, "and never has Caesar not prevailed."

Whatever the case, Cleopatra wanted her brother deposed, or even dead. Over the past few months, she had met with her youngest brother, Ptolemy XIV, a fearful child still, and willing to faithfully follow whatever she said. She would mold him, for he had no advisor around him, and no one to fill him with ideas that would make him a threat.

But Cleopatra had one last demand.

CHAPTER 67

ALEXANDRIA

———————◇———————

With tears streaming down her face, hair disheveled, and spittle flying from her abusive mouth, Arsinoe resisted the men who held and dragged her. She called the officers disloyal cowards, her brother a cockless pig with no dignity, her sister a common whore ready for Roman markets, and behind all this, her advisor a worthless eunuch who should have been left as a beggar on temple stairs, and the citizens a bunch of filthy rats who would burn soon. She vowed terrible revenge on them all for their hand against their queen. She spit at the guards who held her, tried to scratch them, and kicked at them until she was finally bound by her hands and legs, and carried struggling into the palace compound.

In a twist of fate and the machinations of the many actors in this family drama, Cleopatra had suggested to Caesar that Ptolemy could be allowed to go *in exchange for* Arsinoe. She made an impassioned reasoning to a very agreeable Roman, who was anyway used to such hostage-taking, that reducing threats to her and to Rome would have to be done by neutralizing her rebellious siblings one by one. The fed-up Alexandrians were only too pleased to make this exchange, and they conspired with Ganymedes, who saw this as an opportunity to simplify the command situation and side with the boy, who had greater loyalty among the troops that wished to be led by a king rather than an ill-tempered queen. And so, she was seized and carried away and handed to Caesar, who was only too pleased to remove her from the equation.

Caesar then placed her under house arrest and agreed to release the still weepy boy-king.

And then the young King Ptolemy, no sooner had he left the palace walls and joined the army, proceeded to prosecute the war with gusto. He quickly assumed his role as head of the army, with the tactical military command under Ganymedes. The officers, seeing an opportunity to teach Romans a lesson and not thinking about what might happen eventually, dropped the pretense of a truce and prepared to march on Alexandria. And while all this was happening, Mithridates of Pergamum, the nobleman summoned to help Caesar, arrived near Pelusium. The news of this marching army had reached both Caesar and Ptolemy, who both proceeded to act in the way they best thought to handle the situation.

Ptolemy ordered his army to turn towards the Nile and prepare fortifications to stop Mithridates and destroy him. At the same time, having received credible news of Mithridates' arrival, Caesar escaped from the palace with his legions, all loaded onto the remaining ships. With him were the pregnant Cleopatra and the prisoner Arsinoe. Caesar's legions made a short trip west of Alexandria and disembarked on a remote stretch near Chersonensus. Then, with astonishing speed, a hallmark of Caesar's tactics, they marched around Lake Mareotis to rendezvous with Mithridates' forces near the delta.

The armies met midway between Alexandria and Memphis, with the Great River behind them towards the west. Ptolemy's forces were better placed on a hill, with Caesar's men planning their attack from below.

CHAPTER 68

NILE DELTA

CLEOPATRA

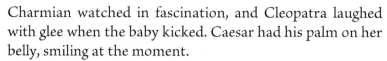

Charmian watched in fascination, and Cleopatra laughed with glee when the baby kicked. Caesar had his palm on her belly, smiling at the moment.

She lay on the relatively comfortable couch in the tent. Bringing Cleopatra here to the battlefield was not just for the sake of her safety, but was also a strategic move. It signaled to Ptolemy's men that a co-ruler stood on the other side. Tactically, all other options–hiding her in Alexandria, moving her elsewhere, sending her away to Rome and so on– were dismissed. The extent of treachery and backstabbing meant that for her to be out of Caesar's immediate reach would put her at risk. She knew it, and he concurred. Finally, they had mutually agreed that even with her being visibly pregnant, the safest place was near Caesar's army.

Caesar had issued formation orders to ready for the attack on Ptolemy's hilltop fortifications. Cleopatra's camp was far away, ringed by a special cavalry and a cohort co-led by Apollodorus and a Roman Centurion. In the worst eventuality that Caesar was losing, a signal would lead to her being taken away to safety. And then whether she would *really* be safe would be a matter for the gods.

"Your child," she whispered as she patted her bulging belly.

Caesar did not respond, but instead gently rubbed his palm on Cleopatra's stomach. "Do you still feel sick?" he asked.

"Sometimes," she said, looking tired and anxious. "My back hurts, and Charmian is not the best massager."

Charmian grinned and Caesar wagged a finger. "You must do better, Charmian!"

"I make Her Majesty hot lemon drinks and honey candy, General Caesar. She complains no matter how I massage!"

"Once all this ends, you can return to the palace under the care of your staff and midwife," Caesar said.

"I hope so, too, Caesar," she said, as she played with his purple cloak. "You rarely talk about your daughter. How was she?"

Caesar paused for a moment. His face softened somewhat, and his eyes looked at a far hill outside the tent. "I did not have too much time with her," he said, "but the few memories with my daughter are much cherished. She was beautiful. Gentle. Julia."

"You can spend more time with our child," Cleopatra said.

Caesar nodded. "Perhaps. And Pompey loved her. He was distraught when she died. I do not want to lose you in childbirth as I lost my daughter," he said with surprising kindness. "The gods never gave me a chance to hold a grandchild."

She took his hand in hers. "You will have a chance with our child. I am a goddess. I am ordained to spend time here. With my people. With you. And with your child."

"And with me too," Charmian said, bringing levity to the conversation.

"And you too, my beloved Charmian," Cleopatra said. "And little Iras!"

Charmian walked to Cleopatra's feet and sat by them, and Caesar looked down on her with stern seriousness.

"Your brother will die, one way or the other. Have you made peace with that?" he said finally.

"It is what the gods have determined. And you have my permission," she said. *There was no other way.*

Caesar leaned forward to peck her forehead. He then stood, regal in his bearing, straight in his magnificent armor and cloak.

"It is time," Caesar said as he bid her goodbye and walked out to prosecute the Battle of the Nile.

CHAPTER 69

NILE DELTA

SABU

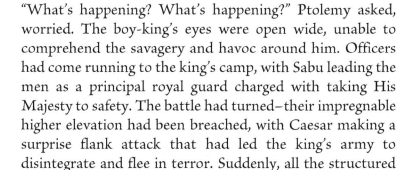

"What's happening? What's happening?" Ptolemy asked, worried. The boy-king's eyes were open wide, unable to comprehend the savagery and havoc around him. Officers had come running to the king's camp, with Sabu leading the men as a principal royal guard charged with taking His Majesty to safety. The battle had turned–their impregnable higher elevation had been breached, with Caesar making a surprise flank attack that had led the king's army to disintegrate and flee in terror. Suddenly, all the structured formations had crumbled, and Caesar's infantry and cavalry had begun to chase the fleeing combatants. Theodotus was nowhere to be found; the bastard had fled the battlefield at the first opportunity.

"We have to run, Your Majesty. Now! Now!" Sabu yelled. He forced the frightened king to throw away his helmet and remove the beautifully appointed royal golden armor. He then forced the king to wear a soldier's bronze breastplate.

Sabu ruffled the king's hair and ripped the diadem. And then, with the king having no chance to protest, Sabu dragged him by the hand to a waiting contingent. Guards surrounded the king and helped him on a horse, with Sabu riding alongside. The boy was terrified. He trembled and had become speechless, looking to Sabu to do whatever had to be done.

They whipped through the madness, rushing down the incline, often trampling their own fleeing soldiers and dodging Roman javelins. Far below, about a mile away, was the river with boats that they could make their escape in.

Bodies were strewn about–stabbed, beheaded, trampled—and the speeding horses, terrified by the din and the grisly ground, sometimes panicked and ran hither and thither, and had to be controlled. The boy-king gripped the rider in front, his face white with terror, eyeing the chasing Roman cavalry and the random group of legionnaires rushing towards the fleeing party.

The ground closer to the river was marshy and riddled with stones and boulders, making it difficult to maneuver the horses. Sabu whistled to the guards to stop so they could disembark and run to the waiting boats. With no Roman presence in the immediate vicinity, Sabu exhorted the boy-king to run with him, and they joined a group of fleeing soldiers and some villagers from a nearby town, all headed to a waiting boat. The king stumbled twice and fell, causing him to scratch his arms and knees and bleed, but Sabu rudely hoisted His Highness back to his feet and rushed him. "You have to run! Run!" he shouted at the king, who was now blabbering.

Sabu shouted at the people around. "Make way for the king! Get out of the way!" he shouted, but many paid no heed as they jostled with each other to get on the embarkation plank. Ptolemy looked like a frightened little boy, nothing like a king. The guards struggled to keep him moving while pushing the crowds away, and they ended in a scuffle, causing Sabu to stab two men and lose one of his own guards, who was dragged away by a group and beaten to death. The mud beneath the feet made it harder to run, and distant Roman slingshots still hit the group, breaking the skulls of the unfortunate victims.

The boat was not very large, and it was already full of men scrambling on it. The oarsmen were getting ready to depart, lest a huge projectile hit them. Once Sabu pulled the boy on board, he quickly retrieved the diadem from his pouch, wrapped it on the boy's head, and began to shout. "The king is on board! Where is the boat-master? Leave! Leave now!"

Since the crowd was mostly soldiers accustomed to command, many quickly fell to their knees, and a few guards managed to cut the ropes to the plank. Someone shouted for the oarsmen to speed up, and the boat, overflowing and strained, began to move. Ptolemy, still in shock, held on to the side as the boat pulled away from the shore. Men were still jumping into the river and begging for them to wait. But they were soon sucked in by the turbid water, which quickly became deep as one progressed from the bank.

As the boat began to move, Sabu inched closer to the king and watched over him. The scene at the bank was as pitiful as it was horrifying. Roman cavalry and some elements of infantry had arrived, and they appeared to mercilessly target the fleeing men, turning the black-brown bank red with blood and hacked limbs. *What happened to Caesar's doctrine of restraint?* Bodies were piling up on the marshy beach, and the boat narrowly missed the javelins flung by the soldiers. Just when the vessel reached mid-river, it turned sharply to avoid a rock and another boat. The clumsily managed turn, no doubt caused by the panic and confusion amongst the oarsmen, caused the boat to tilt heavily, compounding the chaos. Many angry men shouted at the oarsmen and some beat them, while many others lost their footing and fell on each other. The boat heaved again and the right edge rose high, with the weight of the men all on one side. The shouts to balance went unheeded in the ruckus.

Just as these terrible situations surfaced the strangest fears and deep hidden angers, a burly, bearded man who stood by the boy-king's side suddenly launched an attack. "You caused this, you bastard runt! You are getting us all killed!" he shouted. He gripped the terrified boy-king by the throat, and before Sabu could react and break the hold, the man pushed the king up by the neck and threw the screaming boy overboard.

Seeing this, Sabu—a confident swimmer, for he had grown up by the banks of the river—jumped into the water. He gasped, for the water was cold in this third month of the year. Desperate people were paddling around, and some bodies floated downriver.

His Young Majesty Ptolemy not only did not know how to swim, but also his bronze armor was pulling him under. The boy's eyes opened in sheer terror as he flailed and screamed, shouting to cling to Sabu. They struggled in the water, and Sabu realized that to hold the king would mean to die himself in the churning water, and he began to extricate himself from the boy's grip.

Perhaps the panicking king saw Sabu's disengagement as a deliberate act, one of revenge plotted by his sister, for he began to splutter and shout. "Tell my sister I will let her rule! I will not fight with her! Please! Don't leave me!"

He began to wail and cry, kicking his legs and desperately trying to hold on to the rim of the tilted boat. He went underwater twice, briefly, and surfaced spitting the dark, dirty water while trying to scream and implore. But just then the vessel regained balance.

Ptolemy lost his grip.

Sabu watched as the horrified face of the boy, still gasping and spitting, calling his father's name, submerged beneath the dark and muddy waters. And soon, Ptolemy Theos Philopator, *god, Father-Loving*, brother of Cleopatra, only fourteen years old and wearing the heavy mantle of a king, sank to the bottom of the Nile, the great river that took life just as it gave life.

CHAPTER 70

ALEXANDRIA

CLEOPATRA

---◇---

They were all back again at the great temple of Taposiris Magna, a location that not just two years ago was witness to a similar declaration. How much had happened then! She sat wearing the sun disk and cow horns along with a magnificent gold-leaf patterned, specially constructed loose silvery silk gown that mostly hid her now-growing belly. In her hand she held a blue-glass-and-obsidian crook and a heavy bronze flail. Beside her, her timid brother and recently wedded husband, Ptolemy the Fourteenth, sat quietly, wearing a cream *shendyt*. But in his hands were absent the symbols of Pharaonic authority, therefore sending the unmistakable signal to every present dignitary of who the true ruler would be.

The musky chamber smelled of rose, lavender, and burned wood as priests chanted verses. Bronze armors and red plumes dominated one side, and white linen and gold jewelry on the other. Those in the room were split half-and-half between the officers of Caesar's legions and Mithridates' army; and the rest the senior officials, officers, and priests of Cleopatra's retinue. Charmian stood behind Cleopatra, and Iras, having been reunited with them, sat with a caretaker. A reluctant Apollodorus had been sent away to hold Cleopatra's army, still under Metjen and Kadmos' control, and to manage payment and release of the mercenary soldiers.

Apollodorus. Oh, how would she manage her emotions toward this man?

Caesar, dressed in a resplendent purple toga and wearing a laurel wreath (though the conferring of a dictator's title had not been bequeathed to him by the Senate, but did Caesar care?), opened his declaration with a flourish. "And it is by Roman law and my decree that I, Gaius Julius Caesar, Consul of Rome, hereby declare Cleopatra Philopator, and Ptolemy the Fourteenth, the new co-rulers of Egypt, keeping with their father's will and his wishes," Caesar said.

The priests, standing beside the rulers sitting on their thrones, rang their bronze bells and burned incense that filled the room with the gentle aroma of frankincense and myrrh. The senior officials of her administration and officers of Caesar's legions all made great clamor and celebrated the declaration. The smoke wafted through the opening in the ceiling and indicated that Caesar's proclamation was complete, causing the anxious multitudes outside to shout and rejoice that the conflict was finally over. True to his word, Caesar had magnanimously pardoned the Alexandrian mischief-makers, and there was no large-scale retribution. They had now accepted the Roman as master and protector of their kingdom.

Caesar folded the will and looked around. He continued, "It is also Caesar's decree that the island of Cyprus be returned to Egypt, under the royal patronage of Her Majesty Cleopatra. These titles shall remain with the understanding that the new rulers of Egypt maintain cordial relations with Rome and continue to fulfill their responsibilities of a client-state. On my departure, the twenty-seventh, the thirty-seventh, and the forty-third legions shall remain in Egypt, overseeing an orderly transition to peace, and to preserve the sanctity of this announcement."

The audience was surprised at these announcements, and there were several hoots of joy at the mention of Cyprus being returned to Egypt. After all, the island was a Ptolemaic region that had been stolen by Rome years ago, and now Cleopatra had managed to convince Caesar to return it. She hoped that the people saw her hand behind this act.

Cleopatra looked at him. While she resented the idea of Roman troops staying on her soil, she had grown to be fond of this man, even with all his *look at me, I am the mighty Caesar* posturing. Did she love him with unbridled passion? Perhaps not. Did she feel the same flutter at seeing him as she did about Apollodorus? Perhaps not. But his allure was his power, his protection, his wit and wisdom. It was a different type of love for her. One borne of expediency, safety, and ambition. He was kind in private and had stood by her side amidst all the plotting and threats to her life.

She rose from her seat, and so did her brother. The audience, including the Romans and Mithridates' men, knelt as per protocol. Caesar was the only man who remained standing, and Cleopatra bowed to him, and he returned the gesture.

She then addressed the audience. "I, Cleopatra Philopator, Queen and Pharaoh of Egypt, daughter of Ptolemy Neos Dionysos, of goddess Isis, with my beloved husband and brother Ptolemy Dionysos, son of Ptolemy Neos Dionysos, will rule this land and protect its citizens. I also declare Egypt's eternal cooperation with the great citizens of Rome, and my avowed friendship with Imperator Gaius Julius Caesar!"

After the cheering subdued, the king spoke. In a soft, quiet voice, he merely declared, "And I, Ptolemy Dionysos, with my beloved wife and sister Cleopatra, shall rule as a king Egypt deserves. I extend my eternal friendship to Rome."

He looked at Cleopatra for affirmation of his performance. She smiled and nodded to him in reassurance.

Caesar, looking satisfied and happy, walked forward. He had put on some weight, having had the chance to sleep and eat properly, and receiving splendid treatment in true Alexandrian style with spellbinding performances, feasts, and luxurious treatment from masseurs, nail-painters, and stylists. He held Cleopatra's hand in his right and Ptolemy's in his left, and then raised them for a great roar of approval.

Cleopatra smiled inwardly. She had prevailed.

And then she patted her belly. She would call her son Ptolemy Philopator Philometor Caesar, *Father-Loving and Mother-Loving*, a child of two great dynasties that would rule the entire world.

CHAPTER 71

ALEXANDRIA

CLEOPATRA

———◦◇◦———

"You will send for me, Caesar. Will you promise me on your gods?" she asked Caesar as he prepared to leave.

Caesar caressed her face, and then held the baby in his hands. "I will," he said. "I wish for the people of Rome to see you by my side."

Cleopatra smiled. While Caesar was officially the master of many domains, including hers, she now had the freedom to rule as the undisputed queen. She had outlived many of her detractors and assumed the throne while deftly managing to keep Caesar on her side.

But now he had to leave. He had rather reluctantly accepted the child as his own, and she understood his predicament: Roman law did not recognize children of foreign mothers, let alone one born on foreign soil, and he was about to return as conqueror and needed the support of the Senate for his ambitions. Caesar gently held the baby, swaddled in soft linen, and looked down affectionately.

"He looks like me," he said, and she smiled.

With a heavy heart she watched the grand ceremony as the brilliantly disciplined legion marched to the trumpets, with their red capes and plumed helmets moving in harmony as they followed their general. He had kept his promise and left three legions for her, headed by a Roman general called Valentinus. They would be peacekeepers, primarily garrisoned in Alexandria.

With the farewell ceremony complete, Cleopatra returned to her throne room. She walked the magnificent great hall with its crocodile god and falcon statues, exuberant and richly painted walls, soaring Doric columns adorned with lotus and rose patterns, doors guarded by sensually draped pink marble maidens, and five-foot-tall bronze and gold-plated lamps. She looked at the sole high throne on a podium, *hers*, with a smaller chair beside it. Her brother, the now twelve-year-old Ptolemy, was also her husband, though in name only.

She looked at Charmian and smiled. After the battle of the Nile, there was news that King Ptolemy, Cleopatra's brother, had drowned, though no one had found his body. Then, she and Caesar had gone on a tour of the Nile, enjoying people's adoration and watching Caesar as he was awed by the spellbinding Pyramids and the great temples. When her child was born, there was again a great celebration–many said how much like Caesar he was, though she sometimes saw Apollodorus in him. But as Caesar's son she would raise him.

And now, Caesar had left.

Apollodorus? Oh. Apollodorus. What would she do with him? See him? Not see him? Send him away to some far corner? Her fondness for him had not dimmed, but there were now far greater considerations. She had told him many times to find a woman for himself or seek a few affairs, but he had shaken his head politely and walked away. *How can I love another woman after I have been with the most magnificent of them all?* he had said.

What a stubborn idiot.

She would bring Kadmos and Metjen home. Charmian, in her own understated and sweet way, had enquired, very politely of course, if Kadmos would come to serve Her Majesty. Cleopatra had teased her that Kadmos would be sent back, because who would want to keep a brute like that, but stopped the joking before tears welled up in the disappointed girl's eyes. She could see Charmian's anticipation of the big loud-mouth's return.

CHAPTER 72

EGYPT

Theodotus had shaved off his hair and beard. He sat in the rickety cart, driven by a slimy driver who demanded a handsome sum from many who were fleeing Egypt, fearing persecution. The men around him stank; former soldiers, mostly, who did not recognize this high ranked man and gave him no respect. They coughed, spat, itched their balls and farted with no shame. They wiped sweat on him, and their breaths stank. And yet there Theodotus was, hoping to escape to Syria or Judaea and live a quiet life until he had the chance to return again to finish off the bitch queen. As the cart rattled on the dusty, gravelly road, Theodotus plotted his return. Even if it meant years, he was confident that he would prevail.

Arsinoe wept quietly in the carriage. They had tied her hands. *Tied! A Queen of Egypt!* And they were taking her away to Rome. Where was Ganymedes? He was supposed to protect her and get her out of this travesty. What would happen to her at the end of this terrible journey, where she was being dragged like an animal with Caesar's legions? All she knew was that she had stood bold and sought clemency with dignity, and yet they said that her sister—*bitch, bitch, whore like her elder sister, filthy bitch*—had asked Caesar to reject it. Her own sister had given her away to be strangled in a forum. Her father had her elder sister executed, and now her remaining sister was going to murder her. A powerful rage developed in Arsinoe; she was confident that the people of Rome would not allow a balding, dirty dictator to have a beautiful young queen strangled. And then she would come back and have Cleopatra crucified.

Ganymedes fell after he struck his foot on the stub of a sunken mangrove. The grimy smell of wet, seaweed-filled marsh enveloped him, and the brackish water gushed into his mouth. He got up and sputtered, gasping and spitting the dirty water. And they were there, somewhere near, walking in knee-deep water to find him. He heard no sounds, and a gentle relief washed over him as he regained his breathing and looked around. He stood slowly. His feet hurt terribly, and he bled from a laceration between the toes.

Ganymedes limped along a few shaded trees, hoping to escape this marshy patch and find comfort in a nearby village. He found a good spot to sit and rest. He looked around wearily. It was quiet. Perhaps the Romans had finally given up, after all. He had been on the run for months, and he had been too stubborn and stupid to run away from Egypt. He had hoped that he would somehow find his way to the rest of the army and regroup–and then it was too late to get to the borders. He thought he was safe, until they had tracked him down again. He sat nursing his foot and leaned on the tree, cursing his luck.

He had begun to doze off when he heard footsteps. And before Ganymedes could react, something heavy slammed into his head, and the world went dark.

After he woke, it took a while for Ganymedes to come to his sense and take stock of the situation. His skull was tender, and his head throbbed with a dull deep pain. They had tied him to a pillar near the palace compound by the edge of a small cliff. He stayed there, becoming increasingly hungry, thirsty and afraid, as he waited for someone, anyone, to approach him. Why did they not just kill him? Why hold him here?

His questions were answered when he saw a few figures approach him. His heart thudded with anxiety when it became apparent–Her Majesty Cleopatra herself! And along with her was the Roman general Valentinus. He was unsure how to react, and knowing the hand he had played against her, Ganymedes decided to be quiet and leave his fate to the gods.

Cleopatra stood before him. Radiant, recovered, and full of the haughty confidence he had seen in her in the early years of regency and co-rule with her brother, the now-disappeared His Majesty Ptolemy the Thirteenth.

"So, you still live," she said, her voice gentle but without kindness.

"The gods have willed so, Your Majesty," he said, even as his shoulders ached from his arms tied behind him.

"Where is my brother?"

Ganymedes was confused. Were they testing him?

"His Majesty was taken away from the battlefield by his guard. Everyone knows he died by drowning. I was in battle, and then on the run."

She looked at the general.

"My men say Ganymedes had been on the run for months now. They tracked him twice and lost him, until today," Valentinus said.

"Why did you abandon and turn against me?" she asked, her voice again cool and without emotion.

"Her Highness Arsinoe was adamant," he said, knowing there was not much he could say, or that he had a hand in attempting to wrangle power from Pothinus by using Arsinoe as a shield.

"You wish for me to believe that this was all her plan? Oh, Ganymedes. You have seen me as a child and as a regent, and you still take me for a fool. Do you think I have not seen the envy in your eyes or heard the jealousy in your voice when it came to Pothinus?"

Ganymedes said nothing. He knew there was nothing to say. His choices were simple: whether to beg for mercy and find a way to live, or die with dignity, having served his mistress as duty required him to.

"I could be of immense use to you, Your Majesty," he began, and she cut him off.

"Pothinus said the same before he died," she said as a hard edge glinted off her gray eyes. "You have rendered your service, Ganymedes, and I have no use for treasonous eunuchs."

She nodded to the soldiers by his side.

Ganymedes began to pray.

They unshackled and led him to the edge of a short pier that jutted out from the section. Then they tied a large stone to his ankle. Ganymedes knew his fate, but he did not cry or beg. They would leave his drowned bones here as an example.

And when they threw him into the sea, Ganymedes' last thought was that he hoped the gods would bring him back to life, and leave him whole in the next.

Cleopatra walked to the edge of the pier and looked out to the beautiful blue sea. It was tranquil outside, but many matters bubbled like molten rock in her mind.

Not all unrest in Alexandria and the countryside had quietened. Many senior officers from Achillas' troops had vanished to the countryside, no doubt still plotting.

Treasonous priests and administrators still skulked about in the darkness. The coffers were almost empty, and tax collection was in disarray after the mess of the last two years. She had a claim on Judaea and Samaria, which were also Roman client-states, and Caesar had been unwilling to consider handing them over to her. Her curiosity was also piqued by a curious papyrus scroll in the great library which spoke of a corridor of gold under the Great Pyramid; it would be an exciting find, and would also help with the financial pressures. No one knew yet if her brother was actually dead.

She was now the undisputed Queen and Pharaoh of Egypt. And critically, with the support of Rome's most powerful citizen, which meant that any wandering eyes in the east would keep them away from her direction.

She would make sure her brother, co-ruler and husband, knew not to cross her.

She would bring Metjen and Kadmos back to counter any growing influence of the Roman general garrisoned in Egypt.

She would bring the renegade administrators and officials to account for their actions.

And she would make sure that those who betrayed and abandoned her would pay.

And then, with Caesar by her side, and his son as heir, she would rule the world.

The time for games was over.

CHAPTER 73

SOUTHERN EGYPT

———◇———

The men gathered at late evening in the hut located in a desolate area near Thebes, far away from curious eyes and messengers of the kingdom. Six men and a boy, no older than twelve. The one they called 'the big man' hosted them for the evening.

The big man examined the fearful-looking teenager carefully. He pressed on the boy's cheeks, then pulled his hands forward to take a look. He asked the boy to breathe in and out, and checked his skinny torso. He ran his fingers along the boy's ribs and his thick black hair. He made the boy stand to his full height and breathe in, and measured his height. Then he asked the boy to open his mouth wide, and examined his teeth and gums.

"Fits the look," he said to the men who sat nearby. They smiled with approval.

"Parents?" a wise-looking, genial older man asked.

"Dead. We made sure," he said, and they all sniggered. The boy stayed quiet; his eyes sorrowful.

"Go ahead, boy. Now. Speak a few sentences in Greek," the older man said, his voice soft and encouraging. Kind.

"Anything?" the boy asked, wiping his palms on his thigh. The big man had struck those palms several times with a bamboo stick to ensure compliance.

"Yes. Anything."

The boy's tinny voice blurted a few inane phrases about mountains and rivers, but all in impeccable Greek.

"He still has a peasant's accent, but I can work with it," another man said. He had a scraggly beard and very Greek features. He also had a soaring voice with which he impressed this cabal.

"Will he follow all our instructions?" the fourth man asked. He was a bi-lingual Egyptian, a very senior man in Her Majesty's administration in Alexandria.

The big man waved the bamboo stick back and forth and swung it, causing a sharp crack as it struck the floor. The boy flinched, and they all laughed.

"Be strong, boy. Were you not beaten enough at school? I had welts on my back every other day. Stop behaving like a girl," the man scolded him.

The boy stifled a sob and stood quietly.

"What is the news of the queen?" the older man asked.

"She is in control now, but her relations with the priests and senior officials is still weak," the administrator said. "But she will no doubt look to purge the ranks."

"We must bide our time, but not wait so long that her grip tightens like a lion's jaws on a weak buffalo," the older man said.

"And do we think we can manage the Roman garrison? What do we know of this General Valentinus?" the big man asked.

"Old school. Very rule-driven. Rigidly principled. Will only do what was prescribed by Caesar. Very gifted and stubborn," the administrator said. They knew that this man had his eyes and ears in Alexandria.

"How is his relationship with the Queen?" the older man asked.

"Do you think I live in her bedroom and squat in her bathroom?" the administrator snapped. "I don't know. What little we have learned is she keeps a distance from him, and he goes about his job of protecting her and keeping Alexandrian peace."

"What about your man, Kadmos? Will he join us?" the administrator asked the genial old man—an accountant, he called himself, but an astute organizer of mercenaries and a hand behind much mischief in Syria and surrounding regions.

The old man, Fabricius, smiled. "He probably thinks I fled the fetid camps, and he seems enamored with that girl by Cleopatra's side. We may need to neutralize him before we take control of my men. And Apollodorus, of course."

"Let us return to the subject at hand," the administrator, Unasankh, said. He turned to the Greek man beside him. "Theodotus, how long before the boy can be paraded as if he were Ptolemy?"

"A few months," Theodotus said. His eyes burned with the fire of revenge. "It requires some training before this boy can be convincing. There is no doubt that Cleopatra will have her spies keep an eye out for threats to the throne, including pretenders."

This cabal had formed in the months since the battle of the Nile, and now, with Caesar long gone from Egypt and Cleopatra alone at the helm, a wonderful opportunity had presented itself.

And Theodotus would finish what Pothinus could not.

END OF BOOK I

THANK YOU FOR READING

I would be immensely grateful if you took a few minutes to either rate the book or leave a review if you enjoyed it. This makes a huge difference to new authors like me. You can go to https://jaypenner.com/review for easy links.

I hope you enjoyed reading this book! What happens in the next? Well, we're going to meet the quirky but dangerous Herod and the impetuous Mark Antony, for starters. Grab *Queen, The Last Pharaoh Book II* to continue the saga.

Want to virtually visit the locations mentioned in this book through a cool Google Earth flyby? There's something really exciting about going to the locations and imagining what it might have been like two thousand years ago. Go to https://jaypenner.com/maps and ONLY visit the Book I map (because the callouts may have spoilers). I hope you find it informative and fun.

You will find detailed notes at the end of the third book addressing many questions–about the characters (who was real and who was not?), the events (Cleopatra's meeting of Caesar, Achillas' and Pothinus' deaths, Arsinoe's imprisonment), and the timelines.

By the way, did you wonder about *Eurydice*, mentioned by Cleopatra as one she was inspired to learn languages from? Check out my highly rated Whispers of Atlantis series–exciting books that take you to a world around the times of Alexander, and to the time when Cleopatra's ancestor, Ptolemy Soter, founded the Ptolemaic dynasty.

Until next time!

-Jay

JAY PENNER

Stay Connected!

Join my popular newsletter

My website: https://jaypenner.com

Follow me on: The Amazon author page

Or my page on: Facebook

Or write to me at hello@jaypenner.com

REFERENCES

The following works provided helpful historical references and commentary on the life of Cleopatra.

1. Cleopatra, a Life, by Stacy Schiff–Little, Brown and Company

2. The Parallel Lives by Plutarch, Loeb Classical Library edition–Life of Caesar, Pompey, and Antony (writing eighty to a hundred years after the events of this book)

3. Civil Wars by Julius Caesar, Loeb Classical Library–Book III (contemporary)

4. Alexandrian Wars, possibly in the name of Julius Caesar, Loeb Classical Library–contemporary

5. Showtime–The Hunt for Cleopatra's tomb

6. Cassius Dio, Roman History, Loeb Classical Library (writing about two hundred years after the events in this book)

7. Cicero's Letters to Atticus, Project Gutenburg, Translated by E. O. Winstedt